The Deep

The Deep

by

Helen Dunmore

HarperCollins *Children's Books*

First published in hardback by HarperCollins *Children's Books* 2007

HarperCollins *Children's Books* is a division of HarperCollins*Publishers* Ltd,

77-85 Fulham Palace Road, Hammersmith, London W6 8JB

www.harpercollinschidrensbooks.co.uk

1

Isbn-13 978-0-00-720491-5

Isbn-10 0-00-720491-4

Printed and bound in England by Clays Ltd, St Ives plc

This book is proudly printed on paper which contains wood
from well managed forests, certified in accordance with
the rules of the Forest Stewardship Council.
For more information about FSC,
please visit www.fsc-uk.org

Mixed Sources
Product group from well-managed
forests and other controlled sources
www.fsc.org Cert no. SW-COC-1806
© 1996 Forest Stewardship Council
FSC

Why you will love the Ingo books

Ingo

"Ingo has a haunting, dangerous beauty all of its own."
Philip Ardagh, *Guardian*

"The electric thrill of swimming with dolphins, of racing along currents, and of leaving the world of reason and caution behind are described with glorious intensity."
Amanda Craig, *The Times*

"Helen Dunmore may have a few drowned readers on her conscience, so enticing and believable is the underwater world she creates in Ingo." *Telegraph*

The Tide Knot

"Intensely compelling." Amanda Craig, *The Times*

"Dunmore's graceful style is what makes the unbelievable believable here... this is more than just an exciting fantasy." *Independent on Sunday*

"Dunmore creates a story that races along like the currents the children travel on. Total submergence in her watery world is unavoidable." *Bookseller*

CHAPTER ONE

It's April, and the sun is warm. I'm sitting on a rock with Faro, way out at the mouth of the cove. The water below the rock is deep enough for Faro to swim, even now when it's low tide. I scrambled out over the jumble of black, slippery rocks to get here.

The sun glitters on the water. Everything's so bright and alive and beautiful. I'm back in Senara, back at our cove, back where I belong. Faro and I have been talking for ages. Not about anything special, just talking. That's one of the best things about Faro. We start a conversation and it flows so easily, as if we're picking up each other's thoughts. Sometimes we are.

Faro's tail is curled over the edge of the rock, and every so often he pushes himself off with his hands, and plunges into the transparent water to refresh himself. The muscles in his arms and shoulders are very powerful, and he can pull himself up again out of the water and on to the rock again without much effort.

Faro can't stay out of the sea for too long. The skin of his tail, which is usually as glistening and supple as sealskin, grows dry and dull. Faro says that if the Mer get too much sun on their skin it cracks, and then they get sun-sores which are hard to heal.

But I'm sure that Faro's able to stay out of the sea longer these days. Maybe it's something to do with Faro growing older, and more resilient...

My thoughts drift away. Luckily, Faro's one of those people you can be silent with, too. He hauls himself up on to our rock again, dripping and glistening.

A new summer is about to begin. For my brother Conor and me, there'll be days and days of swimming and sunbathing and long evening walks with Sadie. Sadie loves swimming, too, and with only her nose above the water she looks more like a seal than a Golden Labrador. In the evenings we'll build driftwood bonfires on the sand, and have barbecues where we cook mackerel which we've just caught off the rocks.

I don't want to think about the past. I want to live *now*. But no matter how hard I try, the memory of the flood in St Pirans keeps coming back. Floods change people, even after the water's gone down. You don't feel safe in the same way, once you've seen fish swimming in and out of the car-park gates, and houses like caves full of salt water.

Conor and I have never talked to anyone about what happened to us the night of the flood, when the Tide Knot broke. Nobody would believe us, anyway.

The Tide Knot is sealed again. The sea can't come raging in over the land.

But I shiver. I know Ingo's power.

We moved back to our cottage here in Senara in January. That was one good thing that came out of the flood: our rented house was an uninhabitable wreck. And Mum didn't want to live in St Pirans any more. She thought we'd be safer back in Senara, high up on the cliff.

If you've never been in a flood, you can't imagine what St Pirans looked like afterwards. The streets were full of mud, sand, rocks and every kind of rubbish. Wheelie bins, smashed cars, street signs, hundreds of plastic bags, soggy sofas, wrecked computers, TVs with shattered screens, filthy clothes and books turned to mush. There were waterlogged oranges everywhere. You wouldn't believe there could be so many oranges in one town. There were lots of dead fish too, stranded when the water fell.

The smell was the worst part. The whole town stank of rotting food, rotting seaweed, dead fish and sewage from broken pipes.

There were muddy tide marks on the houses higher up the hill, but ours was completely underwater during the flood so it was dirty all over. There was even a branch of seaweed sticking out of the chimney. Our front door hung off its hinges. All our possessions had swilled around in the flood water. Some had disappeared, and most of the rest were ruined.

Mum was really upset about losing our photo albums. Conor and I searched through piles of stuff, trying to find them, but in the end we had to give up. We did find just one framed picture of all the family, face-down in the fireplace under a tangle of seaweed. In the photo Mum and Dad were standing close together, with Dad's arm around me, and Mum's arm around Conor. It was taken a few years ago, and it was always Mum's favourite.

But after Dad disappeared, nearly two years ago now, she put the photo into a drawer.

The photo frame was smashed, but the photo wasn't damaged. Conor and I dried it carefully, then we gave it to Mum.

That was the only time Mum cried. But she said she was being stupid, because she had us safe and who cares about photo albums if you've got the real thing?

She hasn't got Dad, though. She still believes Dad drowned nearly two years ago. When she talks about him, it sounds as if that part of her life is closed. I'm scared that her boyfriend Roger is slowly and surely taking Dad's place.

I sit bolt upright at the thought, clenching my fists. Faro gives me a quizzical smile.

"Do you want to fight, little sister?"

"Sorry, Faro, it's not you, it's just something I thought of..."

"Watch me instead. I'm going to do underwater somersaults."

He dives in a pure, fluid line. I'll never, ever be able to dive like that, no matter how much I practise. And those somersaults – his body is a blur, whipping the water into foam. Round and round, faster and faster until he breaks the surface, tosses back his long hair and calls triumphantly, "Did you see that, Sapphire?"

"It was great, Faro."

He climbs out of the water again, and settles to watching sea anemones in a tiny pool on top of our rock. Faro can watch rock pools for hours. So can I usually, but not today – my thoughts keep pulling me back.

So we came back to our cottage in Senara. The Fortunes, who were renting our cottage, moved out when they heard we were homeless. They've rented another cottage nearby. Gloria Fortune came round on the first day we were back, with an apple pie. She knocked politely on our kitchen door as if she'd never lived here at all.

Everybody in Senara brought us furniture and food and clothes and blankets, as if we were refugees. It's true that all our clothes were gone, and we didn't have money to buy new ones, but I didn't want to wear other people's old stuff. Mum got an emergency payment from the insurance, so now at least we've all got new trainers and a set of new clothes each.

The restaurant where Mum worked has closed, like all the other restaurants in St Pirans. Mum's got a temporary job at the pub here in Senara, four evenings a week.

We're home again. We are really home.

Sometimes I can hardly believe those words. I wake up and expect to find myself in the little bedroom with the porthole window in St Pirans. But here I am, in my own bedroom with the ladder leading up to Conor's attic. I feel something I can hardly describe. It's like when you panic because you're late and it's Monday morning, and then you remember that it's half-term. It's like the sun coming out. *Home.* All the sounds and smells of our cottage are just right. I know where all the scuffs on the furniture have come from. I know why the living-room door doesn't shut properly (because Conor smashed into it when he was learning karate). I know which birds sing in the tree outside the kitchen door. Every object in our cottage is like part of the family.

The Fortunes hadn't changed much inside our cottage, but they did loads of work in the garden, getting it ready for spring planting, just as Dad used to do. I'm planting stuff every day now, all the things Dad used to plant: carrots and lettuces and tomato plants up against a sunny southern wall, and some strawberry runners that Granny Carne gave me. She gave me lots of seeds, too. Granny Carne doesn't ever buy seed in packets, from shops. She saves it all from year to year, she says. She has seed you can't get nowadays.

Dating back to the sixteenth century, I expect, I wanted to say, but I kept my mouth shut. You have to show respect to Granny Carne. Besides, it makes me dizzy when I try to think of all the time Granny Carne must have seen. All those lives coming and going.

Granny Carne went on carefully sorting seeds and putting them into brown wage envelopes marked in her strange, spiky handwriting. Finally she said, "If you can't feed a family from a plot of land as good as you've got here, there's something wrong with you."

She bent down and crumbled a clod of earth between her fingers. "Respect the earth and give it back what it needs, and it'll always feed you," she said. The birds sang loudly, as if they agreed. Granny Carne touched an apple branch. "He'll be covered with bloom this year," she said. "Look at the buds."

I hadn't noticed how many buds there were, fat and ready to burst into flower. Or were they really there before? I wasn't certain. I stared hard at Granny Carne's brown fingers, which looked as if they could bring life out of a dead branch if they wanted to.

"Yes, this branch will be bending down with fruit come September," murmured Granny Carne, and then she left the apple tree and went over to the rowan that grows near our door.

"Do you know why this tree's here, my girl?"

"No, Granny Carne," I answered meekly.

"Your ancestors had the good sense to plant the rowan close by their threshold, because they knew the rowan keeps away evil. The rowan's a powerful tree, Sapphire, full of Earth magic. Never hurt the rowan, or cut it down without great cause. Let it live out its natural life in peace, and the rowan will always give you its protection."

I stared at the rowan with new respect. It's not a big tree. No tree grows tall up here because the winter gales blow them sideways and the salt stunts their growth.

"No evil shall pass this threshold," muttered Granny Carne, with one hand on the trunk of the rowan.

Evil? What evil does she mean? I thought, and fear jagged through me.

"Put your hand on the bark, my girl," Granny Carne urged me. I lifted my hand. But it felt as if a wall of solid air lay between me and the rowan. I pushed hard, but I couldn't get through it. My hand dropped to my side.

"I can't touch it, Granny Carne."

Her fierce owl eyes swept over my face. I thought she was going to be angry with me, but then her expression changed.

"Is it that you don't want to, or that you can't?"

"My hand won't. There's a barrier." I looked down at my hand nervously, and then back at Granny Carne.

"Granny Carne, it's not... it's not because I'm evil, is it? You said that no evil could get past the rowan tree. Is that why I can't touch it?"

Granny Carne's wrinkled face looked meditative. "No, my girl. Most likely it's the Mer blood in you that won't touch the strong Earth magic of the rowan. Not that the Mer have much love for any tree."

"Why not?"

"Maybe because trees are rooted in the Earth. You remember this, my girl. It's not evil that separates Earth and Ingo, it's difference. But there are plenty who want to make evil out of difference. Be warned, Sapphire."

Her face was set and harsh. She stared into my eyes as if she was searching for something.

"Be warned, my girl," she repeated, and a shiver like the flood-memory shiver ran down my back. "Go careful, on Earth and in Ingo, when you meet those who seek to make their power out of the differences between us all." Her voice had risen, as the wind rises before a storm. Suddenly it dropped again. "I'll leave you to get on with your planting now," she said, and turned her back on me.

"Granny Carne—"

But she was gone, striding up the lane as if she were as young as Mum, and not as old as... as old as...

The rowan tree?

The hills?

Roger's living in our cottage, too. Well, not completely – he's got a studio flat in St Pirans as well. But he's spending most of his time here. He sits in Dad's chair at our kitchen table, just as I was always afraid he would.

Roger wants us to have a boat. He says it's crazy not to when we've got such a good mooring down at the cove. And Conor and I are both old enough to be sensible. The fact that our dad disappeared when he was out in the *Peggy Gordon* shouldn't be allowed to stop us from ever having a boat.

I know that this is Roger's opinion because I happened to hear him talking to Mum when I was digging in the garden and they were talking in the kitchen. Mum didn't agree.

"Give me time, Roger," she said. "I know you mean well, but I can't bear the idea of them taking a boat out on their own. The weather changes so fast. I can't risk losing them."

Roger said, "You hold on to those kids too hard, Jennie."

"Do you think I don't know that? But Sapphire can be so impulsive. So wild. So like..."

"Like her dad?"

"Yes."

"You can't change that. Sapphire's pretty tough. Look at the way those kids coped during the flood. God knows what they went through that night. They're good kids. You think about it, Jennie. I know where I could get them a boat. A real little beauty."

The trouble with Roger is that you can't hate him for long – even though I want to hate him, for not being Dad...

"You're thinking about that diver again," says Faro. I jump, and nearly fall off the rock. Faro grabs my arm.

"I wish you wouldn't break into my thoughts," I say crossly.

"You let me," he says.

It's true. I can keep Faro out of my mind completely if I want to. I only have to put up a mental portcullis, like the ones that guarded the entrance to castles in the olden days.

"Roger's not just 'that diver', Faro. He's my mum's boyfriend."

"Is he still your enemy?"

"I don't know. I used to hate him. I still *do* hate him sometimes..."

"I could deal with him for you," says Faro, as if it's the most normal thing in the world. "Next time he's in the sea, I can be there also." He flexes his shoulders, and the muscles ripple.

"*No*, Faro." Sometimes it seems that Faro might do anything.

He frowns darkly. "Your enemies are my enemies, Sapphire."

But just at that moment something distracts him. There's a flurry of foam on the calm water about a hundred metres out beyond the mouth of the cove, in deep water. Mackerel maybe. Or perhaps – perhaps even a dolphin...

Faro leans forward, watching the water intently as if

he's reading it. The surface breaks into a shower of glittering drops. I think I catch the shadow of a tail under the clear water.

"It's a dolphin, Faro."

"No. It's one of my people."

My heart thuds. One of the Mer. One of Faro's people.

"It's not my sister," murmurs Faro. "No, it's a signal. I must go."

He turns to me, his eyes glowing with excitement. "Wait here. Don't move."

And in a second he's gone, pushing himself off the rock, slipping beneath the surface in one smooth, strong dive. I watch him swim deep, his tail driving him out towards the mouth of the cove, and then he disappears.

I wait. I know he'll come back. Faro always does everything he says. I look up and see a scud of cloud coming in, covering the sun. It's past low tide now. Soon the water will be rising. I mustn't stay too long or I'll get caught by the tide. Soon it'll be time to climb the steep, familiar path over the rocks, back up the cliff to home.

Conor's in St Pirans, helping our friends Patrick and Rainbow to clean out their cottage, which is right on the beach. The full force of the flood hit it, and they've lost everything, even the windows and doors. Everything inside their cottage was smashed to pieces.

Conor took Sadie with him because Rainbow was desperate to see her again. She loves Sadie. Thinking about Rainbow makes me feel guilty because I haven't seen much of her since we moved back here. She wants to be friends, and I want to be friends, too, but it's complicated. I keep thinking, would Rainbow still want to be my friend if she knew the truth about me? If she knew that I had Mer blood and half belonged to Ingo? If she could see me sitting on this rock, now, with Faro? I'm afraid Rainbow might blame me for what Ingo did to St Pirans that night.

It's all too complicated. I'm not going to think about it any more. Mum and Roger are buying stuff over in Porthnance. I didn't use to be allowed to come down to the cove without Conor, but I'm older now, and Mum hasn't said anything about it since we've been back. And anyway I'm not on my own. I'm with Faro. No one could keep me safer in the sea than Faro.

At this moment, Faro's head breaks the surface, sleek and shining. He pushes back his hair.

"Sapphire! Come quickly!"

"The water's freezing, Faro. It's only April. I've got human blood as well as Mer blood, remember? I'll get hypothermia."

Faro shakes his head impatiently. "Come *on*, Sapphire. I'm not talking about the swimming that humans do. Come to Ingo with me."

To Ingo. I won't feel the cold there. The water will envelop me, and feel like home. I'll dive beneath the surface, through the skin of the sea, and my lungs will burn just as Faro's burn when he enters the Air. But not too badly. Like Faro, I don't feel the change so much these days. The sea change. A thrill of excitement runs through me. But I still hesitate. Time in Ingo isn't like our time. I might be in Ingo and think only an hour had passed, while it could be a whole human day. Mum has had enough fear and worry. Conor and I haven't been into Ingo since the night of the flood. We've kept close to home.

"Quickly, Sapphire! My friend is here, waiting. There's an Assembly."

"What's an Assembly? Is it like a Gathering?"

My heart quickens again. When I was in Ingo with Faro last autumn I saw crowds of the Mer in the distance, their beautiful cloaks of shell and net glimmering around them, on their way to a Gathering. It sounded like a wonderful party, but Faro wouldn't let me go. I didn't even get close enough to speak to the Mer. But maybe this time I will. I'll get to know Faro's people. Maybe I'll have a cloak, too—

"No," says Faro, "a Gathering is for pleasure. An Assembly is more... more serious. My friend has been sent to summon you."

"Summon me!"

I stand up on the rock, and draw myself to my full height. "*Summon* me, Faro? Who is he to summon me?"

Faro looks up at me, and I look down. I feel the power in him. Mer power, strong as a magnet. But I feel the power in me, too, rising to meet his. I'm his equal. We stare at each other, and neither of us looks away.

At last Faro says, "They're asking you to come, Sapphire. They need you there."

"That's not what 'summon' means, Faro."

"Maybe that was the wrong word. Don't be angry." A persuasive smile flickers on Faro's face. "Come, Sapphire. Come."

I look behind me. The white sand of the beach, and then rocks and boulders rising almost to the lip of the cliff. The way home. I look back at Faro's face, and then beyond him to where I think I see a shadow waiting, deep in the water. One of Faro's friends. The Mer want me to go to an Assembly.

Maybe this means that the Mer are letting me deeper into Ingo now. An Assembly... If it's for something serious, as Faro says, maybe Saldowr will be there. Surely they'd need him there, because Faro says Saldowr is the wisest of the Mer. I want to see him again. I hope the wound in his shoulder has healed. He was so badly hurt in the struggle to seal the Tide Knot again that I was afraid he would die.

So far, even though I've been to Ingo many times, I've only met Faro and his sister Elvira and Saldowr, and seen the shadows of other Mer swimming in the distance. There are bound to be a lot of them at the Assembly. Hundreds, maybe. And I'll meet them face to face.

Excitement pulses in me like a rising tide. Senara, Mum, Conor, Sadie are already shrinking in my mind.

They're just as clear, but small and distant, like images at the wrong end of a telescope. Ingo is holding out its arms to me.

"I'll come," I say, and I swing my arms forward, and dive from the rock.

CHAPTER TWO

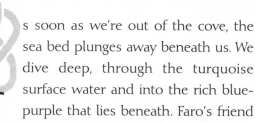s soon as we're out of the cove, the sea bed plunges away beneath us. We dive deep, through the turquoise surface water and into the rich blue-purple that lies beneath. Faro's friend swims ahead. I watch the swish of his tail from side to side as it drives him through the water. Sometimes I think he glances back to see if we're following, but I'm not sure.

The power of Ingo sweeps through my body and I race after him. I could never swim this strongly in the human world, up on the surface. My body cuts through the water. I feel as sleek and fast as a seal, and I'm not tired at all, even though we must be more than a mile out from land already.

Now there's the first tug of a current. It seizes us in its strong arms, and drags us southward. Slowly at first and then faster, faster, until the water flies past us and the sea bed below us is a blur.

But no matter how fast we go, Faro's friend is still ahead of us. There he is, just visible, riding the current's crest. He's not going to let me catch up with him. Faro could, easily, but I'm not fast enough.

"Why won't he wait for us, Faro?"

Faro's white teeth show in a teasing smile. "He's shy of you, Sapphire."

"He can't be!"

"You're human, don't forget. Morlader's not like me. He's never spoken to a human, or even seen one up close. Most of the Mer are like that. You don't realise how unusual I am," he adds with self-satisfaction.

"Why?"

"Why what?"

"Why are you different from the others?"

Faro frowns. "You wouldn't understand, Sapphire. It's a Mer thing." Streams of bubbles play over his face, half-hiding it. He's close, but he looks far away. *A Mer thing.* His words hurt, but the water of Ingo surges around me, and my own Mer blood tingles with excitement. How fast is this current taking us? How far? We must be miles and miles from land now. It's like flying underwater. I've never travelled so fast in Ingo, but I'm not afraid. I'm elated. How can Faro think I won't understand?

"I'm not *all* human, Faro," I say. "You know that."

Faro turns to me. His hair flows past his shoulders, plastered to his skin by the force of the current. His eyes scan my face, intent, anxious – and maybe even a little fearful. He isn't hiding from me now. Suddenly I remember the first time we met.

"*You* weren't ever shy of me, Faro."

"No."

"Why weren't you? You're Mer too."

A strange expression crosses Faro's face. "Yes," he says, more hesitant than I've ever heard him, "yes, of course I'm Mer. But Sapphire, there's something— Look out!"

He grabs my hand and hurls us sideways out of the grip of the current, just missing a jagged spear of rock. In the calm water, he lets go of me. There are white marks on my hand where his fingers dug into the flesh. I could never have got out of that current on my own. Faro's strength is almost frightening sometimes – but he did it to save me.

Faro looks shocked. "It nearly got us. I must have been dreaming. I can't believe I let that happen."

"Scary," I say weakly as I try to calm the pumping of my heart. Usually Faro is as quick as a fish. He senses danger at the first shadow of it. That rock would have killed us, and we only missed it by a few centimetres. If Faro hadn't dragged me sideways, I'd be drifting down to the sea bed now, my body broken and bleeding. For the first time, I really understand that only a second separates life from death, and it's very easy to die. My heart thuds so hard I can feel it in my throat.

Faro rubs his hands over his face, as if he's wiping away a nightmare. He takes hold of my hand, lifts it, and examines it. There are the marks of his nails, too, in my skin. My hand is bleeding.

"I didn't mean to hurt you, little sister," he says.

"I'm all right. We could have died, couldn't we? I think you saved my life."

Faro glances around quickly as if someone might overhear him. "This place could eat us alive and still be hungry," he whispers. "Its spirit is bad – *drokobereth*. We must hurry."

I glance around fearfully. Now the rocks look as if they are clawing the water, reaching out for prey.

"Where's Morlader gone?"

Faro points ahead where the rocks rise up sheer, towering into an under-sea mountain range. I thought that the Bawns near our cove were huge, but these are ten times higher. They are bleak and barren. They look as if they've crowded together deliberately, so there won't be a way through them. They don't want us here.

"Morlader has gone ahead of us, to the Assembly," says Faro.

"Where's that?"

"Farther on. It's no use being afraid of the mountains, Sapphire. There's no other way except through them."

"I'm not afraid!"

"Of course you are," says Faro. His face is very serious. "And so am I."

"If it's so dangerous, why do the Mer hold their Assemblies on these mountains?"

"Not *on* the mountains: *in* them. Our Assembly cave is deep in the heart of the mountains. Our ancestors chose it, because we could hide from our enemies there for a thousand years if need be. We could defend ourselves with only a handful of warriors."

"What enemies?"

Faro glances round again, quickly, cautiously. "We can't talk about it here. Come on, Sapphire. It's not solid rock, there's a way through. We'd be safer approaching from the south, but we haven't got time to swim all the way round now."

"Do you know the way?"

"Of course," says Faro. I'm sure I can hear doubt in his voice, but there's no choice. We've got to go on.

"Careful, " whispers Faro. "Even a scratch from these rocks can turn to poison." We swim forward very slowly, gliding cautiously around the razor-sharp flanks of the rocks.

Before long the rocks have closed around us. Ahead, the rising mountain blocks our sight. There's no clear water anywhere, only channels between dangers. I've never felt cold in Ingo before, but these rocks cast an icy shadow. There is no sign of life. No flickering fish, no glowing sea anemones, no graceful herds of sea horses. There isn't even any seaweed clinging to the rocks. The valleys are empty and the peaks bare. Below us the sand is dark, ashy grey.

We swim on, barely disturbing the water. Now the

rocks on either side of us look as if they've been split open by a giant hammer.

"The tides did this when they broke loose," says Faro, steering me past a shattered fang of coral. We slow down even more, so that we can ease our bodies through the wreckage without getting trapped in it. Besides, I don't want to disturb these waters, for fear of what might come out.

"Why can't we swim higher up in clear water?" I whisper.

"We have to go this way," says Faro. "Mind your hand, Sapphire! That's where the eels have their holes."

I snatch my hand back, shuddering. So there *is* something alive here. Roger told me once that divers have to watch out for conger eels. They live in crevices like these. If they get your arm in their jaws, they won't let go. What else is hidden away in the holes and crevices?

"Search every crook and granny," I murmur.

"What?"

"It's meant to be 'Search every nook and cranny' – Conor got it wrong when he was little and so we always say it like that."

"Why would you search a granny – you mean, your mother's mother?"

"Never mind, Faro, it's not important."

It's like trying to tell a joke at a funeral. Everything is so eerily silent. The split rock glimmers like oil. At the corner of my eye something flickers.

"Faro!"

But when I turn my head, there's nothing.

"Faro, I'm sure someone – something was there."

A flash of alarm crosses Faro's face.

"Just keep swimming," he whispers in my ear. "Pretend you haven't seen them." He takes my hand and pulls me with him. "Don't look back."

I wasn't going to look back. I swear I wasn't. But somehow my head turns, and the flicker of movement behind me becomes real, solid—

"Faro, look! Look at her!"

"*No*, Sapphire!"

"But she's so beautiful!"

So beautiful. She's sitting on the knife-sharp edge of the rock, but it doesn't seem to hurt her. Her shining hair drifts around her shoulders like a cloak of glass. Her smile glows with welcome and her arms are open wide as if to embrace us.

"But, Faro, she's Mer. She's one of your people. Why won't you look at her?"

Her eyes fix mine. They are huge and hungry. She wants me. She wants me to come to her.

"*She's not Mer!*" says Faro, his voice full of revulsion.

"Just look for a minute. She's so lovely," I plead with him.

"All right then, Sapphire, *you* look at her if you want to! *Look!*"

Her beautiful face, her sloping shoulders and swirling hair – her—

"*Look*, Sapphire!"

She twists her body free of the rock. She pushes off with her hands. She's coming towards us...

Where a tail should be if she were Mer, where legs would be if she were human, there is a claw. A single claw, steel blue and gleaming. An open claw that snaps as the creature swirls towards us—

Faro raises both hands, fingers crossed, and touches them to his forehead. The creature stalls in the water.

"Get behind me," he mutters, "and whatever you do, don't look at it again." Very slowly he begins to swim backwards, still holding his hands in place and shielding me with his body. I scull myself backwards with trembling hands, keeping my eyes fixed on Faro's back. I won't look at – at *it* – again. It's not going to make me look at it. A faint sound drifts through the water. *Clack. Clack.* The claw, I think. It's opening and shutting the claw, getting ready to snap—

"Don't be scared," murmurs Faro. "Feel behind you." My back is against the wall now. A sheer, gleaming wall of rock that blocks our way.

Clack, clack.

Surely the sound is fainter now?

"Faro – Faro – has it gone?"

"Wait."

We hang still in the water, backs to the wall, and wait.

"Don't look, Sapphire. It's not safe yet."

Clack, clack.

It's almost gone. At last Faro's shoulders slacken with relief. His hands drop to his sides.

"It's gone back to its hole," he says. "But we've got to be quick. There'll be more of the Claw Creatures around here and I can't hold off more than one at a time."

"Can't we swim straight up the rock, Faro?"

"No. We've got to go through. There's a passage here somewhere. I used to know where it was, but since the Tide Knot broke, everything's changed. Even the routes we've used for a thousand years. Come round this way, Sapphire. Squeeze through. That's it. Good, the Claw Creatures can't get in here."

We're in a small cave. The back of it is blind, and there's no passage through the rock.

"We'll rest here for a while," says Faro, and closes his eyes. It's very gloomy in the cave, but there's enough light to see how drained he looks.

"At least now you know never to look at one of the Claw Creatures," he says lightly.

"If you hadn't been there—"

"Shall I tell you what would have happened, little sister?"

"No, don't. I can guess."

We are quiet for a while, resting. I wonder how much farther we've got to go. Faro says that everything's changed in Ingo since the Tide Knot broke.

"But the tides went back," I say aloud.

"Ingo is slow to heal."

Like the human world, I think. St Pirans is shadowy in my mind now, but I can't forget the destruction of the flood.

"*Ingo er kommolek,*" I say suddenly, without realising that I'm going to speak. Just as suddenly I remember where those words came from. The dolphins spoke them, that day last autumn when they came into the bay, and we were out in the boat with Mal's dad. But the words were different then… *Ingo er lowenek*… was that it?

My brain doesn't know what the words mean, but something deeper in me understands. There's a shadow over Ingo now. Grief and destruction have spread through Ingo like currents of rushing water.

"*Ingo er kommolek… kommolek… trist Ingo… trist, trist Ingo…*"

Faro is staring at me.

"How do you know those words, Sapphire?"

Power rises in me again, as it did when I was standing on the rock, back in our cove.

"I learned them from the dolphins."

"You're coming on, little sister," says Faro in his mocking way. "You are becoming a daughter of Ingo."

His words thrill through me.

"Sometimes I think that won't ever happen. Just when I feel I'm part of Ingo, I'm pushed away again."

"I don't push you away."

But there's a lot you never talk about. How little I know

about Faro's history – and I still feel I can't ask him quite ordinary things like where he was born, who his parents are...

"Sapphire?"

"What?"

"Wake up. It's time to move on."

CHAPTER THREE

We come out of the cave, and stare up the sheer face of the mountain. It's just as forbidding, but now there's a challenge in it, too.

"Morlader must have found the passage."

"Yes," Faro agrees.

"But then why didn't he wait for us?"

Faro shrugs. His eyes are dark and grim. "You think all the Mer are one family, Sapphire. But it's not as simple as that. Sometimes we... we *test* one another."

"You mean Morlader's testing us to see if we can find the way?"

"Not Morlader alone," says Faro. "He's been sent, and told what to do. And I think I know who sent him. Come, little sister, we have to take this path."

He points around the shoulder of the rock face. We edge along it, keeping close to the rock without ever touching it. Faro takes my hand and steers us both onwards with barely a flicker of his powerful tail. The rock is no longer barren. Weed clings to it, and in crevices there are limpets crusting its smoothness. Long trails of weed catch at my feet. It's a dark, smooth green, like bottle-glass. It hangs from the rock in swaying curtains, so thick that we can't see through them.

"The entrance is here somewhere," says Faro. He lets go of my hand, pushes aside the curtain of weed, and vanishes.

"Faro!"

"Come on, Sapphire, it's this way."

His voice sounds muffled and hollow. Where is he? Gingerly, I touch the weed. I'll have to push my way through it, and I don't want to. It's like going into a trap.

The weed sways like an animal being stroked. Suddenly the fog that hides the human world when I'm in Ingo clears for a moment, and I see Sadie standing in a patch of sunlight. Sadie! Thoughts of her flood my mind. Her warm smooth coat, her brown eyes, the way she scans my face to work out what I'm saying. Dear Sadie. My hand falls to my side. What am I doing here? Her eyes plead with me to come home. Why am I pushing my way through a slimy curtain of weed?

"Sapphire!"

Faro sounds farther away now, and impatient. He's going on. He's not waiting for me. I can't get left behind here on my own – but I can't go in. Rocks and icy shadows and cold unfriendly water press in on me. *Get out of here*, a voice says in my brain. *Get out now, while you still can.*

Suddenly I hear another sound. It's very faint, but as soon as I hear it a prickle of terror races over my skin.

Clack. Clack. Clack.

I'm imagining it; of course I am. But Faro's not here to help me now. *Don't look back, Sapphire. Don't risk being trapped by that beautiful face and that lethal claw.*

Clack. Clack. Clack.

It's coming closer. Frantically I scrabble at the curtain of weed, trying to find an opening. The weed resists, then suddenly it parts and I fall through it.

It's dark in here, a shadowy greenish murk. I blink, and slowly my eyes adjust. There's Faro, about a hundred metres ahead. The rock face curves inward at the bottom, and the weed hangs down, creating a secret space.

"Quick, Sapphire! Here!"

I swim forward, and see a narrow hole in the rock. It must be the opening of the passage Faro wants us to go through. It's just wide enough for our bodies, but we won't be able to swim. We'll have to use our hands to pull ourselves through. But it's so narrow – what if we get stuck?

"Hurry!" says Faro in an urgent whisper. "They'll scout up and down the weed, searching for us. They're stupid, so they probably won't find us. But you can never be sure. Come on. I'll go first."

"But, Faro—"

"It's the only way. Come *on*. They can't come into the tunnel because their claws get jammed."

His eyes are bright in the gloom as he squeezes my hand. "It takes us to the Assembly chamber. I know it does. Trust me, Sapphire."

He swims down to the hole and grips both sides with his hands. With a sinuous, supple movement he squeezes his body in, and disappears.

It's all right for you, I think angrily. *You've done this before. And besides, you're Mer.*

My heart is beating fast again. I'm frightened but I push the fear down. In a place like this it's not safe to show weakness. That creature with the claw can't get into the passage; Faro said it couldn't —

Clack. Clack. Clack.

Am I really hearing it?

Stop it, Sapphire. Don't think about the claw.

Faro's tail has vanished. I've got to follow him.

I swim down to the tunnel entrance and scull the water as I try to peer inside. It's very narrow. I can only just fit in. There's hardly any light at all. My fingers look ghostly.

Do it, Sapphire. You've got to go in.

I reach for the entrance of the tunnel. My hair floats around my face, blinding me for a second. What if my hair gets caught and I'm trapped?

I shut my mind, swim down, feel for the sides of the tunnel, and haul myself in.

I can't see anything. My body blocks out the light behind, and Faro must be blocking the light ahead.

"Faro?" I whisper. I don't dare call out. Anything might be listening. A conger eel would love to coil itself away here, and wait for its prey. Maybe there's a labyrinth of tunnels leading away from this one. Tunnels full of hidden creatures. Octopuses, giant squid, crabs and eels—

"Faro!"

I'm not making a sound. I'm trying to reach Faro with my mind. Where is he?

Hurry up, Sapphire. Human toes are a rare treat for conger eels down here.

He's heard my thoughts. I've never been so glad to be teased in my life. Somehow Faro turns the conger eels into cartoon creatures. But under the teasing, I sense that Faro's afraid too. Not of eels or octopuses, but of something deeper. Something formless, shadowy. A flicker of his fear brushes over my mind and I shudder.

I'm not going to let fear win. I'm going to fight back, like Faro.

Those conger eels don't care about toes, they're after your tail, I shape my thoughts to tell him. I know how proud Faro is of his strong, supple tail.

I'd like to see them try. One blow from my tail and they'd never move again. Feel your way along the rock with your hands, Sapphire. If you find a hold you can pull yourself along.

He shows me a mental image of what he is doing. His strong hands grasp the sides of the rock and propel him forwards.

I reach out cautiously, but the sides of the tunnel aren't slimy, as I feared. They're just smooth, and hard, and unforgiving. My nails scrape for a hold. I pull myself forward a little, then my hold breaks. There's just enough room to put my hands down by my sides. Palm outwards, my hands push and propel me forward.

But now the tunnel's getting narrower. If I'm not careful I'll get stuck with my hands wedged by my sides. I won't be able to bring them up to protect my face.

Don't panic, Sapphire. If you panic in here you're in real trouble.

Very cautiously I roll on to my side, and push backwards until I'm pressed against the tunnel wall. Carefully, I work my right elbow loose underneath me until my right arm comes free, and then I roll and do the same for my left.

You've done it, I tell myself. *You kept calm and worked it out. That's what you've got to do if you're going to get through the passage.*

It feels safer with my hands stretched in front of me. I can't move as quickly, but I can shield my face. Faro's quite a way ahead now. He must be moving more easily than me, with the force of his tail to push him on. My head knocks against the roof. *Slow down, Sapphire. Take it easy. Faro's bigger than you and he didn't get stuck.*

My foot catches on an outcrop of rock on the tunnel roof. For a desperate moment I struggle to pull it free, but it won't go the right way. The rock's holding on to me. It won't release me.

I've got to think. Think. *Use your mind instead of going into a blind, blank panic. You won't ever get free if you struggle; it's like pulling a knot tighter.* Maybe if I push backwards a little, it'll take some pressure off my foot.

Very gently I push back against the sides of the tunnel until the grip on my foot eases. I wriggle my foot sideways, and the rock lets me go.

I mustn't let it catch me again. I scull hard with my hands to bring my body down as close to the floor of the tunnel as possible, and then I edge forwards with my feet together. I won't kick any more, in case I get trapped again.

It works. I'm moving, slowly and steadily. But there's no time for relief. I've got to catch up with Faro. If I lose him—

What if the tunnel divides and I don't know which way to go?

It's cold as well as dark. It feels as if the tunnel walls are breathing out a dead, freezing mist. Every time my fingers touch the rock they get more numb. Got to keep moving. Faro's up ahead; I know he is even though I can't see him. I can't even find him with my mind. *Keep going, Sapphire. Pull yourself along. One handhold. Another handhold.*

Keep going. The water feels cold and lifeless, but it isn't really. You're still in Ingo.

My worst fear is that the tunnel's going to squeeze shut, closing me in. I could never find my way backwards, all the way to the entrance. I'd get stuck, and then I'd be trapped in the tunnel for ever.

As if the tunnel senses my panic, it starts to crowd me. My hands scrabble for space. My feet kick against the tunnel roof.

Faro!

There's no reply. My thoughts bounce emptily around my mind. Faro has left me. I'm alone.

A wave of panic wipes me out. The rock bulges, crushing me. My fingers scrape at the surface but this time I can't move. The tunnel has got me and it's never going to let me escape.

But as the tide of panic roars, a small, quiet voice speaks deep inside me. I don't know if it's my voice, or Faro's. *Think, Sapphire. Use your brain. You're not trapped as long as you think.*

I remember how I freed my foot. *Ease backwards. Don't struggle, because it only ties the knot tighter.*

It's one of the hardest things I've ever done. When you're trapped, every cell of your body screams for you to fight free. But I've got to do it, because even Faro can't help me now. He's up ahead, waiting for me, I'm sure he's there, but the tunnel's too narrow for him to turn and pull me free.

Somehow just the thought of Faro waiting makes the rock face move back a fraction. The roof of the tunnel doesn't press down quite so hard.

You survived the Deep, Sapphire. None of the Mer can survive the Deep, but you did it. This isn't so terrible, compared to the Deep.

That's when I first see the light. It's a tiny greenish glimmer, so faint I'm not sure at first if it's real or not. As I watch, another tiny light springs out on the rock face, like a signal. *Don't be afraid. We're here with you.*

Like fairy lights. But they can't be fairy lights because there's no electricity down here. I peer through the darkness and then I see them. They are small, worm-shaped creatures, clinging to the rock. The glow of light comes from their heads. As I watch, another point gleams out, and then another. They light the passage, showing the way onwards.

"Thank you," I whisper, and the lights glow more strongly, as if the little creatures have heard and are glad to help me.

Slowly, slowly, the rock lets go of me as I relax. I'm easing myself forwards again. There is clear water between the rock and my body. I carry on doggedly pushing myself along. A few centimetres, a few more. The tunnel is curving round to the left, and surely it's growing much wider now...

There's a shimmer of light ahead, and a shape, moving—

A conger eel!

No. A familiar shape, strong and supple and like a seal's tail. Faro's tail. He's swimming up ahead of me.

"Faro!"

"Little sister, I was beginning to wonder what had happened to you. I tried to reach you with my mind but all I could find was rock."

I swim up alongside, so overwhelmed with relief that I'm afraid I'll cry if I try to talk. Faro turns and smiles impishly.

"So those conger eels didn't eat you up after all."

I laugh feebly.

"You're bigger than me, Faro, however did you get through so easily?"

Faro shrugs. "We're used to it. Our bodies know their way through rock passages. As long as you don't think about it, you'll always get through."

The tunnel's opening up like a flower from a stalk. In the distance there's a murmuring ripple of sound. Faro takes my hand.

"Wait, Sapphire."

We float, listening. The light is even stronger now, and I see that the sides of the tunnel aren't black at all. They are a deep, rich ruby red. It looks as if the tunnel is carved out of a huge jewel. Faro's face glows with reflected light.

"We're close to the Assembly chamber," he whispers. "Listen. You can hear my people."

So the murmuring ripple isn't the far-off noise of the

sea. It's the sound of Faro's people, gathered together.

"How many are there?"

"Hundreds. Maybe thousands. Listen to the echo. You can tell that the chamber is full."

"What are they doing?"

"Waiting."

"What for?"

"For us, of course. Or strictly speaking, my dear little sister, for *you*."

I stare at Faro in horror. "You're joking."

"They've been travelling for days to get to this Assembly."

"How do you know? Morlader only just came to – to fetch us."

"I know the ways of my people," says Faro proudly.

For a second I even wish that I was back in the tunnel again, talking to the worms. I try to imagine stepping out in front of hundreds – maybe thousands – of Mer. How disappointed they'll be when they see that I'm just an ordinary girl, with no special powers at all.

"They've got it wrong, Faro. They can't be waiting for me. Let's go back—"

"What? Back through that tunnel? You've got to be joking. Even for me it was a close thing."

"Were you scared, Faro?"

"Me? Scared?" His eyes glitter indignantly. "I was – *extended*, my dear Sapphire."

"So was I. Very extended indeed."

The murmur of voices seems louder now. I try to imagine what they look like, all those hundreds and thousands of Mer gathered together. Suddenly I'm curious as well as nervous. I've always wanted to meet the Mer face to face. Faro's people. Maybe my people, too, in a way.

"Will my father be there?" I ask abruptly.

"No."

"Why not? He's Mer now, isn't he?"

"He's still recovering."

"Recovering! You didn't tell me he was ill."

"You knew that he was hurt when the Tide Knot broke. His body felt the anger of the tides."

"But I thought he'd be all right by now – I didn't know it was serious. Why didn't you tell me? What's wrong with Dad?"

Faro touches his right arm, just above the wrist. "The bone was broken here. He had broken ribs too, and cuts and bruises all over his body where he was hurled against a rock. My sister's teacher has been healing him. She is a great healer."

"Oh."

I feel sick at the thought of Dad being hurled against a rock. I know what it's like when a current seizes hold of you. It must have been terrible to be caught in the full force of the escaped tides. I knew Dad was hurt because he didn't come back to help us in the flood, but I didn't realise how bad it was.

"And his mind is heavy," goes on Faro quietly, as if he's confiding a secret.

My father is *trist*, I think. My father is *kommolek*. The words are like shadows on my heart.

"Yes," says Faro, reading them, "you are right, little sister. His mind troubles him more than his body."

I wish I could reach Dad with my mind. I wish I could say to him, *Hold on. We haven't forgotten you. Conor and I will do anything to get you home.*

But Dad can't hear me.

I listen again to the murmur of voices.

"What about Mellina? Will she be there?"

"She may be. I don't know."

If she is, I'll see Mellina face to face at last. The Mer woman whom my father loves. The woman who enchanted him away from our home, away from Mum and Conor and me and everything in the human world.

I wish I was away in Ingo...

Mellina sang that to Dad, and he believed it. He wished for Ingo, and his wish came true. When I saw Mellina's face in Saldowr's mirror she looked young and soft and gentle. But I'm not going to be tricked by her. I'm going to find out the truth, and tell Mellina that she's got to let go of Dad, and allow him to come home.

"All right, Faro. Let's go in."

We swim to the edge of a thin screen of rock. I tread water to steady myself. Warily, keeping my body in hiding, I peer around the side.

It's a vast underwater cavern, as big as a cathedral. The walls curve inwards and they're carved into tier after tier, like rows of seats in a theatre. I wonder if the sea gouged out those tiers, or if the Mer carved them.

And there are the Mer. Hundreds of them, as Faro said. Maybe thousands. They are as real and solid as a football crowd, and as strange as a dream. Their tails glisten. Their long hair streams in the water, half veiling their bodies. Some are wearing shining cloaks of net and pearl, others bodices of woven seaweed.

The source of the light is above us. The light of the open sea filters down to the heart of the underwater mountains. For a second I think of the sun and its light, then I lose my grip on the thought. The human world feels as distant as China or Paraguay.

I stare around the chamber in wonder. The far wall shimmers with phosphorescence. The skin of the Mer glows too. There's a tinge of blue in their skin that isn't like any colour I've seen in a human. The same blue sheen ripples over their tails. I've never noticed that colour in Faro's body. Maybe the light of the cave changes everything. They look so foreign, and so beautiful.

"My people," says Faro, with such pride in his voice that I turn to look at him. His shoulders are braced, his hands are clenched into fists, and his face is stern.

"My people," he repeats, "and I will give my life to defend them. You are the only human who has ever seen such an Assembly."

"I'm honoured," I answer quietly.

Faro's face flashes into a smile, then he says urgently, "Sapphire, promise me that you'll listen to them. Even if – even if what they ask sounds impossible."

"I promise, Faro."

We swim slowly forward, out of our concealment. First one head turns, and then another. A ripple of sound flows through the chamber.

So many pairs of eyes, fixed on me and Faro. So many faces scanning us, taking in every detail. It's like being on stage, except that I don't know the play, or what my part is.

Now everything's still again. The water in the chamber is as clear as glass. There's nowhere to hide, even if I wanted to hide. But I don't. I swim forward. At long last I'm here, in the company of the Mer.

They stare at us, waiting. The atmosphere is tense with expectation. What are we supposed to do?

"Come farther forward, Sapphire. They want us to go into the middle of the Chamber. There, above the Speaking Stone."

He points to a stone set in the floor of the cave. It's pearl coloured, with veins of green and blue and crimson, like the veins in an opal. But it can't be an opal. No precious stone could ever be that big.

"Follow me, Sapphire."

We swim to the centre. It feels as if our bodies barely disturb the water. We're part of its stillness. When we reach the Speaking Stone, Faro dives and touches it with his hand, as if he's touching it for luck. As he rises again he says to me, "Dive down, Sapphire, and touch the Stone."

"Why?"

"It makes us speak more clearly."

I dive down, and touch the stone lightly. I'm expecting to feel some charge of power in it, like the power that surged in the Tide Knot, but it's just a stone.

A tall Mer man with a strong, hawk-like face uncoils his body from the front rank of seats, swims forward and holds his hands out to us, palm up.

"Greet him, Sapphire," whispers Faro, and I hold my own hands out in imitation. Faro does the same. With a quick, easy flick of his body, the man dives to touch the Speaking Stone, then swims back up to where we are. His hair swirls around his shoulders.

"I am Ervys, Morlader's uncle," he tells me. "We are sea rovers. We gather news from all the oceans, and bring it to our people wherever they are. You are welcome here. I have come to share with you the thoughts that I have, and the thoughts of our people. These are painful thoughts, dark and violent. You would not want them in your head or in your dreams, and so I will not pass them into your mind. We will speak our thoughts aloud at this Assembly.

His eyes are fixed on me. They are very clear. I've never seen human eyes with that silvery light in them. He looks more – more *Mer*, somehow, than either Faro or Elvira. More Mer than Saldowr, even. I push the thought down, to consider it later. I need to concentrate. All those faces, all those eyes. But somehow the fact that we are floating above the Speaking Stone makes the hundreds of watching Mer a little less intimidating.

"These are dangerous times for us all," says Ervys, "since the tides turned and the Deep awoke. Or since the Deep awoke and the tides turned."

Suddenly I'm impatient. After such a journey, I don't want to hear clichés. I know that these are dangerous times. I know all about the aftereffects of the flood. They are like the aftershocks of an earthquake, and no one could fail to notice them. *The tides turned and the Deep awoke.* What's that really supposed to mean?

My impatience must show on my face because Ervys says sharply, "Do you expect me to deliver all my thoughts in a moment?"

"No," I say meekly, but I don't feel very meek inside. Faro shoots me a warning glance, and I remember my promise. "I'm a friend of the Mer. I'm ready to listen," I say, and this time Ervys's face relaxes.

"You are very young," he says, looking at me with a certain doubt in his expression. "But we have been told that you have a gift. Saldowr tells us that you have visited the Deep."

I feel the hush in the chamber, the tension stretched out so tight it might snap at any moment.

"Yes," I answer, "I visited the Deep, before the tides broke."

A gasp runs around the chamber, followed by a murmur of voices. Ervys turns and raises his hand. Silence falls.

CHAPTER FOUR

I wish I had Conor by my side. Ervys is looking at me so intently. What does he want? His face is hungry.

The eyes of all the assembled Mer are fixed on me. It's like standing on a stage with all the lights on you. The silence is eager. If only I knew what they wanted from me. I glance sideways at Faro for support, but he's gazing down at the Speaking Stone, his head bowed as if in respect for the Assembly.

Maybe Ervys is waiting for me to speak first. If Conor were here, he'd know what to say.

"You visited the Deep," repeats Ervys at last. "I was told that this had happened, but now I hear it from your own mouth. It seems... beyond our beliefs. Saldowr himself cannot enter the Deep. And yet it opened to you. Tell me how you did this. Tell me what force you used."

"I – I don't know."

Ervys throws back his head. His hair eddies around him. "You don't know!" His voice is full of disbelief.

"It just – it just happened. I was in a rogue current. It threw me off. It threw us all off. I couldn't see Faro or Conor. They were dragged away from me... I don't remember all of it," I say slowly. "Maybe I was knocked out. When I woke I was in the Deep. It was so dark..."

My voice trails off. I should never have started talking about it. The memories claw at me. Everything is coming back. The crushing darkness and silence of the Deep. The weight of my hand when I tried to move it, as if my hand was made of lead. I was trapped, a prisoner of the Deep. If I hadn't met the whale who rescued me...

"But you lived," goes on Ervys sternly, like a teacher trying to find out what you've really been doing when he's out of the classroom. "If Saldowr had not told us it was true, how could we believe it? How could a human do what none of the Mer can do?"

Suddenly my fear is swept away by anger. How dare he doubt me? How dare he think I owe him anything? The Mer want something from me. That's why Ervys sent his nephew to fetch us. But Morlader didn't even guide us safely here. He went ahead and abandoned us. We had to struggle through that tunnel on our own. What if Faro hadn't found the way? I'd never have guessed that the tunnel entrance was hidden behind that curtain of weed. Those Claw Creatures could have got us.

Why do the Mer have to make everything so difficult and complicated? And now, after all that, they still refuse to trust me. The way Ervys is interrogating me, you'd think I'd committed a crime and was lying about it.

I clench my hands into fists, and dig my nails into the palms of my hands. I try to guess what Conor would say if he were here. Conor would keep his head and think clearly to the heart of what was happening. Conor doesn't lose his temper and lash out like me. People listen to him.

I must be like Conor now. I can't blurt out my anger. I must make it speak clearly, so that the Mer have to respect what I say.

Wait, Sapphire, wait. Let the silence stretch. Ervys needs something from you. All these Mer are here for a reason. Take control. You don't have to let Ervys question you as if you're on trial.

"It's true that I'm human," I say at last. My voice is reedy, but at least it doesn't tremble. "It's true that I'm not in my own world here. You knew I'd need a guide to find my way to this Assembly."

"I sent my nephew to guide you."

"But Morlader went ahead of us, out of sight. We had no guide."

"Faro knew the way."

"Not well enough for our safety. Was it a test, Ervys?"

I look straight into his eyes. He frowns, and for a moment I'm afraid I've gone too far and his anger is going to flare out. I don't look round, but I sense that Faro's watching me closely now. He's on my side, I know it for sure. Faro is Mer, but he is no friend of Ervys. The tension between me and Ervys stretches as taut as a guitar string. Then, slowly, Ervys's face cracks into a smile.

"Saldowr gave us a true picture," he says slowly. A ripple of relief goes around the chamber. They were worried, too. Does that mean the other Mer are afraid of Ervys? "Saldowr told us, 'These human children look as helpless as seal pups on a rock. Don't be deceived.'"

"Where is Saldowr?" I ask eagerly. "Is he all right? Has he recovered?" Surely the wound Saldowr took on the night the Tide Knot broke must have healed by now. Saldowr is so powerful. His magic is as deep as the ocean, just as Granny Carne's is as strong as a rock. Even if no one else can heal him, Saldowr must be able to heal himself.

Ervys doesn't reply. Instead he nods at Faro, asking him to speak. To my surprise Faro dives down and touches the Speaking Stone a second time, as if he needs more strength, and then turns to face the Assembly.

"You all know that Saldowr is my teacher," he says proudly. I suppress the thought that the Mer seem to spend a lot of time telling each other things that they already know. Faro is deadly serious.

There's a murmur of agreement. Suddenly a broad-shouldered man leaves the front rank of seats and swims down to the Speaking Stone. As he swims up to face Ervys, challenge flashes between the two Mer men. Then he turns to Faro.

"You are Saldowr's *scolhyk*," he says, "his student and

more than that. You are his follower. You are not his son in the flesh but in all other things you are Saldowr's heir." His gaze travels over the ranks of the Mer. "Am I speaking the truth?"

The ranks of Mer sway as if a strong current has swept into the chamber. Many clench their hands together, and hold them out towards the speaker as if they're offering support to his words. But I can see some who look sullen and angry, and sit back with their arms folded. *Ervys's followers*, I think.

"You are speaking the truth, Karrek," says Faro calmly. "I am Saldowr's *holyer* and his *scolhyk*. You all know how Saldowr is now. He cannot leave his cave. His wound refuses to heal."

"I have not visited Saldowr, but I have been told this," says Ervys, as Karrek swims back to his place. "But tell us, Faro," he goes on smoothly, but with an underlying eagerness in his voice, "is there more we should know? Is Saldowr's condition worsening? I hear rumours that he may be readying himself for the journey to Limina—"

"No!" cries Faro. "Never! Never, Ervys!"

Ervys waits again, as Faro's cry dies away in the huge space of the chamber. Limina... that's where the Mer go when they're ready to die. Faro took me there once and I remember how the old and the sick waited on the white sand, patrolled by guardian seals. Faro told me that they were waiting for death. Limina is very peaceful – even beautiful in a way – but it's on the other side of life.

Once the Mer cross that threshold, they can't come back.

Saldowr mustn't go there! Saldowr holds the secrets of the past and the future. What would happen to Ingo without Saldowr? How can Ervys even think of suggesting that Saldowr might be ready to go to Limina?

"Everyone goes to Limina one day," says Ervys, as if he's read my thoughts. His voice is calm but the words are like a clash of weapons. What does he mean? Is he trying to suggest that Saldowr is not so special, that he is just one of the Mer like any other? But that's not true. I know in my bones that it isn't true. Saldowr has power – he has magic that Ingo needs.

"Saldowr is the Keeper of the Tide Knot," says Faro boldly, as if that answers all arguments. But even I know that it doesn't, not now that the Tide Knot has broken.

Sure enough, Ervys continues smoothly, "But the Tide Knot did not hold. Can Saldowr help us now, when we have to face the – consequences?"

Faro's face is dark with fury. "Who is there to take his place, Ervys?" he demands. The question flashes through the chamber like the blade of a sword. The Mer begin to mutter. Ervys holds up his hand.

"We are not here to debate Saldowr," he says. There's nothing wrong with the words, but the meaning behind them is another weapon-thrust. Ervys is hinting that Saldowr can be put aside. He has lost his power, and decisions can be made without him now.

"Then what are we here for?" I ask. Both Ervys and Faro stare at me in surprise, as if they've forgotten I'm here. "What *are* we here for?"

Ervys folds his arms.

"We are here because the Kraken is awake," he says.

Again the ranks of Mer lift their hands. This time they cross them as Faro did in the face of the Claw Creature. Their crossed hands touch their foreheads, hiding their faces. Their index and second fingers are crossed too.

"Raise your hands, Sapphire," says Faro urgently. "Ward off the evil."

I begin to raise my arms, but it doesn't feel right. Why am I doing this? I look at Ervys and Faro, who have crossed their own hands. I shake my head, although they can't see me. "The Kraken," I say, tasting the ugliness of the word. "Who is the Kraken?"

For a long moment, no one answers. Very slowly the hands uncross, and the Mer settle back as they were before.

"The Kraken lives in the Deep," says Ervys. "He sleeps, and while he sleeps the Deep does not trouble Ingo. As you know, none of us visits the Deep. None of us has ever seen the Kraken. But we know that he has woken before, in the time of our far ancestors."

"How long ago?"

"About ten life-spans."

Ten life-spans... how long would that be? Six hundred years, or maybe seven hundred. But suddenly I realise that I don't even know how long the Mer live. I've been assuming that they live as long as humans, but maybe that's a mistake. They might live a hundred and fifty years – or fifty.

"What does the Kraken do when he wakes?"

"Don't you know?" asks Ervys, in a voice that says, *Can you really be as stupid and ignorant as that?*

"Nuclear warhead," I say. Ervys stares at me in bewilderment. "Chemical weapons," I go on.

"Sapphire, what are you saying?" asks Faro.

"Don't you know?"

There's a silence, and then Ervys gets the point. Again his face stretches unwillingly into a smile. "The Kraken is a creature of the Deep," he says.

"A monster?"

"We Mer have never seen the Kraken," says Ervys carefully, as if even to put the Kraken into words is dangerous.

"But then what – what kind of thing is it?"

And why is it so frightening? I want to ask, but I don't dare. The atmosphere bristles with terror. The Mer sit as still as if they've been carved into their seats.

Faro says, "Some say that the Kraken is like us. That he has Mer blood. But he belongs to the Deep, and the Deep has taken his Mer nature and made a monster of him. No one can look on him, Sapphire. The sight of the Kraken would freeze your blood and make your body as cold as the dead."

"But if none of the Mer have ever seen the Kraken, how do you know that he's a monster?"

Ervys puts up his hand to silence Faro, and takes control. "The Kraken was seen once, in the time of our ancestors, when he came up to the borders of the Deep to claim what was his. Our Guardian saw him in a mirror, and since then the Kraken has never even been glimpsed. He cannot endure to be seen. He struck our Guardian with a cold curse that took a hundred moons to heal."

"Guardian… do you mean Saldowr?"

"Saldowr!" says Ervys, and this time he can't hide his jealousy and contempt. "I am talking of what happened ten life-spans ago. What was Saldowr then?"

A mutter of protest rises in the back of the chamber. Faro clenches his fists. I know Saldowr *could* have been there. Ten life-spans might be nothing to Saldowr, just as hundreds of years seem to be nothing to Granny Carne. But Ervys doesn't want to believe that Saldowr has such power.

How much support has Saldowr got here? No one stands up to challenge Ervys openly. I wish they would. I wish I could. I'm hot with anger inside, but I daren't let Ervys see it. Not yet. I'm not strong enough, and this is Ervys's territory. Even Faro says nothing, although his head is thrown back and his eyes blaze through the water.

"But if the Kraken stays in the Deep, and the Mer don't go there…" I say hesitantly. I can sense the fear but I still don't understand why it's so strong.

"You speak from ignorance," says Ervys.

This is too much. I don't care if he's on his own territory. I don't even care that his arms ripple with muscle and one blow from his tail could kill me. I'm not letting him get away with this.

"So would the Mer speak from ignorance, if they came into the human world," I answer him. "Even you, Ervys. You asked me to come here. I've visited the Deep, which none of you have. If you want my help, why not explain things to me instead of telling me how ignorant I am?"

I'm out of breath by the time I've finished, and scared of what I've said, but still glad that I said it. I wait for Ervys to explode, but he doesn't. He looks at me measuringly.

"I see how you were bold enough to go into the Deep," he says at last. "Listen. There are things we prefer never to speak about, but we must put them in open words now. The Kraken has the power to destroy our world. The thunder of his voice can split the sea bed, release the tides, destroy Ingo, and send flood and terror even into your world. When the Kraken broke the Tide Knot he was barely whispering. We cannot wait for him to roar. He must be calmed. He must be put back to sleep. And there is only one way to do it."

"What – what way?"

There is silence in the chamber. Even Ervys doesn't

seem to want to answer. A tense silence, crawling with dread.

"Only one thing can send the Kraken back to sleep," says Faro, in a low, toneless voice. "A boy and a girl must be sacrificed to him. This is what happened in the time of our ancestors."

A low moan ripples around the ranks of the Mer. I don't want to believe it. Surely it can't be true. The Kraken hasn't woken for hundreds of years; Ervys said so. Stories get distorted. Maybe there was an epidemic of a sickness which killed children, and the Mer believed that they were sacrificed to the Kraken. Dad used to say that's how all legends start. *They have a seed of truth in them, Sapphy, and the seed grows as the story gets passed from mouth to mouth.*

For a second the thought of Dad is so strong that it's like hearing his voice. And then I remember the baby. Dad's new family. My little half-brother, fast asleep in his cradle of rock, so peaceful and trusting. A Mer baby with a Mer father who's left the human world. Just as in the old legends…

That legend was real, though, wasn't it, Dad? It grew and grew until it swallowed you up. Maybe the Kraken is real too. I want to believe that it's a myth that has grown into a monster because of the dread that the Mer have of the Deep. But perhaps it's true.

A boy and a girl…

"They are taken to the border of the Deep, to the

point where the Mer can go no farther," says Ervys. The pain and horror in his voice makes me feel a stab of reluctant sympathy for him. "They are left there for the Kraken. This is what happened in the time of our ancestors."

But how could anyone give their children to a monster?

The thought floods my mind and I don't know if I've said it aloud or not.

"No one loves their children more than we do," says Ervys, "but unless we sacrifice to the Kraken, then the whole people will die. Not just the Mer, but all who live in Ingo. Unless we can find another way."

All who live in Ingo... Dad's face floats in my mind. I scan the ranks of the Mer, searching. Some of them must know Dad. Maybe Mellina's family are here, too. It gives me the strangest feeling. Do *they* know if Dad is happy or unhappy here? Would they know if he wanted to leave Ingo and return to the human world? Conor thinks the Mer are keeping Dad here against his will. I want to believe it too, but sometimes it's hard. If only I could be as sure as Conor that Dad is waiting for us to bring him back to the human world...

Suddenly Ervys's final words take hold in my mind. *Another way.* What way does he mean?

"We know from the whales who visit the Deep that the Kraken is growing impatient," Ervys goes on. "The breaking of the Tide Knot was not enough for him. If we are to put the Kraken back to sleep, it must be done quickly. If we can find another way – if we can avert the sacrifice – then we will do anything."

"But the Mer can't visit the Deep. How can you put the Kraken back to sleep if you can't get near it?"

"*We* cannot," says Ervys, with the faintest emphasis on the first word. "But we believe there is another way. Farther back in time, more than fifty life-spans ago, the Kraken woke and ravaged Ingo for more than a year. But the sacrifice was never made. Mab Avalon put the Kraken back to sleep."

"Who – what was Mab Avalon?"

Ervys shakes his head. "That memory is not clear. He did not belong to us. He came to Ingo and then he departed for his own world."

"What world was that?"

"After fifty life-spans even we Mer find that memory has dissolved much of what happened."

Fifty life-spans, I think, trying to work it out in my head. If the Mer live about seventy years, as humans do, then that's about – about three thousand five hundred years ago.

"Mab Avalon," I repeat. The name is rich in my mouth. I'm sure I've never heard it before, but it has a strange familiarity. "Ervys… did Mab Avalon come from my world? The human world?"

"He survived the Deep. He returned peace to Ingo. He was Mab Avalon," Ervys intones.

It is so frustrating. I want information, and Ervys just keeps on repeating the same things.

At that moment Karrek swims forward again, plunges to touch the Stone, and comes up to us. This time he faces me and speaks directly to me. "We don't know what world Mab Avalon came from," he says, "but he was cleft, like you. Memory tells us that much."

He gazes into my eyes, his face grave, and then nods and swims back to his place.

Ervys looks thunderous at this interruption, but he quickly covers his anger and takes control again.

"We know that Mab Avalon was able to enter the Deep," he goes on smoothly, as if Karrek hasn't spoken. "We know that after a great battle, he subdued the Kraken. At least once in our history the Kraken has been calmed without the loss of our children."

"You can't ask her to do that," breaks out Faro's voice. And then I understand.

"We are asking," says Ervys.

They are asking... Yes. All those faces turn to me. They're still heavy with dread, but now there's some hope in them too. They're hoping that Ervys is right and that there's a chance I can do what they can't.

Mum always says that people will do anything for their children. They'll walk over fire for them. But what if walking over fire doesn't make any difference? What if it's someone else who can do the only thing that might protect your child?

"But – but *I'm* a child. I mean, why wouldn't the Kraken..."

Think I'm the sacrifice, is what I mean, but I can't get the words out of my mouth. The idea is too horrible to bring into the open. *And I'm most certainly not Mab Avalon*, I want to add. It sounds like a warrior's name from an old story. Someone in old-fashioned armour, carrying a sword. Nothing to do with me, Sapphire Trewhella of Trewhella Cottage, Senara Churchtown, West Penwith, Cornwall... *Why not add The World, The Universe while you're at it*, I think, and nearly giggle in spite of everything.

The Mer have got completely the wrong idea if they think I'm going home to fetch my trusty sword and whack the Kraken over the head with it.

"You are too old to be a sacrifice," says Ervys.

A wave of relief washes through me, and then I notice the strained, desperate looks on the faces of the Mer women. Some of them cover their faces with their hands. Maybe they're the mothers of young children...

Suddenly I'm afraid. Terribly afraid. There are hundreds of the Mer, and I'm alone. And they all want one thing. *People will do anything for their children*. If I don't give the Mer what they want – or if I *can't* do it – then what will they do?

I have never felt so isolated.

And then I feel an arm around my shoulder. Faro is at my side. He turns and looks into my face as if Ervys and the whole chamber of the Mer don't matter at all. He speaks as if we're alone.

"I'll go with you, Sapphire," he says.

"Go where?"

Faro looks intently into my face, my eyes. "Into the Deep. We have to stop the Kraken before it grows so strong that nothing can stop it. We've got to stop the sacrifice."

"But you can't enter the Deep, Faro. You're Mer."

Faro tosses back his hair. "I can try."

He is so brave. He's already been hurt before, trying to go to the Deep to find me. The Deep nearly crushed him, and yet he's ready to brave it again. But it won't work, I know that it won't work. No one has more courage than Faro, but courage isn't enough on its own.

All the Mer are looking at me hungrily. Wanting. Needing. I'm being hit by wave after wave of pressure. But they can't make me do this!

I've got to think clearly. Of course. Why didn't I realise it before? I need Saldowr. And Conor. I've got to talk to Conor.

"I must see Saldowr," I say firmly.

"Saldowr!" Anger leaps into Ervys's face. Quickly he smoothes out his expression. "But what help can *he* give? Saldowr is sick and weak."

Faro makes a quick, outraged gesture at this disrespect towards his teacher. Quite a lot of the Mer don't look happy about it, either. There are frowns and mutters. I lay my hand on Faro's arm warningly. Strength is rising in me again, now that I've got the beginning of a plan. I don't trust Ervys. He wants me to help the Mer, but it's for himself as well. If he can defeat the Kraken by sending him back to sleep without sacrifice, than he'll be famous in Ingo, and more powerful even than Saldowr, maybe—

"I must see Saldowr," I repeat, looking Ervys in the eyes. "Faro and I will go. We need to hear his wisdom."

It's scary to outface an adult and a leader among the Mer. My voice wants to shake, but I'm not going to let it. I'm not going to let Ervys use me to increase his own power. *You want me to help you*, I think, *you want me to risk my life in the Deep. You think that because I'm a human and a child you can make me part of your plan. But I knew Saldowr long before I met you. If I go to the Deep, it won't be for you.*

Ervys's brows knit with anger. His tail lashes the water, lightly, like the tail of a lion when it spots an oryx on the plains. He'd like to pounce on me. He'd like to punish me for daring to take Saldowr's side against his, but he can't. However much he wants to brush Saldowr aside, Ervys can't deny me if I say I need to talk to him. The Mer assembled here are afraid and desperate, and they believe that I'm their only chance. If the Kraken really has woken, they'll do anything to make it sleep again. And besides, they aren't all on Ervys's side.

Faro's eyes glitter. Ervys dared to speak insultingly of Faro's teacher in front of all the Mer. He's made an enemy of him now. I know Faro well enough to understand that he'll do anything to stop Ervys getting what he wants.

"Will you waste our time by consulting a sick healer?" Ervys demands, making his voice ring until the chamber fills with water echoes. "Will you give the Kraken more time to gather its strength?"

His face blazes with conviction. He throws back his shoulders proudly. Some of the Mer are nodding, some even raise their fists in what looks like a salute. But I notice that others look doubtful. Some are even turning away. And there's Elvira, right at the back of the chamber, her anxious, imploring gaze fixed on us. She's afraid too. She doesn't trust Ervys; I know it.

It's not enough just to stand up to Ervys. I'll make an enemy of half the Mer gathered here. They'll believe what he tells them, that I don't care about saving Ingo from the Kraken. I've got to make them understand. Ervys won't listen, but maybe some of these others will.

I jack-knife into a dive, down to the floor of the chamber, to the Speaking Stone. I touch it. The cool solidity of the stone clears my mind. By the time I've swum up to Ervys and Faro again, I know what to say.

"It's true that I went to the Deep," I say slowly, talking not to Ervys now but to all the Mer. "And I came back alive. But it wasn't my own power that did it – at least I don't think so. The Deep let me – it was the Deep that chose not to destroy me. And then there was a whale..."

My heart lightens at the memory of the whale. She was so huge, like a rough-skinned mountain. So motherly. And she had such a terrible sense of humour. The whale didn't have to help me, but she did. She brought me back safe from the Deep.

The Mer think it's just about being able to enter the Deep, but it's much more than that. You have to be able to find your way, once you're there.

"So you see I have to talk to Saldowr. I can't just *decide* that I'm going to the Deep; I'm sure I can't. But Saldowr will know what to do; I know he will. And my brother..."

Conor was the only one who could read the writing that healed the Tide Knot. I can't do all this alone, or even with Faro. I've got to have my brother with me.

"My brother will come to Saldowr with me," I say as firmly as I can. "I must talk to my brother first, and then we'll go to Saldowr."

Murmuring fills the chamber. The ranks of Mer sway as if strong currents are pulling them this way and then that. Ervys watches them, his arms folded, his face stormy.

It seems a long time that the argument ebbs and flows without words, and then a Mer woman with long white hair leaves her place and swims forward slowly, dives to the stone and rises to speak. Her face is lined with age. Ervys bows his head a little, in unwilling respect.

"The child is human," she says. Clearly age doesn't diminish the Mer habit of stating the obvious. But she has a face I trust. "She is human, but we know by her presence here, by the fact that she can live in Ingo like us and not drown like her human brothers and sisters, that she is also Mer. Her blood is mixed, her fate is mixed, her knowledge is mixed."

Every time she says the word "mixed" she sounds as if she's striking stone against stone.

"We see things that are hidden from this child, but she sees what we cannot see. If she says she must go to Saldowr before she can help us, then we must accept her words or risk losing our only hope against the Kraken."

As soon as she's finished speaking, the old Mer woman swims slowly back to her place. There's a ripple of approval. More and more Mer nod their agreement. Suddenly I understand how the Assembly works. They don't vote, they are like a tide moving. And now the tide is running my way. They're deciding to believe me.

Ervys knows it too. The tide is too strong for him to swim against it.

"Let her go to Saldowr then," he says harshly, as if the decision is his. But we all know that it isn't. The power of the assembled Mer has been stronger than Ervys's will.

If Faro weren't in the middle of the Assembly

chamber, I know exactly what he'd do. He'd flip into a series of triumphant somersaults, whirling so fast that all I'd see was the gleam of his tail and the cloud of his hair. As it is, he gives me a quick, sparkling glance which says, "We won."

The decision is made. The waters of the Chamber swirl as the Mer rise from their ranks of seats, and start to swim upwards, towards the roof of the Chamber where light filters down. So that's the way out. Maybe it leads to the south entrance, the one Faro talked about. He said it was easier than the tunnel route we took. I hope so. The thought of going back through that cramped tunnel makes me shiver. I want to get home. I want to talk to Conor.

The Mer stream past me. Their tails flicker and their hair fans out as they go by. They don't talk to each other. No one lingers. There's fear on many faces. They want to get home too, to make sure everyone's safe: the children, and those who are too sick or weak to make the journey to the Assembly.

It's the Kraken who puts so much fear on their faces. He's far away, but he's everywhere in people's minds.

I reach out for Faro's hand. The rush of the Mer swimming past me makes my eyes blur and my head dizzy. So many of them. Young men, old women, groups of Mer who look so alike that they must be brothers or sisters, or cousins. They stream past us. All the faces are tense.

What if I can't do it? What if I can't help them? And I've got to go to the Deep, where the pressure of the ocean makes you feel as if you're being crushed as thin as a piece of paper. And there's no life... only the creatures of the Deep, and I don't know any of them.

And the Kraken. The Deep is his home. It's so dark down there that I won't be able to see him or touch him until I'm—

Don't think of it. The whale, that's who I've got to think about. The whale who looked like a monster with her sides as tall as a cliff. I was afraid of her, but she helped me.

"Sapphire," says a voice close to me. A figure pulls away from the flowing current of the Mer and swims to me. Her hair swirls back from her face.

"Elvira, is Mellina here?" My voice comes out harshly. I can't help it. Why shouldn't I be angry with the woman who stole my father? I push away the memory of Mellina's gentle, welcoming smile, when I saw her face in Saldowr's mirror. Long ago, before the Tide Knot broke and the flood came, and the Kraken stirred in the Deep.

Saldowr, Mellina, my father, the Deep. They're all connected but I still can't see how. It's all happening too quickly. I shake my head to clear my thoughts.

"Mellina," I repeat. "Is she with you?"

"No." Elvira hesitates. "Sapphire, I have something to give to you." She opens her hand. "I carved this. Will you give it to Conor for me?"

It's coral. It's a tiny figure, a young Mer man. The body is perfectly carved, but the face has no features. It could be anyone. There is a tiny hole through the tail.

"Take it," says Elvira. "It's for Conor."

I'm not sure I want to touch it.

"It's a talisman," Faro murmurs in my ear. "It brings good fortune. Take it, Sapphire."

I stare at the little coral carving in Elvira's palm. She smiles at me. "Will you give it to him, Sapphire?"

The carving is so fine. It must have taken hours to make this little figures out of hard coral.

"Please give it to Conor," says Elvira.

Suddenly the thought crosses my mind that the carving might be a charm, with magic in it to pull Conor to her, the way Mellina drew my father from Air to Ingo. Is it safe to take it? I hesitate again.

"Please, Sapphire. It's for Conor's good," urges Elvira. Can I believe her? But if it's a talisman, as Faro said, I can't refuse it. Conor might need it. *Good fortune.* Something tells me that we're going to need all the good fortune we can get against the Kraken.

I've never even heard of the Kraken before today, but something deep inside me recognised his name with a chill of fear. As if long ago, in another life, someone told me about the Kraken, in the way that human mothers tell stories of giants and ogres and witches...

The difference is that the Kraken is not a creature of myth. The fear in the Chamber is real and solid. *The Kraken is awake...*

My hand goes out, and takes the talisman.

CHAPTER FIVE

t's a grey evening, close to darkness, by the time I am out of Ingo. I shiver and stumble as I scramble up the rocks. Faro's gone, and the rough grey surface of the sea hides everything.

Why didn't I leave some dry clothes up on the rocks, above the tide line? *Because you didn't know you were going to Ingo, of course, you idiot.* And now I'm freezing, shaking and shivering as I climb over the grassy lip of the cliff and start to scramble up the path. Bony fingers of last year's brambles snatch at my hands. Up the path, up the track. What's going to happen when I get home? I've been gone for hours. I was sitting in the sun when Morlader came to fetch us, and now it's evening.

I reach our gate, dodge in past the rowan tree and through the door. We never bother to lock the cottage unless we're going away.

I hope no one saw me running up the track with water dripping off my clothes.

"Conor? Mum? Roger?" I call. But I know they aren't there. You can always tell if home is empty, because it has a completely different feeling. My voice echoes as if the cottage is a shell. I hurry up to the bathroom, strip off my clothes, find a towel and rub myself all over until my skin tingles. I'll have to put on some of the hand-me-down clothes I hate wearing. And rinse my wet clothes quickly, to get the salt out of them before they shrink.

Mum mustn't know. I put on an old pair of jeans that's slightly too big for me, and a green top that's about the best of the hand-me-downs. I clatter downstairs with my wet clothes in a bundle, quickly shove them into the washing machine and turn it on to Rinse and Spin.

Conor must still be down at Rainbow and Patrick's, with Sadie. Mum and Roger have been over at Porthnance for hours. They must be buying up the town. Or maybe they're just "getting a bit of space". That's what Roger says sometimes: *Your mum and I need a bit of space.* It's extremely irritating, considering that Conor and I are out of the house most of the day. How much space do they need?

I make a mug of tea and a banana sandwich and carry them to the table. My body is limp with fatigue. It's not swimming that's worn me out – I can swim for miles in Ingo and not notice it. It's the tunnel, and being so afraid, and then the tension of the Assembly and the battle of words and wits with Ervys. At least Faro and I didn't have to come back through the tunnel. We came back the way the Mer usually go. It takes longer, but it's much gentler. I couldn't have faced the tunnel again. It's easier when you do things innocently, for the first time, before you realise how tough they are.

Oh no, Conor's carving is still in the zip pocket of my trousers! I punch the washing machine programme button and drag out the clothes. Water flops on to the floor but I don't care. I unzip the pocket, and there's the talisman. I lay it carefully on the table while I mop the floor, put the clothes back in the drum and restart the machine.

I sit down again. Under the electric light the carving is more beautiful than ever. I study it dreamily, admiring the strong curves of the Mer tail, the flowing hair, the line of the diving body. I know just how he feels as he plunges through Ingo, swooping through the water like a razor blade through silk. No, not really like a razor blade. Ingo welcomes you, and silk would never welcome the blade that cut it. Sometimes I have a very strange feeling that Ingo longs for me just as much as I long for Ingo. As if we need to be put back together in order to be whole. I must talk to Faro about it...

And then my eyes light on the headline of the newspaper that someone's spread out on the table.

"New flood defence scheme for St Pirans!" it shouts. As if anything that humans can do would hold back the tides. I pull the paper towards me to read more, and that's when I realise. It's the *Cornishman*. But the

Cornishman comes out on Thursdays, and it's Wednesday today. This must be last week's paper.

I stare at the date. It's impossible. I blink, but the figures stay the same. I am looking at a newspaper which comes out tomorrow.

How long have I been gone? I've got to speak to Conor. But the flood took his mobile and he hasn't got enough money yet for a new one. I've got to talk to Conor before I speak to Mum, then I'll know what's happening. If I've really been gone for a day and a half, then Mum will have contacted the police and the coastguard and everyone. But there's no sign of that. The cottage is undisturbed. I remember what it was like after Dad disappeared, with neighbours and men in uniforms everywhere, and phones ringing.

There's not even a note for me on the table. Mum would have left a note, surely. She wouldn't have just thought, *Oh well, Sapphy's been gone for thirty-six hours but no worries, I'll go and have a bit of space with Roger.*

I know for sure that Conor went to Rainbow and Patrick's. They might know something. There's a landline number for them somewhere, if their landline is back on yet after the flood...

It is. I find the number in our phone's memory, and to my relief there's a normal dialling tone. After six rings, someone picks up.

"Hello?"

It's Rainbow.

"Rainbow? It's Sapphy. Is Conor still with you?"

"Oh, hi, Sapphy." Her voice is relaxed, friendly, unconcerned. "How are you? Are you coming over?"

"Um, no, not just now – listen, Rainbow, can I have a word with Conor if he's there?"

"Sure, wait a minute, he was here a second ago—"

And I hear Conor's voice in the background, "Rainbow, can I take the phone in the kitchen?"

The phone is passed over. I hear footsteps and the door shutting. He's gone into Rainbow and Patrick's little back kitchen. I hold the phone, listening. Conor doesn't say anything at all, but I know he's there because I can hear him breathing.

"It's me," I say at last. "Are you all right?"

"*Am I all right?*" says Conor quietly and furiously. "What do *you* think, Saph? You've been gone since yesterday."

"I was fine though, Conor, I was in—"

"I know where you were."

"Conor – Mum, does she know?"

"She'll be at work now. She thinks you're here with me. I called her yesterday and said you'd decided to come down to Rainbow and Patrick's and help out with the cleaning. And then it got late and so we all stayed over. But *that's it*, Saph. It's the last time I lie for you. Next time you can tell your own lies."

"Conor, I—"

"I don't want to hear it. Rainbow and Patrick don't know anything. If they meet Mum, and Mum says something about you being here, they're going to think we're both liars. Why don't you ever *think*? Why do you just plunge in and do whatever you want?"

I can't find an answer to this. I look down at the talisman lying on the kitchen table.

"Elvira gave me something for you," I say quietly. I hear a sharp intake of breath.

"What? What is it?"

"I can't really describe it. I've got to see you, Con."

Suddenly there's a flurry of barking in the background. I hear a door burst open, and Rainbow's voice apologising, "Sorry, Conor, Sadie was desperate to get to you. I couldn't hold her back."

The barking grows louder and louder.

"Steady, girl, it's all right, I haven't gone away – get down, you crazy dog – *Sadie!*"

"Let me talk to her, Conor."

"She knows I'm talking to you, that's why she's going nuts. Here, Sadie."

A volley of barks hits the phone. I hold it away from my ear, then when Sadie calms down I say, "It's all right, Sadie girl, I'm here. I'm back. I'm coming to fetch you."

She understands, I know she does. She whines, deep in her throat, with a mixture of pleading and relief in her voice.

"Conor? Conor, listen, I'm coming down now. I'll ride your old bike. I've got to talk to you."

"It'd better be good, Saph," says Conor grimly, "and for God's sake don't forget the bike lights."

I nearly make the mistake of leaving a note for Mum to tell her where I've gone. But just in time, I remember that I'm supposed to have been there all the time. But my clothes are in the washing machine! Mum is bound to notice that. She'll know I was here in the cottage, and not in St Pirans all the time...

I've got to think. Mum's at work, Roger's off somewhere – I've got to make it look as if I never came back to the cottage at all. I check the bathroom, then drink the cold mug of tea, finish the banana sandwich, wash up the evidence carefully and put away the mug and plate. By this time, the washing machine's programme is almost finished. I wait impatiently while it chunters through an endless slow spin. At last the red light switches off and I can open the door. I stuff the clothes into a plastic bag and hide them in the garden, under a gooseberry bush, in case Mum checks my room. I'll put them out on the line tomorrow.

Now I've got to think about how to get to St Pirans. I've got Conor's old bike, but I can't ride through the village in case Mum looks out of the pub window and sees me. Even if she doesn't, someone could easily come in and say, "Just saw your Sapphy biking off St Pirans way."

It's nearly dark. It'll be all right if I wear a hoodie and crouch down low over the bike. There's a grey hoodie somewhere in the stuff we've been given. Even if someone sees me they might not recognise me.

Some hope of that. Everybody knows everybody else in Senara Churchtown. You can't sneeze without someone at the other end of the village asking if you've caught a cold, that's what Mum says.

I'll just have to ride fast. It's much too dark to risk going back to St Pirans by the coast path. I close the cottage door, wheel the bike out of the shed, and set off up the track.

I make it past the pub, past the church, past the little row of cottages that clings to the graveyard, and on up the lane that leads to the St Pirans road. The evening light is thickening. It's almost dark now. My bike light wobbles ahead of me, lighting up the narrow lane and the thick hedges. I pedal hard, but it's a long, steep climb out of Senara, and I have to slow down. At least no one's seen me so far—

One moment she isn't there, the next she is. Granny Carne, stepping out into the lane as if she's been hiding in the hedge, just waiting for me. As if she knew I was coming this way. She raises her hand, and my bike wobbles to a halt.

"Where are you going so late, my girl?"

"Oh, just down to St Pirans to, um… see some friends."

Granny Carne surveys me. Her eyes have a shine on them like an owl's at night.

"Strange," she observes at last. "Your mother told me you'd been down St Pirans since yesterday. And now here you are with your hair full of salt and tangled like seaweed. Gloria Fortune told me she'd seen you coming up the path, coming away from Ingo."

"She can't have said that! Gloria doesn't know that Ingo exists."

"She doesn't know its name, that's true. She said you looked strange, as if you were coming out of a dream. You were coming up from the cove, she was sure of that. She's desperate to get down to that cove, Sapphire. More and more every day she wants it, and if it wasn't for that bad leg of hers she'd have climbed down long ago. You know what she'd find there. But I'm working with the bees to keep her here where she belongs, Sapphire, and don't you go disturbing my work."

This is so unfair. Granny Carne can't really believe that I'm trying to tempt Gloria Fortune into Ingo. I've been so careful. I've said nothing. It's not because I want to hide Ingo from her, but her life will never be the same once she realises that she has Mer blood. What if she disappears, as Dad did?

Granny Carne's amber gaze pierces the dusk as if it was daylight. Suddenly she pounces.

"What have you brought out of Ingo with you, my girl?"

"What – what do you mean, Granny Carne?"

"You have something with you. I can feel it. Something that's not made by human hands."

Of course, the coral carving that Elvira made. That's what Granny Carne means. The Mer figure for Conor. But how does she know? It's hidden away in my pocket. It's as if she can sense there's something close that doesn't belong to Earth.

"Show me," says Granny Carne commandingly.

I get off my bike and prop it against my leg on the grass verge. The handlebars swing towards me and the bike lamp lights up my hands as I reach into my pocket and carefully bring out the talisman, which I've wrapped in one of Dad's old handkerchieves. I unroll it carefully. If I drop the talisman here in the long grass, I'll never find it again.

There's the little Mer figure. He looks more alive than ever. The lamp-light catches the strong curve of his tail and his diving arms. A sudden breeze blows up and the grass shivers. In the distance an owl hoots.

"Show me, Sapphire," repeats Granny Carne.

I hold it out to her.

I hear her intake of breath. She bends over to see more clearly. I can smell her smell of honey and lavender and wood smoke. Her lined, seamed face is stern as she pores over the talisman.

"Do you want to hold it, Granny Carne?"

"No, my girl. It's not for me to hold such a thing. No need to tell me where that came from. So it's not enough for you to go to Ingo now, forgetting Air and Earth and all that belongs to it. You have to carry Ingo with you, even when you come back to us. Don't you see how far away from us you're travelling?"

I'm about to explain to Granny Carne that the carving is for Conor, not for me, but something holds my tongue. Granny Carne sees the Earth side of Conor. She trusts Conor. She even let him talk to her bees. She'll stop me taking Elvira's talisman to him, in case it binds him to Ingo. But I've already told Conor about it, and I know he'll want to have it, because Elvira made it for him. It's better if Granny Carne believes that the little carving is mine.

But I'm not going to lie to Granny Carne. Her eyes would soon search out a lie. I just close my fingers around the carving again, and slip it back into my pocket. I don't bother to wrap it with the handkerchief; I just want to get the talisman out of Granny Carne's sight.

"So you went to Ingo again, and from the look of it you didn't like what you found there," says Granny Carne. Even though I'm trying to hide the purpose of the carving from her, the quietness and the darkness makes me feel that I can confide in her.

"Granny Carne, someone told me a story about a

monster who lives at the bottom of the – the world. It has to have a sacrifice or it will destroy everything. Nothing else can stop it. And so people have to – they don't want to but they have to—"

"Yes," says Granny Carne calmly, "I know that story."

"*You* know it? But how?" How could Granny Carne have heard about the Kraken? She is Earth and Air. I'm as sure as I can be sure of anything that she has never entered Ingo. It's not in her nature. Granny Carne is the opposite of Ingo.

"It was a long time ago," she continues. The bike lamp carves deep shadows on her face. "He lived in the bowels of the earth. Some said he was a man, some said he was a bull. Or he was part-man and part-bull. They said you could hear him bellowing like thunder miles away, whether in anger or in pain nobody knew. For years he would be still and silent, and then he would roar for sacrifice. Unless there was sacrifice, he would shake the earth until their houses were rubble and their families trapped in the ruins.

"So, like you said, Sapphire, they didn't want to but they had to. They had to put him back to sleep, and there was only one way."

Gooseflesh creeps over my skin. The way Granny Carne tells the story, you would think it was happening here, now.

"Stones were put in a bowl," she continues. "One stone for each child in the city. All the stones were white except for one red stone. And then a cloth was laid over the bowl. The parents came forward one by one. There'd be a father or a mother from each family. One by one, they put a hand under the cloth and picked out a stone. The red stone meant that your child was the sacrifice."

As Granny Carne speaks the picture of the past grows sharp, like a landscape when the mist clears. The parents must have trembled with fear as they put their hands under the cloth. You would hardly dare look down at your hand to see what colour the stone was. And if it was white you'd want to jump up and punch the air with joy. But you wouldn't do that, because the red stone was still in the bowl and that meant that someone else's child had to be the sacrifice.

"But why didn't they all join together? They could have fought the monster."

Granny Carne shakes her head. "They couldn't fight the earth-shaker. If they tried, all the children from the city would die when the houses tumbled and the walls fell on them. But if one child was sacrificed on the altar, then the monster was satisfied. He went back to sleep, deep in the earth."

Her words whirl in my head. *"Sacrificed on the altar! But that means – that means those people killed their own children!"*

"It's true that human hands held the knife," says Granny Carne. "A man who had no children, he did it. But no one blamed *him*. It was the monster who brought death to that child. The monster forced the sacrifice."

"But how could they do it, Granny Carne? How can parents let their own children be killed?"

Granny Carne draws herself up to her full height. "Don't you be so sure that the present is stronger and wiser than the past. They did what they had to do. If you'd seen the faces of those mothers and fathers, you'd understand."

If you'd seen the faces... I stare at Granny Carne. She's done it again. She's made it sound as if the past is as much her home as the present. As if she really saw those faces with her own eyes. And perhaps she did. I shiver, imagining Granny Carne ranging back and forth across time, like a owl with all-seeing eyes.

"But the Mer would never do that," I say aloud, remembering Mellina and her tender face as she looked after her Mer baby. "They don't sacrifice their children. It's the Kraken who takes them."

"Yes," says Granny Carne thoughtfully, "and what I'm telling you of is long ago and far away, Sapphire. And now you're back from Ingo, talking of the Kraken. He's awake, then, is he, my girl?" She says it as matter-of-factly as if the Kraken were a dog that had been sleeping by a fire.

"Yes."

"He's been sleeping a long while. It was time, I suppose." She sighs wearily. "So it's all got to be gone through again, has it? And this time they want you to be part of it. But remember this. You can choose, Sapphire. No one can make a path for you and force you to travel down it. No, my girl, no matter how much the Mer charm your heart away, remember that your blood is equal. Half Mer, and half here in the Air with your feet planted on Earth. They sing very sweetly in Ingo, my girl, but don't let your own voice be drowned."

I shiver again. It's cold standing here and my bike's heavy. I'm tired and I want to go home. But I can't go home. If I do, Mum will know I was never in St Pirans. I've got to cycle the miles to town, and face Conor's anger.

"You can come home with me, Sapphire," suggests Granny Carne, as if reading my thoughts.

I can't do that. I've slept at Granny Carne's cottage once, and that was enough. There's too much Earth magic in her white rooms that are folded away under the Downs, with her hives and her vegetable plot, the fire that never goes out and the Book of Life where words fly like a storm of angry bees if you disturb them. I don't belong in Granny Carne's cottage.

"I've got to go to Conor, Granny Carne."

Granny Carne walks with me up to the St Pirans road. My bike wheels squeak and pebbles crunch and rattle. A vixen barks in the distance, and the sea sighs from the bottom of the cliffs. The sounds make the night feel huge.

"Best ride quick now, my girl, before your battery

fades," says Granny Carne. And then she reaches into the pocket of her shabby old earth-coloured skirt. "I have something here for you before you go," she says, and opens her hand to show me a little bunch of shrivelled berries.

"What are they?"

"Rowan berries. Fruit of the rowan tree."

"From last autumn?"

"Maybe last autumn. Maybe longer. I don't call it to mind exactly. Take them, my girl. The rowan brings protection, didn't I tell you that? Conor's got his talisman."

Yes, but that's the wrong way round, I want to protest. Conor's got something from Ingo, that Elvira made. But Conor belongs more to Earth than I do. And now you're giving me something with Earth magic in it, which can't be much use to me in Ingo.

"Go on, take it."

Even my hand is reluctant. The rowan's pushing me away again, as it did in our garden. I don't want to touch it.

"Take it."

I can't disobey Granny Carne. I force my hand forward and suddenly the barrier gives. The little spray of berries is in my palm. The rowan berries are dark and wrinkled, but when I touch them they feel warm, as if the sun is still glowing on them. That's because they've been in Granny Carne's pocket, I tell myself quickly. I put them in my own pocket, although I don't want to at all. Still, I can throw them away when I'm out of Granny Carne's sight.

"Put the berries somewhere safe. Wherever you go, take them with you."

"Even to Ingo?"

"Even to Ingo. Don't ask me the why of it. Keep them safe and keep them hidden. Don't let anyone know that you've got them."

"But won't they go soggy in Ingo?"

Granny Carne laughs. "They've more life in them than that, my girl. My rowan berries are more than a match for salt water."

"Can I show them to Conor?

"Not Conor, not anyone. Keep them safe."

She raises a hand in farewell. One moment she's there, and the next she's melted into darkness. I get on my bike again, and push off. The road is steep and I have to pedal hard just to keep going. I don't look back. The berries seem to burn in my pocket, but I already know that I won't dare throw them away.

CHAPTER SIX

I t's late. Conor and Sadie and I are sitting by the fire. The electricity isn't back on yet in Rainbow and Patrick's cottage because the whole place needs rewiring after the flood. They are using candles and a paraffin lamp, and a solid fuel stove that heats the water too.

I'm sitting on a cushion on the floor, and Sadie's head is on my knee. Her eyes are half shut; she's snoozing, but not really asleep. I stroke her head gently, rhythmically. She didn't like the talisman. She growled at it when I took it out of my pocket and gave it to Conor.

Conor likes it, though. He's sprawled in one of the baggy old armchairs Rainbow and Patrick got from the Salvation Army. They lost all their furniture in the flood. Luckily their floors are stone downstairs, so they've scrubbed clean. Conor has been helping to prepare the walls because they're redecorating everywhere. There's a big can of white emulsion in the corner. Someone donated it, Conor says.

It's very peaceful. I feel a long way from Ingo, even though Rainbow and Patrick's cottage is built right on the shore. That's why it was hit so hard in the flood. A lot of structural work had to be done before they could even move back in.

Rainbow's mum and Patrick's dad aren't here. They're off in Denmark again, where Rainbow's mum was born – at least, I think that's where they are. They came back after the flood to make sure everything was OK, but they only stayed a few weeks. They've got work out there, and they want Rainbow and Patrick to come over to Denmark too. Rainbow was talking to Mum about it one day. Patrick works in a surf shop and studies, and Rainbow does her music and all her other stuff. Patrick wants to be a doctor and he already knows which uni he's going to apply for later on. They want to stay here, not go to Denmark.

They're at a band rehearsal now. Rehearsals go on really late, Conor says. It's a new band and Rainbow's the lead singer. I didn't even know Rainbow could sing. Not sing properly, I mean. I wonder what kind of voice she's got.

I'm tired and the fire is warm. I could just lie down beside Sadie and fall asleep—

"Saph," says Conor abruptly.

"Wha – what?"

"I've been thinking."

I haven't told Conor everything yet. He was so angry when he opened the door. It didn't seem a good time to tell him about the Deep and the Assembly and the Kraken and everything else, all jumbled up with blame and anger. I gave him the talisman as quick as I could, so that he'd think about Elvira, not about what I've been doing.

It worked. I don't think he's angry now. He's frowning, but only because he's studying the talisman so closely.

"I wonder if I can find a chain that's fine enough to go through the hole," he says.

"You mean you're going to wear it?"

"Of course. That's what it's for."

"Conor, what *is* a talisman for?" Faro said it brought good fortune. I wonder if he's right.

"It protects you," says Conor. "It's made for one person and it only works for them."

"How do you know?"

"I read about soldiers in the war who had them. A special medallion on a chain round their necks or something like that. There was a story about a man who was shot just here" – Conor touches his neck below the collarbone – "but he was wearing a holy medal as a talisman and it deflected the bullet. He'd have been killed without it."

I stare at Elvira's little carved figure, nestling in Conor's hand. It doesn't look enough to stop a bullet. "They probably work differently in Ingo," I say.

"I could try that jewellery shop in Market Street..." goes on Conor dreamily, his forefinger stroking the talisman. I want to shake him.

"Conor, before the others get back..."

Conor stretches and yawns. "We'll have to stay here tonight. Look at the detail on the carving, Saph! Isn't it amazing? Do you think Elvira did it herself?"

"Probably," I say sourly, "since she's so talented."

"Look at the expression on his face. I can't believe anyone could carve anything so fine."

The hairs on the back on my neck prickle. "But Conor, there isn't any expression. Look – his face is blank."

"You're not looking at it properly. Shift Sadie off and come round here. You don't get the candlelight down there."

Reluctantly, I shift Sadie's warm, heavy weight off my legs. She whimpers in protest.

"Poor old Sadie – look, it's all right, you can lay your head on my cushion."

The candlelight wavers as I go round to the back of Conor's chair.

"Don't stand like that, Saph, your shadow's falling on it. Move. Look. Now can you see?"

I stare at the smooth face of the carved Mer man. It's blank, expressionless. It could be anyone. But as I watch a ripple spreads over it, like the bulge of the swell under the sea before the waves break.

"There! You saw it, didn't you?"

"Um, I'm not sure..." No. It was an illusion. The face is featureless.

"You know, Saph, it sounds unbelievable, but I think – don't you think he looks a bit like me?"

"No, Conor!"

The words snap out of me, sharp and fearful, before I even know they're in my mind. Sadie bounds to her feet and whips towards us, barking.

"Get down, you crazy dog, get down!"

"She's not crazy. She doesn't like it, that's all. She's scared of that talisman."

I drop to my knees and wrap my arms around Sadie's neck to comfort her. She's growling deep in her throat.

"Come on, girl, it's not going to hurt you."

But Sadie won't stop growling. In the end I have to drag her into the little back kitchen to calm her down. "You stay here, Sadie darling, then you won't have to look at that horrible talisman," I whisper in her ear, before I go back into the living room and shut the door.

"He does look like me," says Conor again, softly and wonderingly as he stares at the talisman like someone staring at a hypnotist's pendant.

I reach out and snatch the carving from his palm and put it in my pocket. "*Now* can we talk."

Conor rubs his eyes the way he does when he first gets up in the morning, then grins at me. A normal, friendly Conor grin instead of the dopey talisman-struck expression.

"So. About the Deep," I begin in a businesslike way, like a teacher giving out homework.

But just then there's a rush and rattle at the door before it bursts open, and Rainbow and Patrick spill over the threshold.

"I was first!" yells Patrick.

"No you weren't. You cheated. Sticking out your foot to make me fall over in the sand doesn't count."

It's good to see serious, responsible Patrick carrying on the way Conor and I do.

"Being first is what counts, not how you get there," announces Patrick with satisfaction.

"I'll remember that," says Rainbow. "Is that really the time? It's nearly midnight. We had such a great rehearsal, Sapphy, you'll have to come along next time. Do you play guitar like Conor?"

"The only instrument she plays is other people's emotions," says Conor, "and the triangle. Go on, Saph, tell Rainbow about your starring role in the primary percussion band."

"Thanks, Con."

"You look as if you could sing, though," says Rainbow. "Can you?"

"I used to sing with Dad sometimes."

"Did you? What kind of songs?"

"Mostly traditional."

Rainbow warms her hands at the fire. "Sing one of them. I'll join in if I know it."

The way she says "Sing one of them" you'd think it was the easiest thing in the world just to stand there and open your mouth and let the song out. As if nobody would ever be shy or embarrassed or think that their singing wasn't good enough. And Patrick seems to feel the same. He's sitting on the hearth rug emptying sand out of his trainers, but he glances up and says, "Yes, let's hear something. Rainbow'll probably know it too."

Songs flit through my mind. Not *O Peggy Gordon*. It's too powerful, and besides it gives away too much. *I wish I was away in Ingo*... no, I can't sing that here. But there's one I can.

"It's an Irish song," I say slowly. "Dad used to sing it at the end of the evening at the pub." I pause, and take a deep breath. It all comes flooding back to me, from when I was little and would be let sit in a corner table with Mum sometimes, when the air was late and smoky, full of laughter and talk. I'd clutch a packet of crisps, and Conor and I would sit still as mice in case anyone remembered about us and ordered us home.

And there was Dad's face, shining and happy. Sometimes he would sing without accompaniment, sometimes he'd play a few chords on the guitar as well. But his voice was the thing. It was full and strong and it had something in it that stilled the talking and the laughter and made faces grow dreamy.

"Go on, Saph," says Conor quietly. "It's *The Parting Glass*, isn't it?"

"Yes."

I draw in my breath slowly. The first line comes out uncertainly, but then my voice steadies and I forget about myself and only remember the song.

Of all the money e'er I had, I spent it in good company;
And all the harm I've ever done, alas 'twas done to none but me;
And all I've done for want of wit, to memory now I can't recall,
So fill to me the parting glass, goodnight and joy be with you all.

Of all the comrades e'er I had, they're sorry for my going away,
And all the sweethearts e'er I had, they wish me one more day
*   to stay,*
But since it falls unto my lot that I should go and you should not,
I'll gently rise and softly call, goodnight and joy be with you all,
Goodnight, and joy be with you all.

When I reach the end of the song I realise that Rainbow hasn't joined in. The words echo in my head. *But since it falls unto my lot that I should go and you should not...*

When Dad sang those words, did he guess that would be his fate? He would rise and go, and we would stay. But he didn't leave joy to us.

The firelight blinks and dazzles. I look down to hide my eyes.

"Why didn't you join in, Rainbow?" asks Patrick. "You know that song."

But Rainbow shakes her head. "It wouldn't have been right. Sapphy's voice is different from mine."

"It's a good voice," says Patrick, "it makes you want to listen."

"Your voice went well with Dad's, Saph," says Conor.

"Yes." Dad's voice was strong, but he knew how to modulate it so it didn't drown mine. I'd forgotten what it felt like to sing with Dad.

No, I hadn't forgotten. I'd just put it out of mind, with all the other things I couldn't bear to think about, now that Dad was gone.

They are sorry for my going away...

Dad could never, never have known how much sorrow his going away would bring to us. I stare into the fire, remembering that night when we waited and waited, and Dad didn't come home. Conor and I sat huddled on the stairs, listening, hoping until there wasn't room for hope any more. Conor grew up that night. I don't know if I did, though. I don't feel any more sure of myself than I used to.

Conor and I shouldn't ever be angry with each other. We should stick together. Ingo has taken our father. We can't let quarrels over Ingo take us from each other.

I lift my head, and smile at Conor. His expression is

faraway and thoughtful, but slowly it opens into a smile. It's the kind of smile that says, *Let's be friends; let's not argue any more. I don't know what we were quarrelling about anyway.*

"You should be in our band, Sapphy," says Rainbow. "What about you, Conor? Do you sing?"

Conor laughs. "You don't want to hear me. My voice is like a frog's. Gribbet, gribbet, gribbet. They didn't even let me into the school choir."

I laugh too. Conor is like Mum. They sound like a couple of bees bumbling along together when they try to pick up a tune. It's quite a nice sound but you really wouldn't call it singing.

No, Saph. That isn't true. Remember. Remember Conor singing to the guardian seals, and calming them with his power. How strong and sweet his voice was then. The memory swirls in my head. I can almost hear the notes and the mysterious words that Conor sang.

My head jerks up.

"But you *can* sing, Conor!" I blurt out.

Everyone stares at me.

"Um, I mean, your voice isn't that bad," I add hastily. It sounds lame. And there's Sadie scratching at the kitchen door. Why are we leaving her out? She doesn't understand it. She gives a plaintive whine.

"She needs to go out," I say with relief. "I'll take her."

"I'll come with you," says Conor quickly.

Rainbow and Patrick are going to get out the camping mats and sleeping bags. I'm sleeping in with Rainbow,

Conor with Patrick. It's strange to be in a house where there are no adults to decide things or arrange things for you. It's true that Patrick is sixteen, but Rainbow is only my age. And yet here she is checking that there's enough milk for morning, and finding a towel for me. It's strange but I quite like it, and Rainbow seems to think it's completely normal.

Conor and I walk Sadie down the silent night-time streets. Sadie walks on my right side, as far from Conor as she can get. She knows that he's got the talisman back, and it's in his left pocket. She doesn't like it, even though she's calmed down a bit now. She bristled when he brushed against her, coming out of the door.

St Pirans is still only half-alive after the flood. You can't see all the damage by the light of the streetlamps, but a lot of families still aren't back in their homes. They are staying with relations, or in bed-and-breakfasts. The town is midnight quiet. The streetlamps make wavery shadows on the walls so that it looks as if someone's hiding there, waiting to jump out. Our footsteps tap on the cobbles, and Sadie's claws patter. We are heading away from the sea, uphill.

"So tell me," says Conor.

"Tell you what?"

"Everything you haven't told me. What really happened when you were in Ingo?"

And so I tell him. It's easier to talk when we're side by side, walking in the dark. For a long while after I've finished, Conor is silent. We walk on to a patch of waste ground and wait while Sadie does her business. When she's finished, we walk on again. Sadie doesn't care how far we go; she's delighted to be out and she keeps glancing up at me as if to say, *Good, you're showing sense for once and not dragging me home after twenty minutes. Maybe I'm getting you trained at last.*

Conor doesn't suggest going back to Rainbow and Patrick's yet, and neither do I. We keep walking, through the dark, quiet town. St Pirans feels as empty as the drowned village Faro once showed me. At last Conor sighs deeply, as if he's come to a decision, and then he says, "You're not going to do this alone, Saph."

"But I've got to. I'm the only one who can go into the Deep."

"We don't know that for sure."

"Faro got hurt just trying. The current threw the two of you aside."

Sadie's walking close now, rubbing against my legs as if the night is suddenly too big for her. She knows when we talk about Ingo, and she doesn't like it. I reach down and pat the back of her neck.

"I'm going to see Saldowr," says Conor. "If there's a reason why you can enter the Deep and I can't, then I want to hear it from him. Even if there's a real reason, we still might be able to find a way. You know what the Mer are like, Saph. They think everything's fixed and it can't change. They're so... so *rigid*. You went into the Deep, therefore you're the only one who can ever go into the Deep. They need you and so you've got to do what they want. Why should they care what happens to you as long as they get what they want?"

"They do care about me, Conor! Faro does."

"Maybe. But you've got to remember, Saph, Faro's not human. He's not a boy with a tail. He's *Mer*. And we still don't really understand what being Mer means."

"We should do."

"You mean because of our Mer blood? All right, I'm not arguing with that, we've got Mer blood. But what does that mean? Think about it, Saph. We were *born* human. Mum hasn't got a drop of Mer blood in her, anyone can tell that. It comes through Dad from our ancestors, and that's way back. We've lived in the human world all our lives. It's like someone whose great-great-grandfather came from Russia to Britain about a hundred years ago. OK, their descendants have got Russian blood, but they probably wouldn't speak a word of Russian and they'd be lost if they ever went to Russia."

"We've been to Ingo."

"Yes, but this is our home."

I'm not going to quarrel with Conor. Deep down I'm sure he knows that what he says is only half the truth. If we're so human, how come our father has chosen Ingo, and become one of the Mer? Conor can argue logically, but the pull of Ingo overpowers logic.

"But Saldowr's easy to talk to," goes on Conor thoughtfully. "And he really listens, too. You know how some people only listen because they want to hear what they already know? Saldowr's not like that."

"Mmm..."

"*You're* not listening, are you, Saph?"

"I am! You were talking about Russia and Saldowr and..."

But what matters to me is what Conor said at the beginning. *You're not going to do this alone, Saph.* Is it really possible? If Conor could come with me, everything would be different.

Conor's going to talk to Saldowr. Maybe they'll agree that I can't make that terrifying journey to the Deep alone. Whatever happens, I'll have Saldowr's wisdom and Conor's courage and loyalty on my side. I know I should be strong, but it's so much harder than you think when you're reading about someone else's dangers and adventures. I want so much to believe that Conor can come with me.

"I think that's why Elvira gave me the talisman," says Conor unexpectedly.

Elvira gave you that talisman because she likes you. Haven't you worked that out yet? I want to say, but Conor goes on, "A talisman is for protection. People used to give them to soldiers going into war. Why would I need protection unless I was going into danger?"

CHAPTER SEVEN

I'm sitting on the doorstep with a mug of tea. The sun hasn't come round yet, but I've got Sadie to keep me warm. Everyone else is still asleep.

I didn't sleep well, and I woke early. My head is still crowded with dreams about the Kraken. In the dreams I was swimming down, down, down through the waters of Ingo. I couldn't see the Kraken, but all the time I knew he was there like a huge shadow, waiting for me. The water grew cold and dark and I was alone, still swimming down, down into the jaws of the Kraken...

I woke up with a jerk. My heart was pounding. I thought I could hear a roaring sound, like the noise of a bull. But it was the sea. I was in Rainbow and Patrick's cottage, that was why the sea was so loud. After that I didn't want to go back to sleep again.

I'm still cold. Sadie knows it, and she pushes closer until her head is on my knees, warm and heavy.

"It was just a dream, wasn't it, Sadie?"

Sadie lifts her head and considers me intelligently. *You want me to tell you the truth?*

"Yes, Sadie, tell me what you think."

Sadie whines, deep in her throat. The short hairs on the back of her neck rise, as if she's seen inside my dream, and seen the Kraken lurking there, waiting to get me.

"No, you don't like it, do you, girl? You'd bite that nasty old Kraken if you saw him, wouldn't you?"

Suddenly I get a picture of Sadie diving down with furious devotion, seizing a shadowy corner of the Kraken with her teeth, and looking at me for approval. I can't help laughing. Sadie looks outraged.

"I'm not laughing at you, Sadie darling. You're the best dog in the whole universe. Come here."

I hug Sadie and she wriggles forgivingly in my arms. I push my dream away firmly. The tide is out, and the surf is breaking in a tumble of white beyond the Island. Sadie and I have already been for a walk, but she can't go on the beach because it's after Easter now. *No dogs on the beach after Easter Sunday.* What gave humans the right to decide that?

Sadie is so warm and comfortable. I think she's going to sleep. I might just shut my eyes for a minute. Conor and I didn't get back until past one, and I was awake again at half past five...

"Sapphire?"

I jump violently and Sadie springs up, barking.

"Roger!"

"Sorry I scared you. I didn't realise you were asleep. Hey now, Sadie, where's the fire?"

Sadie loves Roger. I think she realises that it was Roger who persuaded Mum about me having a dog. She knows he doesn't let her jump up at him, so she stands still, quivering with pleasure, while he strokes her.

"I wasn't asleep, I was just…"

"Resting with your eyes shut. I know. I came down to check on you kids because your mother got worried in the night. She couldn't sleep."

"We're fine, Roger, we just had a bit of a late night, that's all."

Roger's shrewd, penetrating eyes stare down at me.

"I guess you did," he says at last. "Conor still sleeping?"

"Yes. They're all asleep."

"All except you, hey? You know what they say, Sapphy. A bad conscience keeps you wide awake."

I look up at Roger as innocently as I dare. "What do you mean?"

His gaze sharpens. "You may fool your mother, but you don't fool me. You've been up to something, Sapphire."

"What do you mean?" If I don't admit anything, he's got no evidence. He's just guessing. He can't know where I've been. As far as Roger's concerned, I was in St Pirans all the time, with Conor.

"I saw Gloria this morning," Roger goes on. "She was up early too. Her leg was paining her. She reckons she's going to have to have that hip operation soon, whether she wants to or not. She asked after you, said she'd seen you coming up that path from the cove yesterday evening but you didn't hear her call. She said you looked as if you were in a hurry. She asked me if everything was OK."

"Um, did she say anything else?" *Anything about soaking wet jeans and dripping hair, for example, on a cold April evening?*

Roger shakes his head, still looking at me hard. "Nothing else."

So Gloria didn't betray me. She didn't tell Roger that I looked as if I'd been in the sea.

"Fact is, young lady, you *couldn't* have been on that path, could you? Conor told us you were here with him. So was Gloria seeing things? Or is there some other girl who looks like you and can't keep away from that cove any more than you can?"

I wish I could see inside Roger's head and find out what he really knows. Or what he suspects.

"You're up to something," Roger repeats quietly. "I'm sorry to think that you've got Conor lying to cover up for you, Sapphy. I'd have believed better of him."

"Conor's *not* lying to cover up for me!" It's true. Conor's lying to protect Mum, not me. If she knew about the Kraken and the Deep, she'd be terrified. Why can't Roger realise that it's better not to know too much, better not to ask questions, better just to leave us alone? He can't help us. He's too – much too *human*. All he'll do is get in the way.

"You know, Sapphy, I thought you and I were getting to be friends. I wish you'd see your way to trusting me," says Roger. His voice is flat and disappointed. He thinks Conor and I are shutting him out of our lives. Maybe that's true, but he doesn't understand that it's for a good reason.

"Well, I'll be on my way. I can tell your mother I've seen you and you're safe and well, so maybe she'll get some sleep now."

This makes me feel sad, guilty and angry all at the same time. Why does Roger say things like that? I don't want to think about Mum lying awake and worrying over us. I don't want to think about Roger being disappointed in me.

"We'll be back as soon as Conor wakes up."

"Make sure you are."

The early morning brightness is fading. The line of the horizon is sharp: probably it's going to rain. With a pang of regret, I watch Roger walk away up the beach.

Roger thinks I am a liar who doesn't care about Mum's feelings, or about making Conor lie to cover up for me.

Mum thinks she believes that we've been in St Pirans for two nights, safe together. But in the night she doesn't believe it. She's afraid. She feels we're in danger. Mum knows things that she doesn't know with her conscious mind, just as Conor could read the writing on the Tide Rock.

Conor thinks... What does Conor think? He believes that the talisman is a message from Elvira, telling him that he has to go into the Deep, and into danger. Conor believes that he's got to look after me.

Rainbow thinks I am her friend. But I hold so much back from her. I have a lot of secrets that I never share with Rainbow or anyone else in the human world. Can it be a real friendship when half of me is hidden from her?

Gloria Fortune knows I was in the sea, but she didn't say anything. Why not? Usually adults tell each other things like that. Maybe, without knowing it, she's loyal to Ingo.

Faro... Faro's thoughts slip away from me like bright tropical fish flickering in and out of rock crevices. My mind aches with trying to catch them. Sometimes Faro is so close to me that it's as if we share the same thoughts and dreams. So close that we don't need words. He calls me his little sister, and it's true that sometimes I feel as if I've know Faro for ever, and we grew up together. And then suddenly he's a stranger, completely at home in a world where I don't know if I truly belong or not. Faro is unswervingly loyal to Ingo. He won't stop me going to the Deep if it will help the Mer. Would Faro risk my life to save his people?

Granny Carne knew instantly that the talisman wasn't made by human hands. Her senses are as sharp and quick as Sadie's. You can't deceive Granny Carne, even if you want to. I can't get her story out of my head. All those people, lining up to choose a stone out of the basket. Reaching under the cloth, and praying that their fingers would light on a white stone. But someone had to get the red stone. When Granny Carne talked about those people it didn't seem like distant history, safely over, with all the suffering dissolved into time.

I could see them so clearly. Their faces were creased with fear. Their fingers trembled. The children stood watching, some of them too little to understand what was happening, some of them old enough to be as frightened as their parents. The bull under the earth was roaring for sacrifice. Imagine if you were one of the victims waiting to be chosen.

Someone has to get the red stone. Someone has to get the red stone.

The words drum in my head, louder and louder. But just as they are becoming unbearable, Sadie intervenes. She growls softly, deep in her throat. Not an angry growl, but a warning. It's the growl she makes when someone she doesn't know comes down the track past our cottage. It says, "I'm here. I'll protect you. I'm not going to let anything hurt you."

I put my arms around her and hug her soft warm neck. The growl is still rumbling in her throat. I rub my face against her muzzle. You don't ever have to worry about what Sadie thinks. Sadie would never betray anyone she loved. Her kind of love doesn't have any doubts or complications in it. It's as solid as sunlight.

"I'm so glad I've got you, Sadie girl."

CHAPTER EIGHT

Have you ever noticed that the things you worry about most beforehand often turn out easily? Going to see Saldowr is like that. Saturday morning is beautiful. More like June than April, says Mum as she hangs out the washing. I help her with the duvet covers. A blackbird is singing in the rowan tree. Mum's singing too, through a mouthful of pegs. She sounds more like a bumble bee than ever. The washing flaps as Mum hoists the line up high with her clothes-pole.

"There, that's done," says Mum, dropping the spare pegs in the basket. "What a perfect day. You wouldn't think people would choose to spend it in a dark old pub, would you? But I suppose it's lucky for us that they do, or I wouldn't have a job. I'll be back by six, Sapphy."

Mum works so hard. Roger says she doesn't need to. He earns good money and he'd like her to take it easy. But Mum won't agree. She confided in me one evening:

"Roger's very generous, Sapphy, but you and Conor aren't his responsibility. I don't want him to think he's got to support you. Anyway, I like earning my own money. It's good to have your independence, Sapphy, I hope that you'll always have it. Girls these day can do anything they want to. Don't let anything stand in your way."

Mum's eyes shone with fervour. Any moment now she'd start telling me about how I could pass all my exams if I really tried, and go to uni. And then I could get any job I wanted, with proper training. Sometimes Mum gets angry with herself because she didn't do any of these things, and so she's determined I'm not going to "throw away my chances", as she calls it.

But Mum surprised me that evening. I was waiting for her to go on to the familiar "do your homework, Sapphy, your teachers keep saying you've got potential but you won't pass your exams unless you concentrate" routine, but she didn't. She was quiet for a while and then she said, "I depended too much on your father, Sapphy. I didn't realise it at the time, but I do now. It wasn't fair on him."

It was a long, long time since I'd heard Mum talk about Dad like that, in a voice that was thoughtful instead of harsh with grief and anger. As if Dad was a real person in our lives again, instead of someone she couldn't even mention without getting upset about the way he'd disappeared and left us. I waited, but although Mum gave me a quick little smile, she didn't say any more. But it was good. It made me feel that I was allowed to talk about Dad again.

Mum's longing to go to college one day. She's the opposite of me: she can't wait to study hard and do exams. Maybe she'll be able to fulfil her dream of becoming a nurse one day. She sent away for some booklets about nursing training, and she spent the whole of an evening reading them. She even read bits out to me and asked what I thought. I could imagine Mum doing it. She isn't that old, and I think she'd be good at it. But for now we need the money and so she works in the pub.

It was good talking to Mum like that. When she hugged me goodnight, she said, "It's nice now you're growing up, Sapphy. I can talk to you."

"There," says Mum, looking with satisfaction at the washing as it flies high in the air and begins to flap in the breeze, "that lot will be dry in a couple of hours."

This is when Conor comes out into the garden and says we're going down to the cove. We'll make some sandwiches, and take our swimming stuff. The sea is at its coldest in February, and it hasn't warmed up much by April, so for Mum's sake we take our wetsuits. (We'll dump them in the garden shed on the way out. You don't need wetsuits when you're going to Ingo.)

Mum is more relaxed about the cove these days.

Since the flood in St Pirans, she's stopped believing that she can keep us out of danger if she can just keep us away from the sea. St Pirans turned out to be no safer than the cove, after all. She asks about the tides, just as she always does, and we reassure her that we know exactly when high tide is. We'll be safely up on the rocks long before that. We won't get caught out by the rising tide.

"Oh, well then," says Mum, "I'll see you after my shift. Roger should be back by six too. If it keeps on as fine as this, why don't we have a barbie in the garden tonight?"

Have a barbie? Mum is sounding more like Roger every day, and she's never even been to Australia. Roger lived there when he was a child, and even though he's been in Britain for years, you can still hear the Australian twang in his voice.

There's a touch of Australian in his character too – at least, it's how most Australians who come over here seem to be. Really level-headed and easy-going, and good with everything practical. (Maybe if I went to Australia I'd get a shock – there must be some bad-tempered ones who can't even change a light bulb.)

Last month Roger bought a gleaming steel barbecue on which you could cook Christmas dinner for ten. Conor and I are used to building driftwood fires on the beach inside a circle of stones. I like our fires best, but I have to admit that the Super Antipodean (this is what Conor calls it) is pretty good, too.

"A barbie would be good, Mum," says Conor.

"Will you take Sadie with you?" Mum asks.

"I don't think so," answers Conor easily. "It's a tough scramble down for her, and that paw isn't right yet. She'll be better off staying up here."

Sadie had a thorn in her paw yesterday. I took it out and dressed her paw with antiseptic, but she's still making a big fuss about it, limping around and wallowing in our sympathy.

"All right then," says Mum, "look after yourselves. I'll ask Roger to bring back some burgers."

She smiles at us. Suddenly I realise why she looks different. Mum isn't so thin any more. She's lost that pinched look. Her face is rounder... happier...

The cove glitters with morning sunshine. The sand's flat and hard where the tide has gone out. We leave our trainers and the bag with towels and spare clothes up on the rocks above the tide line, and walk in bare feet over the cold sand. I follow Conor's Man Friday footprints. We're the only people here, and it feels as if we're the only people in the world. Neat little waders walk along the sand, looking at us curiously but without fear. There are frills of seaweed, pearly little shells, and then a tangle of oarweed and plastic twine. Above us the cliffs loom, as old and hoary as dinosaurs.

There's a smell of salt and weed and coconut blowing from the gorse on the cliffs.

The whole beautiful morning belongs to us. For a moment I wish we could go back in time, two years back, before we even knew that Ingo existed. We'd play cricket on the hard sand, with a piece of driftwood for a bat, and a ball that Conor brought down in his pocket. We'd swim and explore the caves and I could make a mermaid in the sand, with seaweed hair and shells for eyes. Life was so easy then; or at least it seems easy when you look back. Maybe it wasn't at the time. I used to hate it when Mum and Dad had rows. I used to pull the duvet right over my head and sing to myself so I didn't have to hear them.

But time has moved on. My last sand mermaid was washed away two years ago. I wouldn't make another now that I know the Mer are real.

I am sure that Faro will be out there somewhere in the bright sea, waiting for us, and he is. As soon as I call his name, Ingo seems to race to meet me. Faro's dark head gleams above the waves at the mouth of the cove. He swims in quickly, his tail driving him faster than any human could swim. His face shines with salt water and laughter. It doesn't seem to have hurt him much to come through the skin to meet us.

"Faro!"

He lifts a hand in welcome, cuts through the crest of a wave and swirls to a stop where we stand waist deep in water. The sea doesn't feel cold today. The waves are fresh and alive, pushing against us, wanting us to play. Faro swims round us, lifts his tail, thwacks it down flat on the water and soaks us in spray.

"Good morning, little sister. Good morning, Conor." He smiles, showing teeth that are just a little whiter and more regular than human teeth ever could be.

"Give me five," says Conor. Faro doesn't know what this means, so Conor shows him and Faro's delighted. He keeps on going "Give me five" and slapping hands. You can tell he can't wait to try it on the other Mer. Maybe it'll become the new cool Mer thing to do.

And then it's the best moment of all. We look at one another, and decide without words that it's time. Time for Ingo.

I watch the waves. That's the one. I gauge its height as it rises to meet me, and dive into the cool green hollow beneath its crest.

The wave never breaks. I am in Ingo and the waves go on for ever. I follow the wave down, plunging through its green and turquoise curves, close to the white sand. I swim out, and the water above me grows deeper as the sand shelves, and then the sea bed drops away. I'm at the entrance of the cove. I follow the distant gleam on the sand, down into the deep water.

We are in Ingo. Conor and Faro are behind me, side by side. I glance back over my shoulder. Conor doesn't look as if he's struggling. Maybe he's been able to let go of the

Air more easily this time. His colour is good. He hasn't got the tinge of blue around his mouth that frightens me so much because it means he's not getting enough oxygen from the water. Faro's helping him, of course.

Ingo. Ingo. I reach out my arms and the sea rushes into them. Ingo welcomes us. *Myrgh kerenza.* I don't hear the words but I feel them. Dad called me his *myrgh kerenza*, his dear daughter, and I was angry with him. If I'm so dear, then why did you leave me? Why did you abandon us without a word? But I'm Ingo's daughter for sure.

Yes, Conor's strong in Ingo today, flying through the water side by side with Faro. The water feels so fresh and alive, teeming with bubbles as if spring has come in Ingo too.

"Close your eyes, Sapphire," says Faro.

"Why?"

"It's a surprise."

I close my eyes. Now I can feel how fast we're really travelling, in the westward current Faro has found for us.

"Hold tight."

And then it begins. The current starts to spin us over and over, like leaves in a waterfall. Whirling onwards, downwards, so fast that even my thoughts fly out of me and I'm free of everything but the rush of water. But it's not frightening. It's like being lifted beyond everything you've ever believed you can do.

And then we're there. The current spills us on to the

sand. I recognise this place. The Groves of Aleph, still devastated by the breaking of the Tide Knot.

The Groves are littered with boulders, debris and dead things. But look – there are shoots of green growing out of the torn stumps. These underwater trees have still got life in them. They're growing back. The destruction doesn't look quite so brutal now that a little time has softened it. Ingo can heal itself, I know it can, if it's given time.

But that's not going to happen. The feeling of spring is a delusion. Winter is coming, not summer. Those green shoots will shrivel. A long winter of pain and suffering and darkness will cover Ingo like a rolling tide. The Kraken is awake, and he's hungry. Ervys said that all the destruction we've already seen is just a shadow of what the Kraken is capable of doing.

Ingo has never seemed so beautiful to me as it does today, and it has never seemed so vulnerable.

"How did we get here without passing through the sharks?" asks Conor.

"They haven't returned yet," says Faro, as if this is bad news. "Saldowr is not strong enough to call them back to him yet."

Faro speaks with absolute confidence that Saldowr will grow strong again. But I remember the dismissive way Ervys spoke of Saldowr, as if he was already finished. Even to think of it makes me hot and angry. Who does Ervys think he is, to speak of Saldowr like that? I want to see Saldowr so much, even though I'm afraid that he'll be changed and weakened.

"Is he going to come out to us?" asks Conor. That's what Saldowr did before.

"Saldowr is in his cave," says Faro.

"But the cave was all filled with sand after the Tide Knot broke."

"I cleared it," says Faro.

"You cleared it! On your own?" asks Conor. He looks at Faro with respect. We both remember what Saldowr's cave looked like after the tides had ripped through the Groves. The cave mouth was completely blocked with sand. Faro must have worked for hours – days...

"Yes, I cleared it alone," says Faro proudly. "Who else should serve Saldowr? I am Saldowr's *scolhyk* and his *holyer*. Who else should take care of him and restore to him what is his? If everyone abandons him, I will not abandon him. And soon the sharks will return, and everything will be as it was."

"Do they have to?" I say.

"Of course," says Faro severely. "You must understand, Sapphire, that there have always been sharks to guard the Groves of Aleph."

"They weren't a great success as guardians, though, were they?" asks Conor. "It might be time to try something else."

Faro ignores this. "We must not keep Saldowr waiting," he says.

"But I thought we couldn't go into the cave. Last time we were here, Saldowr said—"

"He cannot move. There is no other way."

I think of Faro's words as we swim to the cave entrance. *Everything will be as it was.* But I don't believe them. It's like thinking that if Dad came home to us, everything would be the same again.

The weed that used to sway gently over the mouth of Saldowr's cave, hiding it, has all been stripped away by the tides. It hasn't had time to grow back yet. There's enough light to see by as Faro swims ahead of us, towards the back of the cave.

I'd expected Saldowr's cave to be magnificent, with glittering sea jewels set into the walls and a high vaulted roof and maybe a carpet of mother-of-pearl. But it's not like that at all. It's completely plain. The walls are granite, the floor is sand. It reminds me of somewhere else, but I can't remember where.

On a shelf of smooth rock at the back of the cave, Saldowr lies. His hair flows out in the water. It has grown longer and greyer since we last saw him. His cloak is wrapped tightly around his body, as if he's cold. Deep in their sockets, his eyes glow through the gloom.

"Welcome," he says, "I have been waiting for you. Come closer."

We swim towards him. In the green dimness his face is haggard. He stretches out his hand to me, and I clasp it. I can feel his bones.

"Saldowr."

"Yes, my child. I'm not a pretty sight, am I?"

"Are you ill?"

"The wound that the keystone gave me refuses to heal. Conor, give me your hand."

I move back, and let Conor take Saldowr's hand.

"My dear son," he says, and I catch a flash of feeling on Faro's face. Is he jealous? "We have work to do. Much work to do, and little time to do it. You know that the Kraken is awake."

A shiver runs down my back. "Yes," I say.

"And you, my child, have visited the Deep, and so the Mer are hungry for you. They believe that you can help them against the Kraken."

How strange. Saldowr talks of the Mer as "they", as if they are separate from him. I'm sure he didn't use to do that.

Saldowr's eyes search my face. How different he is from Ervys. Saldowr is not hungry for me. He doesn't see me as a means to an end. To Saldowr, I am still Sapphire. Myself.

"Will you do it?" he goes on casually, as if it's not even an important decision. Conor puts his hand on my arm.

"Saph won't go alone," he says.

"But, Conor, you know that you cannot enter the Deep." He still speaks lightly, but there's expectancy in his face too, as if he's testing Conor, waiting to see what his reaction will be.

"Who says so?"

Conor's challenge echoes through the cave. Saldowr nods, as if this is the answer he's been looking for. "You healed the keystone," he says. "You read its runes. If your spirit is still as strong, nothing is impossible. But now, Conor, show me what you have in your pocket."

Conor's as startled as I am. I knew he'd have brought Elvira's talisman. I don't think he's been separated from it since I gave it to him. But how did Saldowr know? Can he sense its presence, as Sadie can? Slowly Conor puts his hand into his pocket and draws out the talisman.

"Bring it closer."

Saldowr studies the talisman, but doesn't touch it.

"You can hold it if you want," says Conor.

"No, no. A talisman joins its fortunes to its keeper. Don't let anyone else touch it, Conor, now that it has come into your hands, or its power will weaken. Who carved this?"

"Elvira."

"Hmm. And what do you see in it?"

"It's one of the Mer, diving."

"And?"

"He has my face."

"He hasn't, Conor," I break in, "you're imagining it. Look, the face is blank, isn't it, Saldowr?"

I want Saldowr to support me and make Conor stop seeing things that only he can see. I don't want Elvira to have the power to carve my brother into a piece of coral.

Saldowr turns his gaze to me. "A talisman joins its fortune to its owner," he repeats mildly. "But you need a chain, Conor, so you can wear it openly."

"I'm going to get one."

Saldowr snaps his fingers, and immediately Faro is at his side. "Search at the foot of my couch," he orders. Faro dives to the foot of the couch, and a few moments later he comes up with a gold chain in his hand.

"I thought the Mer never took treasure," I blurt out.

Saldowr raises his eyebrows, "This is not treasure," he says. "It belongs to Conor. Look, Conor."

Conor gasps, and then I see why. I recognise the chain. "It's Dad's," Conor breathes. "It's the chain for his ring."

Dad never wore his wedding ring on his finger. He didn't like the feel of it. Sometimes he wore it on a chain around his neck. Not always, but he must have been wearing it that night.

"You are right. It is your father's. The Mer do not wear gold," says Saldowr, "and so your father gave it to me. He will be glad of this use, and I think the chain will fit the talisman perfectly."

Conor says nothing, but I can tell he's reluctant to take the chain. It's like – it's like inheriting something after a death. But where's the ring? Where's Dad's wedding ring?

"Saldowr," I say hesitantly, "you said that my father gave you the chain, but – but—"

"You want to know what happened to the ring," states Saldowr calmly.

"Yes."

"He gave it also into my safekeeping."

My heart lurches. Mum doesn't wear her wedding ring any more, either. She keeps it in a box.

"You can trust me with it," says Saldowr gently, and I nod, biting my lip. Saldowr turns to Conor.

"Your father would like you to have the chain," he says, and with sudden decision Conor takes the chain, fits on the talisman, and fastens it around his neck. Saldowr was right. It fits perfectly.

"And did no one give *you* a talisman, Sapphire?" asks Saldowr.

I stare at him blankly. "No. Elvira only carved this one."

"So you have nothing? No protection? No secret gift?"

"No," I say, and I mean it and believe it until a moment after the words have left my mouth. *No secret gift.* But there's the spray of rowan berries hidden in my jeans pocket. Not even Conor knows about that. It's not a talisman, it's just... just rowan berries.

But all the same I feel myself flush as Saldowr keeps looking steadily at me. "I see," he says at last. "In that case Conor's protection must cover you both. And where is he diving to, Conor?"

The tiny carved figure seems to hypnotise us all. It is so lithe, so powerful and so fearless. Diving down, down, down, through the bright seas of Ingo and then where the water grows dark and the weight of the ocean makes his body as thin as a sheet of paper and as heavy as lead...

"To the Deep," says Conor.

CHAPTER NINE

"To the deep," repeats Saldowr. He shifts his body slightly, as if he's in pain.

"Saldowr, your wound – isn't it healing?"

"No, my child. Not yet."

"But it will," I say. "It's got to. Can't you see a different healer?"

Conor nudges me, but he can't stop me. "You're not going to—"

"You mean, is it my time to go to Limina? No. I don't think so. I have things I must do before that."

He talks about it so casually. But going to Limina means dying. And how can Saldowr just let himself die?

"You cannot die, Saldowr!" says Faro fiercely. He kneels down, and clasps Saldowr's left hand in his. "You are our memory. Our Guardian. You protect Ingo. You cannot leave us."

"I'll have no choice in the matter," says Saldowr. "But

let's not talk of death. We are here now, and our tasks are urgent. That's what we must discuss."

His voice sounds stronger. Of course he's going to recover. I look at Conor questioningly, and he gives an almost imperceptible nod. It's time. The plan that began to shape in my mind back in the Assembly chamber is fully formed. Conor and I talked it over for hours last night. He said I'd have to put it to Saldowr, though.

"I can't do it for you, Saph. You're the one who's visited the Deep."

"But, Conor, you're much better at talking than I am. You can make people listen."

"No, Saph. You're the one who's been dragging both of us deeper and deeper into Ingo. You can't hide behind me now. You've got the bargaining power, and they know it."

It must be tough for Conor to say that, I thought. He's used to being the leader. I don't think it's fair to say I hide behind him, but it's true that I usually wait for him to do things first, and he's often the one who speaks up for both of us. Dragging him into Ingo, though... What about Elvira and her talisman? Hmm... maybe it wasn't the moment to mention it.

"You could pretend Saldowr was Roger," suggested Conor. "You don't usually have a problem with giving poor old Roger a mouthful."

Poor old Roger! *Hasn't Conor got eyes in his head?* I thought. *Roger's got exactly what he wants: Mum. I'm certainly not going to pity him.* But, showing heroic tact, I said nothing.

It was much easier to make plans in Conor's attic than it is to carry them out. I don't want to risk Saldowr's anger any more than I'd want to risk Granny Carne's. I spoke up in the Assembly chamber. I stood my ground against Ervys. But now I'm face to face with Saldowr, it's hard to explain the bargain I want to make with the Mer. Saldowr is so clear and straight seeing, like a crystal pool that makes everything else look muddy. Maybe, in his eyes, my plan will look like blackmail. But it isn't, I know it isn't. If we want to rescue Dad, this is probably the only chance. We can't miss it.

I listen while Faro explains to Saldowr about the Assembly. Saldowr's face gives nothing away. Even though Faro doesn't mention Ervys's disrespect, I have the feeling that Saldowr knows quite well that Ervys is against him, and trying to gain power among the Mer.

All he says is, "I see that Ervys has become the voice of the Mer," and there's a cool humour in his voice which makes me feel a little better. Ervys may think that Saldowr is helpless because he's lying here wounded, but he's wrong. He has to be wrong.

At last, when Faro has explained everything, there's silence. Saldowr closes his eyes, thinking deeply. How worn and old his face is. There are hollows under his cheekbones.

We're all gazing at him, longing for an answer. I

133

haven't mentioned my bargain yet. Somehow I can't bring myself to do it.

Saldowr's cave is still. Even the breaking of the Tide Knot hasn't completely shattered an atmosphere of peace that feels as if it's taken centuries to gather. Saldowr rules here, no matter how weak he is, and the tides are home again, safe under their rock, sealed by the keystone.

"There's no answer to the power of the Kraken," says Saldowr at last, opening his eyes. Conor frowns in disappointment.

"But we can't just let a monster do what he wants!"

"Did I say that we would? But although we may return the Kraken to sleep, we will never change him. He is not like you, capable of change for good or for evil. He may seem to alter, but his nature is fixed, and that is the Kraken's tragedy."

I'm not interested in feeling sorry for the Kraken. "Well, that's all we want to do, isn't it?" I ask. "Put him back to sleep, I mean. As long as he's asleep, he can't do any harm."

Saldowr smiles faintly. "You are right. I was talking of evil, and how it can never be finally defeated. You are speaking, very reasonably, of the present crisis. Are you willing to go to the Deep, *myrgh kerenza*, knowing what you know of it?"

Now is my moment. Now's the time to set out my bargain. But instead I look into Saldowr's eyes. I stop thinking of Dad. A different picture rises in my mind. A Mer woman with a child in her arms, weeping as if her heart will break. I can't see the woman's face because her hair swirls around her features. The child looks bewildered, and he's patting his mother's face, trying to calm her.

I hear myself saying, "Yes, Saldowr."

"Good." His eyes gleam, and I have a sudden suspicion that he knows all about the bargain.

"But, Saldowr…"

"Yes."

"I'm choosing, aren't I? It's a free choice. I don't *have* to go."

"No one can make you, my child. Not Ervys and all his followers."

"But you *will* go, Sapphire," breaks in Faro. "You are Mer in your heart. You want to help us. You won't let the children be—"

Saldowr's brow wrinkles faintly, and Faro is silent.

"It was a free choice," he answers me.

I take a deep breath. Now that I've agreed, I can say what I want to say. It's not bargaining, it's telling the truth. "But my father never had a free choice, Saldowr. He *has* to stay in Ingo now. The Mer say that it's breaking their law to let him leave. But why should it be? If I can choose to help the Mer, then Dad should have the choice to stay or leave."

Conor moves to stand by my side. "We're not

bargaining, Saldowr. We're not blackmailing the Mer. But our father came to Ingo and he was never given the chance to return. I don't believe he knew the consequences when he was drawn into Ingo by Mellina's singing. If Sapphire and I can choose to risk our lives to help the Mer, then our father deserves that freedom as well. Otherwise he's no more than – well, a prisoner."

"It sounds to me as if you *are* making a bargain," says Saldowr.

Conor's colour deepens, but he says firmly, "You can call it a bargain if you want. I call it fairness."

A glint of humour lights up Saldowr's face. "Sometimes you are very human," he observes. "But think carefully about what you bargain for. You may have to live with getting what you want."

Why does Saldowr have to talk in riddles? I think crossly. *Why can't he just answer yes or no?* We know what we want. Dad, digging the garden on a warm evening, or strolling up to the pub, or taking us out in the *Peggy Gordon*. Well, maybe not the *Peggy Gordon*, because she doesn't exist any more, but another boat that's just as good. And then everything that's happened since he went away will be just like a bad dream. We'll put our family back together again.

Roger wanted to get you a boat. You'll have to do something about Roger, won't you? says an inconvenient voice in my head. *Before you "put your family back together again". And you'll need to wipe Elvira from Conor's memory as well. And what about Faro? Do you want to lose Faro? That might be part of the bargain, too.*

But I'm not going to listen. I can think about all that later. And it's no good Faro looking at me like that, I'm not going to change my mind. If Dad was *his* father, he'd understand.

How gloomy the cave is getting. It can't be anywhere near evening yet – or maybe it can. Time might be flying through Ingo ten times faster than in the human world today. We could be caught by nightfall. "Conor," I whisper, "we'll have to hurry. It's getting dark."

But Saldowr turns his head painfully and looks beyond us, towards the mouth of the cave. "You have a visitor," he says.

The dark is still thickening. I can hardly see Saldowr's features. I look back at the entrance, and now I see that it isn't night that has caused the darkness. Something's out there, blocking the entrance to the cave.

For a horrible moment I think it's the Kraken. No, that's impossible. The Kraken doesn't leave the Deep. Maybe it's Ervys! He and his followers have rolled rocks across the cave mouth, and we're prisoners.

Don't be so stupid, Sapphire. Why would he do that? He wants you down in the Deep, not trapped in a cave.

"What is it, Saldowr? What's happening?" asks Conor sharply.

"A friend of Sapphire's has come to see her," says Saldowr, and we can all hear the amusement in his voice. "Her kind have never ventured into the Groves before. She is rather... large to enter my cave. She wants to see you, Sapphire. No, not you others. You must wait here. You'll have to go out to her, Sapphire. She's waiting for you."

My heart leaps. There can't be another visitor as huge as this. Can it really be her? I plunge past Faro and Conor to the cave entrance and out into the Groves.

Sides like a rough cliff. Vast bulk of a body that's built to voyage safely into the Deep. And looking at me from far above, with pride and recognition, her right eye.

"Whale! Dear whale!"

"Greetings, little barelegs." Her voice rumbles through the water and even though she's barely moving the sand on the sea floor swirls from her pressure.

"How did you know I was here?"

I swim up her side like a mountaineer. Her skin is grooved and carved like an elephant's. If I didn't know her I'd be afraid of her. She's so massive. One flick of her tail could easily destroy a fishing boat...

But she wouldn't do that. No, she's the one who's hunted and destroyed, if the hunters get a chance. She ought to hate humans, but she helped me.

"Ah, here you come," rumbles the whale comfortably. "You're no bigger than a speck of sand, but at least your mother has taught you manners. Never swim up to a whale from behind; that's not the way. It makes us nervous. Here you come – and now I've lost you. Where are you, little barelegs?"

"Under your... I think I'm under your chin."

"Up you come, that's the way. Dear me, can't you swim any faster than that? And now I've lost you again. It reminds me of when my own children were little and used to play hide-and seek-under my jaw."

"Did they?" I can't help thinking that this must have been quite scary. What if the jaw had opened and sucked them in – by accident, of course?

"It seems like yesterday. But they're still my babies, no matter how big they get. The tickle of those little flukes – you never forget it."

"I suppose they must be quite big now?" I scull the water, keeping level so that she can see me.

"Big enough, little barelegs. Your mother must be sad that you do not grow. You should keep your legs together, and perhaps they'll fuse into a tail. The dolphins tell us that it could happen. It's called *evolution*," adds the whale proudly.

I wonder how Mum would react if she were confronted by a daughter who'd evolved into a whale. Maybe my tail could fit into the bedroom, but then the rest of me would fill the garden – and go halfway to the cove…

"I think Mum's all right with things the way they are."

"She knows best, I suppose. I'd like to meet her. We'd have a lot in common, I'm sure."

Hard to imagine what they'd talk about, really. Mum would faint with horror if she could see me now, deep underwater, conversing with a whale. At least, I think she would. But on the other hand, Mum would trust this whale. She would feel the goodness in her. And I have a feeling that the whale is lonely. Her children must have all grown up and gone away. I wonder what it's like to be so huge...

Is Saldowr still keeping Conor and Faro back in the cave? I wish they were here. I want them to meet the whale. I stare back down her vast side, but I can't see them. I wonder why Saldowr didn't let them come. No one could think the whale could hurt anyone.

I swim round until I can look directly into her eye. It's impossible to look into both of a whale's eyes at once – unless, I suppose, you are another whale. You'd be made on the same scale, then.

"I am glad you remember me, little one. I thought you might have forgotten."

"How could I possibly forget you? I'd never have got out of the Deep without you."

"Ah well, we whales have certain advantages of size. It was no trouble," says the whale, and in spite of her hugeness she sounds shy as well as pleased.

This is my moment.

"Do you think – is it possible for you to help me go back to the Deep?"

The whale's dark, thoughtful eye considers my face. "Help you, little one? How will that help you? The Deep is no place for you. I thought you would have learned that."

She sounds so sure that I falter. Maybe she is right. Do

I really want to find myself back in that dark, formless place where I don't even know which way to look for the surface? If she won't agree to take me, then I can't go. No one can blame me. I'll have tried.

Don't be so pathetic. You wouldn't have tried. You'd just have run away. Even if the others never know, you'll know. And just think of trying to meet Saldowr's eyes while you bleat, "I tried, I really did, but the whale wouldn't take me."

"I *have* to go there. I don't want to, exactly, but the Mer need me. It's because of the children and the Kraken. You know..."

The whale doesn't answer. She fixes me with her eye, mild and patient and not at all convinced.

Salt tingles on my palate. I remember what Faro said: *You are Mer in your heart.* Whether he's right or not, I can feel my Mer blood rising. Words bubble on my tongue, and reach my lips. *"An Kraken... an Kraken... nownek. Peryl ha own...* Dear whale, please help me. "

The words tingle in my mouth like electricity. Going to the Deep is still difficult and dangerous – but it's no longer impossible.

"Da yw genev," murmurs the whale, and relief pours through me. It's agreed. She will help me.

The whale moves her head a little. Water swirls and bowls me sideways. I swim back through the waves she's made.

"Maybe – please would you mind not moving so much?"

"Moving so much?" The whale shakes with laughter, but carefully this time, so that the water rocks but doesn't sweep me away. "Your world must be very dull, little one, if this is *moving*. If only I had learned some new jokes to tell you! A basking shark told me one about an angler fish. I wish I could remember the punchline. You should be thinking of jokes at your age, not of shadows and sorrows. Those come soon enough," and the whale sighs.

Jokes! This isn't the time for jokes, especially not whale jokes. "But the Kraken..."

"Yes, dear child," says the whale calmly. "We whales were the first to bring the news of his waking from the Deep."

"But aren't you frightened? The Kraken's a monster!"

"Yes, he is a monster. But what can the Kraken take from me?"

I stare at the whale. Obviously the Kraken can take everything. Why isn't she afraid?

"The Mer say that Mab Avalon put the Kraken back to sleep, a long time ago, and they think I can do the same. Have you ever heard of Mab Avalon?"

"When they were young, my children used to play a game: one would pretend to be the Kraken, another would be Mab Avalon."

"Have you got two children?"

"Yes. A son and a daughter."

"Just like me and Conor."

The whale makes me feel so safe and looked after. She's like a grandma. I wish I could stay with her all day, talking and maybe travelling with her, finding out more about her family and her jokes and her secret sadness.

"I've agreed to take you into the Deep," says the whale, "but understand, little one, you're going into danger."

"I know."

"Do you? Do you really, little barelegs? Have you ever seen the sea running red with blood?" The whale's voice has deepened. "Understand me, little one. I'm warning you because I care for you, not because I want to frighten you."

Just like Mum, I think.

"My brother will come with me. He's got a talisman." It sounds feeble, even to me. What good is a bit of carved coral against a monster who has been terrorising Ingo for thousands of years? Clearly the whale agrees, because she ignores the talisman.

"I will take you. *Da yw genev.* I will protect you as far as I am able."

"Thank you, dear whale. And you'll take my brother too?"

"Yes. I will wait here for you while you go and tell him."

"But – but we aren't going to go *now*. We're just finding out about it all. We've got to go back home – and work out a plan."

"Are you sure?" asks the whale gently. "I think now is

143

the time. Or never. Never is better, perhaps, little barelegs. Never is safer. If I were your mother, I would choose never for you. But if not never, little one, then it has to be now."

CHAPTER TEN

N o time to see Mum again. No time to say goodbye to Sadie. Everything's happening much too fast.

Dad always told me I should never promise anything for the future that I wouldn't be happy to do today. *Some people will promise you the earth for a fortnight next Friday, Sapphy.*

I swim back down, through the entrance and into Saldowr's cave. To my amazement the cave is full of light now, even though the whale is still blocking its entrance. My eyes sting, and then adjust. There are tiny glowing buds of light everywhere on the walls, on the roof, even around Saldowr's stone couch. They remind me of the lights that guided me through the passage to the Assembly chamber, but these are much, much brighter. I can't even see the creatures that are giving out the light, because they're hidden by the dazzle. They make a brilliant green and silver light, cold but beautiful.

Everything has changed while I've been away. Saldowr

is no longer lying flat. He's propped up by cushions of woven weed, and a girl with long hair is bending over him, carefully tending his shoulder. Elvira. Conor's facing me, but he doesn't see me because his eyes are fixed on Elvira. Faro's holding a coral cup to Saldowr's lip. A ripple of laughter reaches me.

I feel a pang of indignation. They're enjoying themselves, while I'm bracing myself to confront a monster. Look at Conor's face. You wouldn't think there was anyone in the world but Elvira. How did she get here? She must have slipped through the gap between whale and cave without me noticing. So it's not enough for her to give Conor the talisman, she's got to follow him everywhere too.

I want Elvira to leave my brother alone. I'm not jealous of her – of course I'm not – but she's too much like Mellina. I don't want anybody stealing my brother away.

"Oh, Elvira," I say coldly as I swim towards Saldowr's couch, "I didn't realise *you* were here. What are you doing?"

"She's dressing Saldowr's wound," says Conor, without taking his eyes off Elvira. "She's made a poultice to draw out the inflammation."

Doesn't he even care where I've been? Anything could have happened to me, for all Conor knows. He doesn't seem bothered about what's happening outside Saldowr's cave. It's enough that Elvira's here, inside it.

I used to like Elvira, but that was before I realised what she's really like. She was a friend on the night of the flood, and she helped me when I smashed my leg against the granite wall. But now I know that all she really wanted was Conor.

The talisman has opened my eyes. Elvira might as well have carved in huge letters: I WANT CONOR TO COME TO INGO AND BECOME MER, JUST LIKE HIS FATHER.

It's not going to happen, Elvira. Being beautiful and helping everybody and making Conor feel that he's the most amazing person in the universe isn't going to be enough. Conor would never hurt Mum like Dad did. Besides, he loves the human world far too much to leave it. There are his friends and surfing and his music...

But Dad had just as much to keep him. Mum, and us, and the *Peggy Gordon*, and his work, and everybody in our village who'd known him since he was born. And Dad turned his back on all of it.

Conor is still admiring Elvira as she smoothes the poultice with feather-light fingers.

"Oh yes, of course, Elvira's a *healer*, isn't she," I say tartly. Elvira finishes with the disgusting dark green stuff that looks a lot more likely to poison Saldowr than heal him, then she takes a pad of sea moss, places it over the poultice and begins expertly to bind up his shoulder again. Her hands flicker deftly. Reluctantly I have to admit that she knows what she's doing.

When Elvira has finished, Saldowr sighs, leans back and thanks her.

"You have good hands, Elvira," he praises her. "You have it in your power to become a great healer one day, if you study hard."

I suppress a smile, because it so reminds me of Mum telling me to study hard, go to uni and get a good career. Adults are the same wherever you go.

But there's nothing to smile about, I tell myself firmly. Elvira and her wonderful hands are just a pain as far as I'm concerned. Elvira glances up and says with annoying modesty, "I know I've got a lot to learn."

Yes, you most certainly have, I think, *like how wrong you are if you think my brother belongs to you.*

"Don't you want to know where I've been?" I demand of everyone. Immediately, I want to bring the words back. I sound like a little kid who's stayed in a hiding-place long after the others have given up hide-and-seek and gone to play something else. I bite my lip. Let them ask me if they really want to know.

Conor tears his eyes from Elvira and looks as me as if he's waking up from a wonderful dream. "Oh, Sapphy, Saldowr said it was the whale who wanted to see you – the same one who brought you out of the Deep."

And you didn't have the slightest curiosity when I came back. You just carried on gaping at Elvira.

"Yes."

Conor waits, expecting me to continue. Faro is watching this little scene with a malicious smile. He's far too quick. He picks up everything.

"What did she want?" asks Conor at last, seeing that I'm not going to continue.

"To see Sapphire, of course. What could be more natural?" teases Faro.

"Whales don't come hundreds of miles just because they want to see you, Faro," I snap. "She knows about the Kraken. She'll take me to the Deep."

Conor picks up my annoyance, though he doesn't seem to realise where it's coming from, and says in a soothing voice, "But that's good, isn't it? It's what we want."

"It may be what *you* want, Conor. It's not you that has to go."

"I told you I'd go with you." Conor's voice sharpens. "Don't pretend you think I'll let you go alone."

"Nor I," says Faro, and now the mocking edge has left his voice. "Both of us will go with you, little sister."

Yes, a fortnight next Friday, I think. *Just wait until you know what we've got to do.*

"She's waiting for me," I say. "She wants us to go now, straightaway. Now or never, she says."

Elvira freezes in the act of wrapping Saldowr's cloak back over his shoulder. "Now?" she says. "But Conor—"

"He'll be all right. He's got your talisman," I say

unkindly, and sure enough I see Conor's hand go up and touch it.

"I'd come with you, Conor, you know I would, but I wouldn't be any use," says Elvira, looking only at him and speaking only to him. "I'd hold you back. That's why I made you the talisman. I can't even go as deep as Faro can. Blood fills my head and my sight goes black," she adds poetically, increasing my irritation.

"I expect it's a Mer thing," I say, and shoot Faro a look. He pretends not to know what I mean.

"I know, Elvira. I understand," says Conor, so softly and warmly that jealousy plunges deep into my heart like the dagger of stone that wounded Saldowr. Why is Elvira allowed to be weak, and everyone's full of understanding and sympathy, while they act as if it's perfectly normal for me to risk my life?

What is the matter with me? I've got to stop this. I've never been jealous of Conor before, and I hate self-pity. I *want* to be strong, so why get angry when people think I am?

Because you're afraid. Of course that's what it is. My stomach is knotted with fear. My frightened thoughts are whisking from one corner of my mind to another, trying to find an escape. Trying to find an excuse not to go. But the whale's waiting for me. We've got to hurry—

"We can't keep the whale waiting, Conor."

"Whales know how to wait," says Saldowr. " The Deep teaches them the art of living slowly. But all the same you are right: for the sake of courtesy we should send her a message."

He claps his hands gently. A few seconds later a shoal of mackerel flashes through the cave entrance. With their stripes of green and blue and silver, they're as beautiful as jewels. They swim to Saldowr, and weave around his head and body in a dazzle of colour while he speaks to them in a low murmur, too low for us to hear his words. The mackerel pattern changes, like a dance when the music changes. Faro whispers to me, "They're learning Saldowr's message. They remember in their bodies and then in the shoal, not in their heads."

The mackerel dance for a few more seconds, and then they're gone, streaming out of the cave.

"She will wait," says Saldowr, "but all the same we must hurry. We have a great deal to do, and not much time. And I think we may be interrupted." He pauses to rest. His hands clench with pain, and Elvira starts forward, but he waves her away. "Faro, fetch my cup again."

Faro raises the coral cup to Saldowr's lips. I catch a glimpse of what he's drinking. It's a dark liquid that looks as heavy as mercury as it tilts to the rim of the cup. Saldowr swallows, gives a sigh of relief and lies back again. There must be a drug in the drink. Maybe it's some kind of painkiller. Saldowr should be resting. He'll never get well.

"Faro, fetch me my mirror."

Saldowr gives orders as if Faro belongs to him, like a

hand or a foot. Faro doesn't seem to mind, in fact he seems to take pride in how quickly he can do Saldowr's bidding. In one long smooth stroke he reaches the other side of the cave, and begins to feel his way along its polished granite wall. His back is turned to me so I can't see exactly what he's doing. The next moment, a crack appears in the wall, and a light shines through it – a blue-green light that fills me with dread. The tides! There must be another entrance to the Tide Knot from Saldowr's cave. What's Faro doing? Doesn't he understand how dangerous it is to give the tides even a chink of freedom?

A stab of panic makes me speak. "But Saldowr, the tides will get out again!"

"There's no danger. All you see there is the reflection of the Tide Knot, not the thing itself. Faro is reaching into my treasury of reflections. They go back hundreds of years," adds Saldowr, with a note of collector's pride in his voice. "I doubt if there's another treasury to equal it, in Ingo or on Earth. That is where I keep my mirror."

Faro reaches in, lifts something out, and then his right hand feels across the rock again, presses, and the crack in the wall slides shut. He handles the secret opening so skilfully that I realise he must have used it many times before.

He turns, and in his hand is Saldowr's mirror. That's where we saw the image of Mellina and our Mer baby half-brother... and Dad. I scull myself backwards a little. I don't want to look in that mirror again. It's too painful. Conor's looking wary too.

"Bring it to me," says Saldowr, and Faro places the mirror in his hand, still face-down. "Come here, Sapphire. Come here, Conor."

He's going to show us something that I don't want to see, just like last time. I hang back as if a current is pressing me against the wall.

"Don't be afraid," says Saldowr. "My mirror cannot see far today. Look."

He holds up the mirror for us to see its face. The mirror is broken, shattered into a star shape. It reminds me of how my bedroom mirror looked, the day Conor smashed it to the floor because he thought I could see Ingo in it. Yes, it's the same star shape. I can't help feeling glad that Saldowr's mirror has lost its power.

"The Tide Knot broke, and my mirror broke with it," says Saldowr. "It has lost most of its virtue and can no longer reveal everything that is stored in my treasury of reflections. But it can still show you your own face."

Any mirror can do that, I think.

"The Kraken cannot bear to see his own face," says Saldowr. "He hates to see it, or have it seen."

"How do you know?" breaks in Conor.

Saldowr raises his eyebrows. "Maybe Mab Avalon told me," he says drily. "The Kraken is safe while he stays in the Deep, because there are no reflections there. Most of Ingo is full of reflections. So this mirror may be a weapon for you. It is not such a potent one as I would wish, but there is some power left in it. Come here, Sapphire. Look into the mirror."

Slowly, reluctantly, I swim to Saldowr's side. Now that I'm close to him in the green and silver light, I can see how weak he looks. He lifts the hand that doesn't hold the mirror, and without being told, Faro raises the coral cup and Saldowr takes another draught. It seems to revive him.

"Move back," Saldowr tells Faro, and then beckons me closer. "Now, look into the mirror."

It's just a mirror, showing me my own face. Nothing special. Except – except for my expression. The eyes in the mirror are troubled and restless. The lips are narrow. I look angry, jealous and afraid. I blush deeply, and lift my eyes to Saldowr.

"I don't really look like that, do I?" I whisper, not wanting the others to hear.

"Usually people clean their faces before they look into mirrors."

"There's no dirt on my face."

"I mean that they choose what they want to see. They see the best of themselves, but this mirror won't permit it. I don't know what you're seeing, Sapphire. No one but you will see it."

I look again. The mirror returns the same face.

"Give it to Conor."

I pass the mirror to Conor. He looks into the shattered

glass, and like me he flushes, deep red through the brown of his skin. I wonder what the mirror showed him, but I won't ask. I wouldn't want anyone to ask me.

"Shall I look now, Saldowr?" asks Faro cheerfully. Saldowr considers him.

"You could look, my son. Are you still planning to go to the Deep?"

"Of course! When have I ever gone back on my word?" Faro throws back his shoulders and lifts his head proudly.

"I don't doubt your courage," says Saldowr.

And nor do I. Faro is brave from his flowing hair to the tip of his strong seal tail. I know that he would risk everything in order to keep his promise. But it's not right. The Mer can't survive there, everyone says that. Saldowr can't let Faro throw his life away on an impossible quest.

To my relief, Saldowr seems to be thinking the same thing. "The Mer cannot enter the deep," he warns.

"But Sapphire has Mer blood, and she went to the Deep."

"Her blood is mixed, and so is Conor's. They belong to Earth and Air, and they belong to Ingo. For this reason they can go beyond what those who are pure Mer can do. Or at least, they have a chance of doing so.

"Do you understand what I'm saying? Do you still want to go with them? Do you still believe that you are capable of it? Ask yourself these questions, my son. Don't look at what you want to believe, but into the truth that lies in your heart, waiting for you to find it."

I don't understand what Saldowr's implying. How can Faro go? It's useless to suggest it. But there must be something else beneath the surface of Saldowr's words.

Faro frowns. A shadow of disquiet passes over his face. "What are you saying to me, Saldowr?" he asks harshly. "I am your *scolhyk* and your *holyer*. I belong to Ingo with every drop of my blood. I would die for Ingo's sake."

"I believe that, my son," says Saldowr. "You belong where you choose to belong, just as I do. Are you ready to look into your mirror? It will answer your question if you let it. It will tell you if the Deep will push you away, or let you penetrate its dark heart."

Faro folds his arms. For a moment it looks as if he's about to challenge Saldowr, and then his arms drop to his sides. "I will look," he says.

"Then take the mirror."

Faro reaches out and grasps the handle of the mirror as if it's a snake that could lash round and bite him. The mirror gleams dully. I can't see the reflection. I only see its effect.

Colour drains from Faro's face until he's ashy pale. He stares into the mirror for a long moment, and then shudders all over. The mirror drops through the water on to the sand of the cave floor. Faro's face is haggard as he mutters, "The mirror is lying."

"My mirror cannot lie."

"It's got to be lying."

"Then, Faro, you cannot go to the Deep."

Faro's face is tormented. He looks round wildly for help, as if he's caught in a trap. I wish I could help him. I know what it's like to see your worst fears in that mirror, as I did when it showed me my father living happily in his Mer life. Saldowr should keep his mirror in the treasury of reflections and never let it out. It's much too dangerous.

"Faro," I say quietly, trying to show my sympathy, wanting him to know that he's not alone. But he ignores me. I reach out my hand to him, but he brushes it away. He throws back his head in defiance as if Saldowr isn't his much-respected teacher, but an enemy, like Ervys. "I will go then," he says in a strained, harsh voice. "I will go. What choice do I have when Ingo calls on me for help? But I will not carry that cursed mirror with me. I will never touch it again."

Saldowr rears up on his couch, hair streaming and eyes blazing. "No more!" he orders Faro. "You don't know what you're saying. You will come to bless my mirror, not curse it. You say you are my *scolhyk*? Then study. Listen. *Learn*. You cannot go back on what you now know."

The words rap out like bullets. Saldowr sinks back, exhausted, and Faro rushes to him, kneels by the couch and seizes his hand as if begging forgiveness.

Poor Faro, I think. Whatever the mirror showed him, he didn't deserve it. He's so brave, and it's clear that the mirror has cut him to the heart. All Faro wanted to do was to help his people. Why does he have to kneel to Saldowr? He loves Saldowr so much. Too much, maybe.

Saldowr lays his hand on Faro's shoulder. "Know yourself," he says in a gentler voice, "that's all I ask." Suddenly he tenses. His hand drops. He's looking towards the cave mouth, listening.

"We have another visitor," he says calmly, "and this one won't wait outside. You may enter, Ervys."

CHAPTER ELEVEN

ad used to say a game of chess was war by other means. He taught me how the pieces moved when I was five. *The kings can't stand next to each other, Sapphy*, he told me, when I tried to make the pieces whizz round the board doing just what they wanted. He got two magnets out of the toolbox and told me to try and push them together until they touched. I couldn't do it. The air seemed to go solid and keep the ends of the magnets apart.

Each king has his own force, Dad explained. *He can't stand to be that close to another force, just like these magnets, Sapphy. You try to push them together, but they don't want to be together. They want their own zone of power. So listen, the idea of this game is to keep your king's force strong. You've got to think like a king with an army.*

This didn't mean much to me when I was five, but it does now.

Ervys comes into the cave like a king, not like a visitor. He has two of his men with him. They don't carry weapons but they bear themselves like soldiers. They're huge, broad-shouldered men with flowing hair and powerful tails. Muscles ripple in their shoulders and arms. They remind me of the grey seals that guard Limina.

I mustn't show them that I'm afraid. I glance at Conor and Faro. Conor's looking at them with cool interest. Faro's face is dark with anger. I feel my way towards his thoughts, and hit a storm. He can't bear the fact that they'd dared to come here. He'd like to kill them for intruding on Saldowr, and for seeing him in his weakness like this. But he knows he can't. His rage swirls and eddies like the tide when it turns. I retreat, out of its range.

I thought it was the light in the Assembly chamber that gave the faint blue tinge to Ervys's skin. But it's the same here, and his followers have it too. Their eyes have the same silvery sheen. A small flick of the tail, and they move closer. Ervys is in front, his followers just behind.

"Saldowr," says Ervys.

"Ervys," responds Saldowr. "And I should greet you too, Talek and Mortarow."

As Saldowr says their names a brief look of uneasiness crosses their faces. Saldowr looks past Ervys as if he's not here, and talks directly to the one called Mortarow. "You remember, Mortarow, how your grandfather served the Tide Knot, as Faro here serves it now?"

Mortarow frowns and glances at Ervys for support, but Ervys doesn't even look at him.

"That was before my time," Mortarow answers. "My grandad passed on to Limina when I was three years old."

"Of course. But you know of it, and I remember your grandfather well. Your family has a long tradition of faithful service to the Tide Knot. I have always trusted in the strength of the sea bulls. Your grandfather and his father before him."

He says no more. He doesn't need to. Mortarow mutters something, and looks down uncomfortably. But Ervys breaks in, "We have come to talk of the present and the future, not waste time on the past."

"You think you have," returns Saldowr equably, "but the present cannot exist without the past."

"I am not your *scolhyk*, Saldowr," says Ervys with a cold arrogance which makes Faro clench his fists.

But Saldowr doesn't react. Instead he smiles faintly and says, "You may have noticed a whale, I think, Ervys, as you entered my cave?"

A stifled snort of laughter comes from Conor, and Ervys glances at us angrily. "Your questions are fit for children, not for a leader among the Mer," he replies angrily.

"A leader among the Mer," repeats Saldowr softly. He draws himself up until his eyes are level with Ervys's. I forget that Saldowr is weak and wounded, and only see the raw power that surges through him. His eyes blaze.

"The Mer have no leaders," he says with quiet fury. "We have learned the danger of that. Leaders lead to division and bloodshed. We have Guardians, not leaders."

"But how have our Guardians served us?" asks Ervys smoothly. His right arm sweeps out in a wide, dismissive gesture. "Can you deny that Ingo is torn and full of grief? Can you deny that we are weak? Can you deny that the Tide Knot broke and almost shattered us? Perhaps, Saldowr, if we *had* had a leader, none of these things would have happened."

Ervys's followers close around him, shoulder to shoulder. Mortarow and Talek look confident again, and even stronger than they did a few minutes ago. Maybe there are more of Ervys's supporters waiting outside the cave.

And then Conor moves too. One clean stroke takes him to Saldowr's side. He looks across at Ervys as if he's Ervys's equal. Faro hesitates for a moment. He's wishing he'd thought of it first. But then he makes up his mind and swoops to Saldowr's other side. They close in, as Ervys's followers have done. Saldowr glances from Conor to Faro. A smile flickers across his face.

"Let us return to the subject of that whale," says Saldowr calmly, putting aside what Ervys has said about leaders. "She's patient, but she can't be patient for ever. She's waiting to take these children to the Deep, Ervys. You know as well as I do that it's our only chance of avoiding sacrifice to the Kraken.

"The whale knows the patterns of the Deep. Even where darkness covers everything, she can still hear her way. There's no creature in Ingo like her for understanding echoes and reading the darkness. You would be lost there, and so would I, so let's not waste our time talking of leaders. Leaders can do nothing against the Kraken in his own territory."

Ervys and his followers subside, and move back a little. But they're only biding their time, I'm sure of it.

"These children," says Ervys, waving his hand scornfully at Conor and me. "We hear a lot about what they can do, but so far we have no evidence of it. It's all words."

"Evidence!" Once again power flashes from Saldowr. "How can there be evidence or certainty in any of this? I don't know what is going to happen, and nor do they. It's a risk we have to take."

When Saldowr says that, the weight of what we've agreed to do hits me. At the back of my mind I've had the hope that somehow Saldowr magically knows what's going to happen, and knows that we're going to come back safely. Otherwise he wouldn't send us, would he? Because he's an adult, and we're children...

You idiot, Sapphire. He's not a teacher, worrying about our safety on a school trip. He's Mer, and Ingo is under threat.

"And I am going with them," says Faro proudly, staring at Ervys with defiance.

"Is this true?" demands Ervys of Saldowr. Saldowr nods.

A strange smile flickers over Ervys's face. "But no Mer can enter the Deep," he observes. "Not even your *scolhyk* and your *holyer*, Saldowr, unless you can break all the laws that govern us. Or unless, in this particular case, for some reason they... don't apply."

There is a long silence. Ervys's followers look puzzled but aggressive, as if they haven't quite understood what this argument is about but are just as happy to fight it out anyway. Faro understands, though. He pushes forward, but Saldowr restrains him.

"Now is not the time," says Saldowr, and then a fit of coughing seizes him. Veins stand out on his forehead as he struggles to control it, while Ervys looks on with that smile of satisfaction deepening on his face.

Faro dives for the cup, and brings it to Saldowr's lips. Saldowr drains it, his fingers shaking on the rim. "And now no more, Faro," he whispers, "no more, even if I beg you for it. I have reached my limit."

I don't know whether or not Ervys hears this. He and his followers dominate the cave, gazing at Saldowr as if the sight of his distress pleases them. How dare they? Who asked them to come here? My fists clench, like Faro's.

"This child has something to say to you," Saldowr says hoarsely at last, and he indicates me. For a moment I've no idea what he means. I'm so caught up in what's happening that I've forgotten all about our bargain. But then Conor nudges me and I remember.

"We've agreed to go to the Deep," I say. Fear makes my voice shaky, but I swallow hard and look straight at Ervys. He's not going to scare me out of saying what I mean. Too much depends on it.

"And so?" asks Ervys coldly.

"In return we ask the Mer to agree to something. Our father is in Ingo. Our father must have the choice to return to the human world."

Ervys frowns deeply, and folds his arms. Immediately Mortarow and Talek fold theirs, too.

"This should have been discussed in the Assembly chamber," growls Ervys.

"There's nothing to discuss," replies Saldowr.

"She's asking us to break the law of the Mer."

Saldowr sighs wearily. "Don't you understand, Ervys, that everything is broken for us already? The Kraken is awake."

Ervys ponders angrily. I'm afraid that he's going to agree with his lips, but not in his heart. I don't trust him.

"This is blackmail," he says at last. "I agree to it because I have no choice. Let my followers be my witnesses. Talek, Mortarow, witness that I agree under duress."

"It's not blackmail!—" I begin hotly, but Saldowr won't let me speak.

"You are testing my patience, all of you, as well as the patience of the whale. You're not in the Assembly chamber now, Ervys. The time for talking is over."

Maybe it's just old habit that makes Ervys and his

followers fall silent. But it's an ominous, waiting silence. I cling to the hope that Ervys has decided not to cross Saldowr's will openly now, while he still needs us.

Ervys is strong. Muscles bulge in his arms and shoulders. He is in his prime and he can afford to wait. His expression says that he'll get what he wants, if not now then soon.

If Saldowr dies, we'll have no protection from Ervys. *If Saldowr dies…*

No, it can't happen. We won't let it happen. If we go to the Deep – if we stop the Kraken – then Ingo will be itself again. Everything will be as it was, and Saldowr will be as we saw him the first time: tall, strong and more alive than anyone.

The whale is waiting. All the time, I can feel her presence in the back of my mind. Her huge body with its skin that's wrinkled like an elephant's. Her box-shaped head and the teeth which would frighten me if I didn't know her. *We don't eat your kind, little one.*

Her vast tail with the flukes that could knock a boat out of the water. Her sonar that can find a giant squid at the floor of the ocean, thousands of metres down. And her huge heart. Conor showed me in one of his books that the heart of a sperm whale weighs as much as two men. I think of the heart inside her, pumping and pumping, getting ready for the dive.

I look across at Ervys. How big is *your* heart? You claim that you're doing everything for the sake of the Mer, because Saldowr's weak and he can't save his people any more. And so you're the one who's going to rescue them from the Kraken, and get the glory of it. The Mer will be so grateful that they'll give you anything you ask for. They'll make you leader all right.

They're too close. Saldowr and Ervys shouldn't be as close as this. You can feel the pressure of it, like two magnets pushing against each other.

What's Conor doing? At a murmur from Saldowr, he's dropped behind Faro. Suddenly I see that Conor has the mirror in his hand. He's not looking into it, but he's rubbing at the metal back. Polishing it.

"Give me my mirror, Conor," says Saldowr. Conor passes it, and as Saldowr takes it the metal flashes like lightning in the summer sky. The dull metal is suddenly brilliant. Ervys and his followers raise their hands in the gesture I remember from the Assembly chamber: hands up, fingers crossed as if they're warding off evil.

"I see you've cleaned my mirror for me, Conor," says Saldowr. "All these years we've never managed to get a shine on it, have we, Faro? Perhaps it was waiting for this occasion. Waiting for *you*, Ervys, do you think?"

Ervys says nothing.

"Yes, I think so... I believe my mirror knows that you are here. It wants to see you, Ervys."

Ervys lets his hands fall to his sides again. Reluctantly, his followers do the same. You can see that they don't want to. They're rattled now, uneasy, glancing at Ervys to see what to do, and then at Saldowr.

"You've come here uninvited," says Saldowr. "You've cast doubts on these children's courage. Let's see *your* courage, Ervys. Look into my mirror."

A little gap appears in the water between Ervys and his followers. Yes, they're separating themselves from him. Shrinking away. He's too clever not to see it, and know what it means. He swims forward.

"Your mirror doesn't frighten me," he says.

It's obvious that it does. His colour has gone. His lips are set in a tight line. But even so he reaches out his hand.

"Look into it well," Saldowr tells him, and turns the mirror to face Ervys.

The water seems to turn to ice around Ervys. Slowly his hair lifts as if a current is drawing it, until it stands around his head in a halo. His eyes glare into the mirror, fixed.

"So stand there, Ervys," murmurs Saldowr, "stand there and let my mirror teach you."

How stupid I was to believe that Saldowr was like a benign wizard in a children's book. Ervys has trespassed, disrespected the Groves of Aleph and Saldowr's own cave. He taunted Saldowr with his weakness. He brought his followers to swagger here. He challenged Saldowr, and Saldowr didn't challenge him in return.

Ervys must have thought he'd won already, and that Ingo was his. But Saldowr has done the most terrible thing of all. He has shown Ervys himself. Ervys looks as if he's been turned to stone. His followers raise their hands, shielding their faces.

"No," Saldowr commands them, "you must look at Ervys, unless you want to take his place."

He wants them to see Ervys humbled. They know it, and Ervys must know it. Talek and Mortarow most certainly don't want to take Ervys's place, so they gawp at him obediently. A smile of triumph curls on Faro's mouth as he too stares at Ervys, but I look away.

At last, after long minutes, Saldowr removes the mirror. Slowly Ervys's tortured grimace fades into a more normal expression. He shudders all over, and then with a huge effort he regains himself. He gives Saldowr a look of such hatred that I'm chilled. The hatred flashes around the cave like cold fire, over me and Faro and Conor, even over his followers. He hates us all, because we've witnessed his defeat.

"I have looked into your mirror, Saldowr," he hisses, "and one day, I promise you, you will look into mine. All of you will look into mine."

Fear licks over me. I believe him. He will bide his time, and one day his chance will come.

"Now leave us, Ervys," says Saldowr quietly. "These children must make ready for their journey."

CHAPTER TWELVE

The whale is like an ocean-going liner, ready to depart. She wants us to tuck in behind her flippers for the dive, so that the rush of the water won't sweep us away from her. She'll have Faro and Conor on one side of her, and me on the other for balance.

"You must lie close to me, little barelegs," she tells me. Her huge affection laps round me. "Think that you are a part of me."

I remember how we rode with the dolphins. You can't ride on dolphins as if they're bicycles. You have to let go of being separate and relax against them until it feels as if you're sharing the same skin. Perhaps it's like that with whales, too.

None of us knows how long we'll need in the Deep. None of us knows what we're going to do when we find the Kraken. It's like staring over a precipice. It makes you feel sick and dizzy.

But Saldowr's wise, and he's the one who is sending us. He wouldn't throw our lives away for a one in a million chance.

Conor says sperm whales only dive for about an hour. Males can dive longer than females, so maybe my whale won't even be able to do an hour. He's not sure that it'll be long enough, when you think that we've got to find the Kraken and somehow make him sleep again. *Somehow!*

"We have to trust the whale's judgment," Conor says. "Maybe time in the Deep is different from time in the rest of Ingo, just as human time is different from Mer time. Why would she take us if she knew we wouldn't have time to do anything? There's no sense in it, if we're bound to fail."

Conor sounds so logical. I suppose he's right. *Bound to fail. Bound to fail.* Our chance of success feels so slender. All we've got is Saldowr's mirror and the talisman. Oh, and don't forget a handful of rowan berries. When you add it all up, it's not impressive.

Don't think of that now. Think of one stroke at a time. I'm not going to say anything to the others about my doubts. It's bad enough for them to be going to the Deep for the first time. At least I know what to expect.

"Faro, are you sure? Are you really sure?" I murmur, just before we separate to swim to shelter behind the whale's flippers. Conor has swum ahead a little way to find a length of weed to bind the mirror to his leg.

Faro's eyes look like black holes in his white face. He tries to smile his old teasing smile, but it's no more than a shadow. He looks shocked and angry, not afraid. It's something to do with the mirror, and what it's shown him about himself. The cursed mirror, he called it. Suddenly I'm afraid that we're forcing Faro into a danger so terrible he can't possibly survive it. He's not like us. Our mixed blood gives us a chance.

"Please, Faro, don't do this," I beg him. "You can't throw your life away."

His eyes glint. There's no warmth or friendliness in his expression. "Didn't you understand what Saldowr was telling me?"

I stare at him. A flash of understanding passes between us, from his mind to mine, and then I know why Faro is coming to the Deep. Why he's able to come.

A wave of his pain and shock hits me. He can't believe it, he doesn't want to believe it. He, Faro, always so proud of being pure Mer. But the mirror is too strong. You can't escape the knowledge it gives you. It has sunk into Faro and changed him. I reach out to him, but he shrugs me away.

"Not now. Leave me alone, Sapphire."

Conor has bound the mirror to his leg so securely that it's almost hidden by straps of weed. He has the talisman safe around his neck. The little diving figure still frightens me. Why does Conor think that it has his face when it's so obviously Mer? Nothing seems certain any more. I used to know what was human and what was Mer. Faro was Mer, everybody in St Pirans was human, and I was half-and-half. Now the boundaries are shifting, and it frightens me.

Those rowan berries seem to burn through the cloth of my pocket and into my skin. Maybe I shouldn't have brought them. They belong to Earth. They might harm me in Ingo. Granny Carne wouldn't have known if I'd left them behind.

What was it Saldowr said to me? *But you have no talisman, Sapphire.* I'm sure he knew about the rowan berries in my pocket. But I wasn't going to admit I had them.

I hope Saldowr will never be angry with us in the way he was with Ervys. Ervys looked at if he was trapped in a nightmare. He couldn't wake up until Saldowr let him.

Faro and Conor must have reached the other side of the whale by now. I've just got to wait. I hope they're all right. It's dark tucked in behind the whale's flipper, but it feels secure.

We're moving now, slowly gliding our way out of the Groves of Aleph. There's no one to say goodbye to us. Saldowr couldn't leave the cave, and Elvira's staying with him. Ervys, Talek and Mortarow must be miles away by now. They couldn't leave fast enough.

I still wish we hadn't been there to witness Ervys' nightmare. He'll punish us for it. He's the kind who'll wait and wait and get his revenge when you've stopped expecting it.

I wonder if I can hear the whale's huge heart beating? If I put my ear against her skin... No, there's nothing. Her heart's such a long way away. It's strange to be almost part of someone this big. How careful the whale has to be as she manoeuvres herself out of the Groves into free water. Her flippers move gently, steering her, grazing the underwater trees as she goes. I peer out into the water and weed rushes past. The water feels shallow, compared to her hugeness.

"Are you all right, little barelegs? Do my flippers move gently enough for you?"

"Yes, dear whale, I'm fine."

She doesn't seem too concerned about Faro and Conor, even though she was willing to take them to the Deep as well. Maybe she feels closer to me because of the way we first met, in the Deep. She was a warm-blooded fellow mammal in all that cold-blooded darkness. I think she must have felt the same.

I wonder what it would be like to be a whale's daughter? *Of course I'd miss Mum*, I think hurriedly, feeling guilty. Mum has gone shadowy in my mind, the way she does when I'm in Ingo. Even darling Sadie has become distant. I can't remember the exact tone of her bark. I know I love her, but I can't find the feeling.

We're travelling faster now, close to the surface. I tuck

myself in as tight as I can. I daren't peer out now in case the racing water grabs me.

And then the whale's huge body loses speed as it breaches the surface. She rocks from side to side, wallowing. Her speed dies to nothing, and she blows. I feel it all through her body. I picture the column of water shooting into the air from her blowhole. Where are we, I wonder? Miles out to sea, I'm sure. Maybe a fishing boat is in range, and the men will see the whale blow. Dad used to say it was a sight that took your breath away.

It's the power of the creatures, Sapphy. We're nothing next to them. When you're out on the bare ocean and you see a whale breach and blow, you've seen glory. I'll take you down south beyond the Scillies one day and we'll watch for whales.

The fishermen would expect to see other whales because sperm whales live in groups. But my whale is alone, always alone.

Dad and I never made that journey. There wasn't time.

The whale's got to gather her breath for the dive. She's not talking any more. How could she think of conversation when she's preparing to plunge down hundreds of metres – maybe thousands? I lay my face against her rough, pruney skin. *Dear whale, dive well. Dive deep.*

It must be like this for astronauts when they're waiting for the countdown, strapped in their seats. It's too late to go back. All the exits are sealed and everybody's watching and waiting and hoping.

Ingo's watching and waiting and hoping. My stomach slithers. *Too late to go back now. Too late now.* I wonder if some of the Mer have followed us and are watching, from a safe distance, their hair flowing around their shoulders and their faces eager to catch sight of the dive.

Elvira won't be there. She'll stay at Saldowr's side, trying to heal him. She hugged us all before we left, one by one. Even me. Elvira has one of those faces that gets even more beautiful close up. She put her arms around me as if she really cared what happened to me. I forgot to be jealous of her for at least a minute, until she hugged Conor with her beautiful long Mer arms, and they kept on murmuring to each other until Saldowr had to say that it was time to go.

Astronauts must be so scared. I suppose they hide their fear because of the TV cameras. No, more likely it's because the other astronauts would see it. Conor and Faro and I didn't show one another that we were scared. I wish I was going to be with them all the way down, but it's impossible. The whale has to dive straight. Three on one side and none on the other would send her crooked. Conor has to be with Faro. It's his best chance.

I open my mind and try to hear Faro's thoughts, but with the bulk of the whale's body between us I can't pick up anything. I hope he and Conor are all right. They don't know the whale as I do. I hope they can feel her kindness.

A ripple of energy surges through the whale's body.

Something's about to happen. I don't want it! I want to get off. I want to go home.

You must be brave, Sapphire. Be brave.

It's probably my own voice, but it calms me. The hot thudding in my head eases. I relax into the shelter of the whale's flipper. I make my body melt against her rough skin, just as I made it melt against the dolphin's back. She's getting ready. She's going—

A rush of power pours through the whale. She holds still for a second, and then I'm head down and sealed between flipper and body as the world turns and everything I've ever thought or known rushes away from me.

The whale dives.

The Deep. We are in the Deep. There's no light and it's cold and full of echoes. I'm as thin as paper. I can barely move my hands because they are so heavy. I know this place. Fear pours over me as it did the last time I was here and I fight it down. You can't panic here. If you let yourself panic, you're lost.

The Deep. The Deep. Darkness so thick that you can't even believe in light. The weight of the whole world pressing down on us. But I'm with the whale, and I'm safe. I hear her echo system as she feels her way forward. She knows where she's going. The Deep is an open book to her. For the whale, this is familiar hunting ground, not a desert of lonely blackness.

"Keep still, little one. That squid may hurt you. I would eat him, but it would slow our journey."

There's a frenzy of echoes as the giant squid glides past us. I shiver, and nestle deeper into the whale's shelter. I've no desire to meet a giant squid.

"A fine mouthful," says the whale regretfully. "Do you like squid, little one?"

"Um, no, I've never eaten it," I lie, in case the giant squid is listening. But the echoes fade and he rolls away into the darkness.

There's no dark like this in the human world. "Conor? Faro?"

Nobody answers. My voice seems to go nowhere.

"Where are they?"

"They don't speak to me as you do, but I feel that they are there."

"Are they all right?"

"They are warm things in a cold world, little one. Their blood hurts them. But they are living. I feel that they are living."

We move slowly onwards through a forest of echoes. Sound is like light here; it's the only guide there is. I wish I could make sense of all the echoes as the whale does. It hurts my ears when she searches the water with her sonar.

"Another squid," she says.

"Do stop and catch it if you want to."

The whale rumbles, "My promise to Saldowr is worth more than that, child. I must take you to the Kraken."

"Won't he – won't he hurt you?"

"He has no quarrel with me," replies the whale calmly. "Now be silent, little one, I must listen with all my power. We are coming closer, and I must find my way between two mountains."

We move on slowly, cautiously, sounding for echoes. They bounce furiously. I knew that the Deep had mountains, but not what it would be like to find a way through them, steering through jagged invisible rocks, listening for the echoes to thin out and show clear water ahead. What if the whale gets caught? What if the whale hurts herself?

My ears ring. The echoes vibrate and sound hammers through my skin, my flesh and down to my bones. I can't think, I can't see and I can't hear. All I feel is sound. The pain of it batters me until I can't bear it for another second, and then it gets worse and I'm still hanging on, praying for it to end. Now the sonar echoes wham my head like slaps from a giant hand. I curl up, trying to find shelter. I'm going to die of sound. It's going to blow me into atoms.

The noise is so loud that I'm dissolving into it. I tunnel deep inside myself, because it's the only place I can find to hide.

I don't know how long it lasts. I come back slowly,

throbbing from the noise attack. I shake my head, not daring to believe it. Someone has turned the volume down. The echoes aren't battering me any more. The noise is still loud, but it's finally fading away behind us.

"We have come through the pass, little one," booms the whale.

Through the pass... We're mountaineering, thousands of metres below the surface. A pass is a narrow way through high crags. No wonder the echoes were so terrible as they thrashed back and forth off the harsh surfaces of the rock. Maybe the sides of the mountain were so close that I could have reached out and touched them. But the spaces are growing wider now. The echoes keep on fading. I picture the whale sailing out into clear water.

We're slowing down. Soon we are barely moving. We hang, wrapped in darkness. What's going to happen now?

"This is as close as I can come, little one," says the whale. Her voice barely disturbs the water. Maybe she doesn't want anyone to hear her.

"Where are we?"

"We are close to the Kraken's lair. There's little time. I can help you on your way, and then I must rise to breathe."

Horror crawls over me. She's going to abandon us in the Deep. I thought she was going to stay with us. How can we survive down here without the whale? When I was in the Deep without her before, I didn't even know which way I was moving. And I'm sure we didn't go so far down then. There was still a tinge of light, just enough for me to see the whale.

But it's completely dark now. Darker than it ever gets in the human world. It's like being wrapped round and round in a cocoon of black cloth that covers your mouth and nose and ears, and then picked up and turned until your head whirls and you don't know which way is the surface and which the sea bed.

I fight my panic down. Conor. Faro. I've got to think of them. The whale can't leave us here. We'll all die and then no one will ever be able to put the Kraken back to sleep.

"But, whale – dear whale – if you leave us here, we'll never find our way home. We'll be lost in the Deep for ever."

A faint, cautious chuckle shivers the whale's sides. "Of course I shall come back for you," she whispers.

"But you'll never find us again."

"I am a hunter, little one. You must trust me. I shall find you. Now come out, and swim over my body until you reach your companions. Keep within touch of me."

Leaving the shelter of the whale's flipper is one of the hardest things I've ever done. I want to stay there, curled tight in the only shelter I know. Reluctantly, hesitantly, I feel my way through darkness that is so thick it feels as if I could pick up handfuls of it. There's the curve of her flipper. There's the slope of her back. That's where I must swim up, and then down to the flipper on the other side, where Conor and Faro are waiting.

I cling close to the whale's rough, pitted skin. My arms and legs can barely move because the water is so thick and the pressure of the Deep so enormous. I'm glad I can't see myself. It feels as if the Deep has flattened me out to a shadow.

I struggle on, one hand touching her curved back for safety.

"Can you go faster, little one? I must breathe soon."

My heart thumps heavily in my body with the effort of moving. The upward curve of the whale's back seems to go on for ever, and then at last it flattens, and I begin to feel my way down the other side.

"Forward a little," whispers the whale.

The Deep is pushing me away from the whale's body. I cling to her as I scull my way down her other side, not daring to kick in case it takes me away into the blackness that waits everywhere.

"Stop. You're there."

My feet find the outward shape of her flipper.

"Conor?" I whisper, "Faro?"

No one answers. My heart fills with dread. Perhaps the dive has killed them. Perhaps the whale only thinks they're still tucked behind her flipper, when really they've been swept away into the Deep.

I feel my way cautiously around the flipper. My foot kicks something and I almost scream aloud, and then a voice says furiously, "That's my tail, fool."

"Faro?"

"Sapphire, is it you? I thought you were a creature of the Deep."

"Didn't you hear me call your names?"

"Our heads are ringing."

"Where's Conor? Is he all right?"

Conor's voice comes so faintly that I can't hear the words.

"Oh, Faro, he's hurt!"

"No, it's just that we can't tell if we're shouting or whispering. We're deafened."

"Conor!" I find his hand, and clutch it. I'd recognise the feel of Conor's hand anywhere, even here at the bottom of the world. He squeezes it back, and my heart fills with relief. He's alive.

"Hurry, little one. All of you, come forward. I will make a wave to take you to the Kraken's lair."

I feel the boys slowly easing their way out. The whale's voice follows me, "Are you all right, little one? Did my dive hurt you?"

"Not the dive," I whisper. "It was the noise."

I still can't hear my own voice clearly. It's muffled, as if I'm talking inside my own head. The weight of the Deep presses on me. *Mustn't think of it. Mustn't think of the heaviness of the water, or how far away the surface is.* Even if it wasn't dark, to see it would be like staring up from the bottom of the tallest skyscraper in the world.

No, farther than that. How far can whales dive? Sperm whales are one of the deepest divers, I do remember that.

Don't think of it.

I drag my mind away, like I'd drag a baby from the edge of a cliff.

We work our way forward along the whale's body in slow motion, as if we've got heavy weights pulling on our arms and legs. I keep hold of Conor's hand. As long as we're together, as long as we hold on tight to each other, we'll survive. Faro must be on the other side of Conor, holding his wrist and giving him strength and oxygen.

We're moving along her broad flank. I try to remember what the shape of a sperm whale's jaw is like, because we'll need to negotiate our way around it. She's dead still, hanging there in the water, waiting for us.

Her head's like a box, I know that. Sperm whales look like the kind of whales children draw. I wonder if her jaw is open. What if her teeth mistake us for food?

Don't be stupid, Sapphire. She's got much more knowledge than you, down here in the Deep. Her sound system knows where we are and what shape we are. Everything's clear to her, although we humans are like prisoners who've been bound and hooded and then told to identify objects wrapped in a black velvet bag.

But she's going to leave us. We're going to be on our own. She says she'll come back for us, but maybe there won't be any "us" to come back for by the time she returns to the Deep.

The whale's voice comes like the sough of the wind. So big a creature can't really whisper, but she's doing her best. "Move forward. Move forward. You must leave my shelter now."

"But how will we know when we've reached the Kraken's lair? It's so dark. You can't see anything."

"You will know. He makes lairlight. We whales don't speak of it in the higher world."

We must be directly in front of the whale now. Inky dark stretches ahead of us. We've got to push off from her protecting bulk, and survive alone in the Deep.

"Move forward, and then I can help you on your way." We edge forward. Conor's hand grips mine reassuringly, and suddenly, for the first time since we entered the Deep, I hear his voice.

"Saph?"

"Conor!"

His voice is squeezed by the pressure of the Deep, but it's unmistakably my brother's voice.

"Are you OK, Saph?"

"I'm all right."

"My ears have stopped ringing. I couldn't hear anything before."

The whale is behind us now. If I stretched out, I wouldn't be able to touch her. *Don't go*, I plead silently. *Don't leave us alone in the Deep.*

Maybe the whale picks up my thoughts. Her voice curls into my ear in a murmur that's so low it's almost inaudible. "If you want, little barelegs, you can come back with me."

I want to so much. It's like being about five years old and rushing out of school to throw your arms round your mum and hide your face in her skirt. I want to hide in the whale's safety and blot out the memory of the Deep. If only I could go with her and never, ever come back again.

But I'm not five years old. And I'm not alone. There's Conor, and Faro. They trust me. I was the one who agreed with Ervys that I'd go back to the Deep. They came because I did.

"No, dear whale. I can't come with you. I have to stay here."

"Stay here..." echoes the whale. "I keep forgetting that you are not mine. But if you were mine you would never have left the surface —

"I shouldn't have said that," she adds in a hurried, guilty whisper. "I don't know what came over me... But you won't tell Saldowr?"

"Of course not."

"How I wish I could remember a good joke, to send you on your way."

"Never mind," I say gently, "perhaps next time."

The others don't seem to have heard our conversation. It's as if the whale and I have got a private wavelength. Just as well. What if Conor had heard her tempting me to leave him and Faro behind in the Deep?

"I must rise," says the whale in a faint voice that would be a sigh if there were any air in the Deep. "Whatever happens, I will come back for you. And now hold tight and wait for your wave."

A stir begins in the dark water. She's turning. We clutch hands. It's the wave coming. The wave the whale's making for us. I peer behind me but can't see anything. I think I know what she's doing. Her vast tail is moving from side to side, lashing the water. The wave will rise and race, growing in height and power as it rushes at us and lifts us and throws us with the speed of an arrow towards...

CHAPTER THIRTEEN

There's light ahead of us. It's a dead, numb light, like neon filtered through nylon. It pushes out greedy fingers into the Deep, searching, reaching out for us.

Now the darkness of the Deep feels like a friend. This is the kind of light someone would make out of nightmares and evil thoughts.

"It's lairlight," I whisper.

"What?"

"Lairlight. That's what the whale called it. Light where there shouldn't be any light. The Kraken makes it."

The whale's wave was much too powerful. It's brought us straight to the Kraken's lair. I turn, and for the first time since we left the Groves of Aleph I can see Faro and Conor's faces. They look as if they've been hit by an enormous force that bruises from the inside without leaving marks on the skin. Faro's face is drained by exhaustion. Conor looks battered but determined.

"Do you think he's there?" I whisper.

"Of course he's—"

"Of course of course of course," says another voice, light as a feather and silky smooth but with the same greed in it that shines through the light. "Of course I am here to welcome you, *myrgh kerenza*." The voice gives a sycophantic giggle. "Isn't that what they call you? Have I got it right?"

"How do you—?"

"Oh, I have my messengers. You think the Kraken has no friends? You think everybody hates me? No no no no no no no. That's not how it is at all. And you've brought your friends to play with me. How nice."

His voice noses its way towards us like an octopus' tentacle. I press close to Conor, but Conor pushes me gently away and swims forward a stroke.

"Show yourself, then," he says calmly. "How can you be our friend if we can't see you?"

"Oh no no no no no no no no. It doesn't work like that. *You* have to come and see *me*."

Faro has moved to Conor's side, and I swim forward too, through the leaden water. Every instinct in my body is telling me to turn and flee as far as I can.

"You only have to come towards the light. It's not difficult," says the Kraken.

The Kraken's lairlight fingers flicker and make sudden darts at us, but the force of the Deep thrusts them back before they touch us. The Deep seems to be on our side now, protecting us. As long as we stay clear of the lairlight, maybe the Kraken can't hurt us.

But in that case, little sister, what have we come here for? I'm so close to Faro that even the Deep itself can't block his thoughts from me, and they come alive in my head. *Why have we risked the Deep if we're not going to fight? We can't put the Kraken back to sleep by hiding from him. Saldowr gave us a mission.*

Faro's fighting spirit gives me courage. He's right: we mustn't forget why we've come. Remember the white stones, and the red stone. The little Mer children who don't know anything about the Kraken yet. We're here because we want to make sure that they never will.

You have to come towards the light.

The Kraken was taunting us, but he was right, too. We have to brave the lairlight.

Faro's braced, ready for action. I wish I could look as calm and determined as Conor does. Lairlight stabs towards me, and I flinch.

Towards the light. Towards the light.

The decision is made without words. We move forward. If we thought any more, we'd never do it. Slowly, we swim side by side until the first of the lairlight fingers touches us.

It doesn't hurt. It's all right. We didn't need to be so scared.

Suddenly I can't remember what we're doing here. What's the point of it? My mind and heart are as heavy

as my limbs. Darkness sweeps into my head. Conor...
Faro... they're a thousand miles away, behind a wall of
black, icy glass. I see them and hear them but I can't feel
anything. What am I doing here? Why did we ever think
it was important to stop the Kraken? No one can stop
the Kraken. The Kraken is real and everything else is false.
Even Saldowr... Saldowr...

My mind struggles, trying not to be swamped. Faro is
trying to reach me. *It's the lairlight, Sapphire. It's the lairlight.
You've got to fight it.*

He's right, I realise slowly. It's the lairlight painting
blackness into my mind and killing all the thoughts
except the ones it wants. But maybe the lairlight knows
the truth. Maybe all those things, like riding with the
dolphins and talking on the rocks with Faro, were just
dreams. Stupid dreams that you cling on to because
you're so afraid of the truth.

Fingers of light flicker over my skin. They're probing,
penetrating—

Faro's right. Got to fight them. Like octopus' tentacles.
You have to – you have to peel them off.

Slowly, with an enormous effort, I summon up my
strength. I won't let the lairlight kill my thoughts. I'll think
of the whale. Her huge, rough body. Her kindness. The
way she found me in the Deep and rescued me. She
didn't need to do it; she just did it because her heart is
twice as big as her body.

No, jeers the lairlight, *that whale's a big soft old fool who only likes you because she's stupid enough to muddle you up with one of her own brats.*

I'll think of Saldowr instead. His wisdom, and the way he believes in us.

Believes in you? He's desperate, that's all. You're not Mer so he's quite happy about throwing your lives away as long as there's a one in a hundred chance of helping his precious Ingo.

The dolphins. The rush of our journeys with them through the sparkling water. Dolphin language and dolphin intelligence and dolphin loyalty.

This time the lairlight hesitates for a few seconds before it shoots back. *Humans are always mushy about dolphins. That doesn't stop you killing them, does it? How many dead dolphins were washed up on your beaches last year? How many choke to death in tuna nets? How the dolphins must hate you.*

My mind is gasping. I can't think of any more thoughts to fight the lairlight. But at that moment Faro twists me to face him. His face is torn with pain. The lairlight must have got deep into his mind, too.

"Got to – help each other, Sapphire! Think together. Stronger together. Think of the reef."

My thoughts join with Faro's. We're in the sunwater, not far below the surface, gazing down into the beauty of an offshore reef. Weed sways gently. A cloud of striped baby fish separates and the fish spurt into rock hollows. Coral glistens and a wrasse glides by. Starfish stretch out their arms, mussels open to the taste of salt water, jewel anemones cling to the rock. Filtered green and turquoise light dances over everything. And there's a leatherback turtle in the distance, chasing a school of jellyfish—

What a pathetic idea of heaven – a few old rocks with fish swimming in and out of them! sneers the lairlight.

But this time I don't listen. That voice can yammer away as much as it likes, but the beauty of the reef is much stronger. In my mind Faro is with me, smiling and strong, sculling the water so he stays in place against the tug of the current. Our hair flows around our faces, tangling. I'm hoping to see the velvet swimming crabs that Faro told me were around here somewhere...

The lairlight retreats, whickering maliciously to itself. It is still touching me, but it can't get into me any more.

But I've forgotten about Conor. He's in the lairlight too. Has it overwhelmed him?

"Conor, think about Elvira!"

"Think about Elvira?" Conor sounds surprised, and completely normal. "What for?"

"It'll get the lairlight out of your head."

"What do you mean?"

Faro and I stare at him in disbelief. "Didn't you feel it?"

"Nope. Nothing."

"Oh."

So while I was struggling, nearly drowning in the lairlight's influence, Conor was perfectly all right.

"That is so unfair," I murmur.

"What?"

"Nothing, Conor."

"He's too good to live, that's his trouble," grumbles Faro.

"Too good to live... what a fascinating concept," repeats the spoiled, silky voice of the Kraken. "So you don't like my lairlight. What a pity. What – a – pity. Some people can't live without it. But even so, see, you have entered into it. And here I am again. Peekaboo!"

I start violently. Water swirls round me like oil. Something jumps in the corner of my eye. A man? No. There's a seal's tail, as strong as Faro's. One of the Mer? But the Mer can't live here. The tail vanishes, but now a sea serpent coils and stretches through the water towards me. On my left a shark's jaw opens, showing row after row of jagged, brown-edged teeth. I flinch to the right, but there a purple Portuguese man-of-war stretches out its tentacles. Ahead of me, a cloud of piranha fish feasts on a lump of rotten meat. I look behind me and a Mer man stands wrapped in a cloak like Saldowr's. But it's not Saldowr. It's Ervys, arms folded, watching me with a cold sneer.

Conor and Faro see them too. Faro raises his crossed arms over his face to ward them off. Conor plunges to my side and holds me close.

And then comes the worst thing of all, which makes me cry out in horror. The giant sea slug that used to live in my nightmares when I was little, and wake me up shaking and shivering. From the mouth of the sea slug comes a faint, giveaway little giggle. The kind of titter you might get from a clever bully who's pulled a trick you don't understand.

"It's him," says Faro through gritted teeth. "They're all him. He's a shape-shifter."

The shapes flitter and fleer around us, whirling until we're dizzy.

"They're not real," Conor says, gripping me tightly, and it sounds like a prayer. "They can't hurt us, Saph. Look at me, not at them."

I do as he says, and even though my own fear is reflected in his eyes, I feel calmer. We're in this together, the three of us. The Kraken can change shape as much as he wants, but he's only got himself. And, looking at Conor's face, I see something else. The talisman, hanging from his neck. Maybe it was the talisman that helped Conor into the Deep. Maybe that's the limit of the talisman's powers... but it's just possible that it can do more. For a second, in the lairlight, I believe that I can see features on the face of the diving figure.

"Conor, look, your talisman!"

His hand goes to it automatically. His fist clenches tight over it, and then he releases his grip and I realise that he was right all along. Conor saw from the beginning what I'm only just starting to notice. The diving figure has Conor's face, even though he is Mer. I don't know what this means, but I'm afraid. If this is a portrait of my brother then what does it mean? Is it a portrait of what *is*, or only of what might be?

195

My thoughts break off. Conor is gathering himself. Power is flowing into him, as it did when he faced the guardian seals, as it did when he read the runes that made the keystone heal itself. He raises his arms against the weight of the Deep, as if he's invoking something.

A shiver runs through me. This is my brother, but at the same time it's not the Conor I know. It's someone who reaches beyond Conor, and can do things that my everyday brother couldn't even imagine.

"In the name of our Mer blood," says Conor in a voice that's like a chant. "In the name of our human blood. Mer and human, I command you to come forth."

Everything stops. The shapes vanish. The world stops jittering and becomes calm. The wicked little Kraken-voice is dumb.

He's done it, I think. *He's stopped the Kraken's mouth.*

Silence hangs. My mind is numb. I don't know what to think any more. Can Conor really be strong enough to defeat the Kraken with just a few words? I want to believe it, but somehow it feels too easy. Faro and I float motionlessly, waiting and hoping. Conor's arms are still upraised. The silence lengthens, lengthens, like a drop of oil ready to fall from a spoon.

And then there's a tiny giggle. My heart sinks. It's the Kraken; it's got to be. No one else could put so much malice into a sound as small as that. The Kraken giggles again, then finds its voice. It's only a thread of a voice at first, but as soon as I hear it I know that the Kraken hasn't changed. How could I have expected Conor to overcome a monster who has been prowling the Deep for more than fifty life-spans? Life isn't like that.

The Kraken is back, and full of bravado. "Not quite good enough, my friends," it mocks us. "Here I am, back again. Peekaboo!"

In spite of all his courage, Conor's shoulders slump as his arms fall to his sides. Despair sweeps over all three of us. The nightmare circus is starting again. The shapes close round us, taunting us, hunting us down.

"I did my best, Saph," mutters Conor.

"I know you did."

The Deep makes hollow echoes out of our voices. We'll never defeat the Kraken. We'll die here in the Deep and the Kraken will still be laughing at us.

I was so stupid. I kept expecting other people to rescue me. The whale, or Faro, or Conor. But it's not going to happen.

"Let's have another game of hide-and-seek," giggles the Kraken, and then it skips to vanishing point. It's gone, but I know it's not really gone. This is just a breathing space.

I've got to think faster than this. I've got to shake off the clinging tendrils of lairlight that still slow me down. No one's going to help us. We've got to help ourselves. We've got nothing else.

I thought I'd got rid of the lairlight, but it's still in my head. It wants me to give up. I've got to force it away and then maybe I'll think of a plan.

I make a huge effort. I remember diving through water the colour of jasper. I remember dolphin voices. And Saldowr smiling at me, saying, *You did well, myrgh kerenza*. Those things are real.

My mind clears like a landscape under a sweep of sun. And I see it. The mirror.

"Conor! The mirror! We forgot about the mirror."

A jellyfish tentacle sweeps across my face, and I cry out. The next moment I see a claw, clacking its way towards me through the lairlight.

"Conor!"

"Quick," mutters Conor, fumbling with the strapping that holds the mirror, "Saph, help me."

Conor pulls at the kelp to release the mirror. His fingers fumble like lead sausages, struggling against the slowness of the Deep. I tug and tear, breaking my nails on the tough kelp stem. The mirror's metal back appears, then its handle. I grab it, and pull the mirror free of the strapping. Down here in the Deep the mirror has grown ten times heavier. I can barely lift it.

Even in the dismal, oily lairlight it flashes brilliantly. My eyes dazzle, although I'm not facing the mirror. But the flash catches Faro. He claps his hands over his eyes. The mirror-blast has struck him full in the face.

"I told you that mirror was cursed," he mutters.

"Faro! Are you hurt?"

"Blinded me – wait—"

Faro puts out his hand, pushing me away. His tail lashes with the pain of the mirror burn. *Don't let him be blind, don't let him be blind*, I plead in my head.

"It's coming back. I can see you now. Don't look so scared, little sister."

"Let me see."

Faro allows me, and I look into his eyes. They're bloodshot, but the life is back in them. "Oh, Faro, I was so scared."

Faro looks gratified. "That mirror's definitely cursed," he says, and shakes his head as if he wants to shake away those seconds of fear when we both thought the mirror might have damaged his sight for ever.

But the Kraken is back again. This time it skitters up to us in the form of a shrimp. I let my hand drop so the mirror is behind my back.

"It's only silly little me again," it says, coy and ingratiating, but the water throbs with a hundred tons of hatred, malice and rage. "I don't get many visitors, so I try to put on a good show. Now remind me, why is it you came?"

Is he going to stay a shrimp? Yes, it seems he is, for the time being anyway. A little, harmless shrimp. Why would anyone want to hurt him?

Stop that, Sapphire. Think your own thoughts and don't let the Kraken into your head.

I'm still holding the mirror. Its weight drags my left hand down. It would be so easy to let go of it. That's what the Kraken wants. Why not let him have what he wants? He's only a little, harmless shrimp with quivery whiskers and a cute tail – he's not going to do any harm—

He's a Kraken. A monster. He devours children.

"You're the Kraken," I say aloud. "You kill Mer children."

The shrimp convulses with laughter. *"Kill children!* Wherever did you get that ridiculous idea? Kill children indeed. If people want to bring their children to the threshold of the Deep and *abandon* them, and then blame it on me, what can I do? It's always the poor old Kraken who gets the blame. It's been the same since time began. As soon as a person like me tries to make a better world, you find someone else pointing the finger and calling him a murderer."

The shrimp's self-righteousness is horribly convincing. I glance at Conor uneasily.

"He's lying," says Faro. "Can't you hear the slime of lies in his voice?"

For a flash of a moment a monstrous Claw Creature swells up, and then the Kraken is a shrimp again. "Don't worry," he says meekly, "I'm used to being misunderstood."

"That's just as well," says Conor. The Claw Creature bulges like a threatening phantom for a thousandth of a second, and then the Kraken brings himself under control. I try to look as if I haven't noticed anything.

"I don't think you should be so harsh to the Kraken,

Conor," I say. "Maybe he's right, and we're not being fair to him. Think of all the stuff we were told about what a monster he was. But how could an innocent little shrimp shake the sea floor so that half of Ingo is destroyed? How could a harmless creature like that hurt a child? It's obvious he can't. Look at him."

Faro and Conor turn horrified, disbelieving faces towards me. The shrimp gives a skip of joy.

"At last, someone who understands me."

I stare at the thing and have to hold myself rigid to stop my body shuddering all over with revulsion. I'm on the Kraken's wavelength now. I understand him. The bile of his barely suppressed rage and cruelty seeps through the lairlight and sickens me. But I swallow down my nausea and continue earnestly, "I'm sure the Kraken's only trying to help the Mer really. They just don't understand him."

Faro hisses through his teeth, as if he can't believe what he's hearing, but Conor's watching me narrowly.

"Saldowr's supposed to be so wise," I go on, "but he doesn't know everything. Anyway, people are already saying Saldowr's past it."

I wait for Faro to erupt, but nothing happens. Conor has laid a restraining hand on his shoulder, but Faro doesn't need it. He's picked up what I'm trying to do, and his eyes glow with excitement.

"Past it," squeaks the shrimp, its voice vibrating with glee and spite, "past it past it past it. I knew it would happen! Saldowr thinks he's so great, but he couldn't fight the Tide Knot, could he? Could he could he could he could he?"

"No," I say, making myself sound regretful and ashamed. "We thought he could do anything but, well, we were wrong. And I think *he* was wrong about *you*. He just didn't want us to be friends with you because you're more powerful than he is. But – but we do."

"You want to be my friend? Really really really really? More than anything? But what if you're just a little human wiggle-waggle-wiggle-tongue who'll say anything if it gets you out of a tight place? Words words words words words. What if you're trying to trick the poor little Kraken?"

The shrimp zigzags in front of me until my eyes hurt from trying to follow it. "What if what if what if what if?" it needles me, hovering a few inches from my nose. I frown, and then clap my hand to my forehead as if I've just come up with a wonderful idea. The shrimp darts away, still whining like a mosquito.

"Listen, we can prove we want to be friends. Friends give each other presents, don't they?"

"Presents!" shrieks the shrimp.

And before he can repeat it a dozen times I say quickly, " Yes, presents. We brought something into the Deep from Saldowr's secret treasury. He doesn't know we took it but – oh well, I don't suppose he'll mind really. It's not as if we're stealing it or anything. Anyway, even if he does he can't do much about it." I force my features into an ingratiating smile. "Because – because of all the misunderstandings there've been between us, I'd like *you* to have it. As a present."

"His treasury!" The shrimp is having a lot of trouble hiding its triumph. "My dear girl, you shouldn't have. Shouldn't have shouldn't have shouldn't have." The shrimp releases a trill of titters. I don't know which is worse: the Kraken's horrible glee, or his venomous spite.

"Conor tied it to his leg to hide it from Saldowr. Look. Here it is. We've brought it all the way to the Deep."

With all my strength I lift the mirror, keeping its back to the Kraken. This time there's no flash, but even so the shrimp shoots back through the water, out of the lairlight and into the dark of the Deep.

"It's a mirror," I say in a soft, luring voice, "Saldowr's mirror. It's the only one like it in the world. No one's supposed to look into it. Typical Saldowr. He always wants to keep the best things for himself."

Silence. No response. The Kraken's seen through me. He knows it's a trick.

I fight back a wave of despair. The whale gone, Conor's power failing, the Kraken shape-shifting and laughing at us before he closes in for his revenge. Nothing's working. There's nothing left for us to do.

No. Don't think those lairlight thoughts. We've got to keep fighting. We've got nothing to lose now.

"Saph, hold up the mirror so he can see it," murmurs Conor.

I lift the heavy mirror again, up through the dragging water. My wrist aches as I move it from side to side slowly, tantalisingly, always keeping the mirror face down so that the Kraken can't see it.

"Saldowr's mirror," I muse as if to myself. "He'd be so angry if he knew we'd stolen it away and brought it to the Deep. He always keeps it in his treasury, because whoever looks into the mirror gains the mirror's power – that's how we were able to come to the Deep, of course. This mirror doesn't show *you* – it shows what you could become."

"Saph!" stage-whispers Conor ferociously, "You shouldn't have said that!"

"It's OK, Con, no one heard."

The silence changes. Now it's a waiting silence, full of temptation. The Kraken is greedy, but he's cunning. Maybe he suspects that we can be cunning, too.

At last, slowly and slyly, a shrimp's antenna pokes through the darkness into the lairlight. "Coming, ready or not," giggles the Kraken.

And there he is. He's still in his shrimp shape and I wonder why he's not shape-shifting any more. Maybe it's something to do with the mirror – or maybe the Kraken enjoys being a shrimp.

"But I don't know what might happen if someone as powerful as the Kraken looked into the mirror," I say.

"He's so strong already, maybe it wouldn't be a good idea."

"Give it to me." The voice snatches, forgetting to be coy.

"You're too light," I say, "the mirror would crush you. I suppose I could hold it up for you to look in, if you like."

"If I like. *If I like*. Oh no no no no no no no. I don't like at all. I don't like doing what I'm told one single bit, because it makes me ask myself why people are telling me to do it. Why why why why why? *You* look in the mirror first, *myrgh kerenza*, and we'll see what happens. And *I'll* look over your shoulder, just to be sure, before I look for myself."

I stare at the Kraken in horror. Look into the mirror here, now, in the Deep, without Saldowr's protection? With the Kraken tittering at my shoulder? I can't do it. I won't do it. Saldowr said the vision was only meant for one person, and no one else could spy on it. And what if the mirror flashes again and blinds me, maybe for good this time—

"I'll do it," says Faro casually, "if it will set your mind at rest."

"You! You – you *Merboy*. How can anything *you* see in the mirror be of interest to me?" asks the shrimp haughtily.

"You're right, I don't suppose it will be very interesting," says Faro, keeping his voice as light and easy as if he's teasing me in the sunwater on a summer's day. "It's not going to show *me* any glory. I'm not worth it. Just a common Merboy who's never done anything special in his life. But at least then you'll know how the mirror works."

The Kraken is still suspicious. "All this talk about mirrors," he chitters. "I should have killed you hours ago. You're taking up my time and I don't like that. Oh no no no no no no."

"If only I could look into the mirror when the Kraken does," I say to Conor. "Imagine what he could become!" The Kraken pounces, and swallows the bait.

"Merboy first, Merboy first. Let's get *him* out of the way. He can have a look and then he'll find out what the mirror's power has in store for *him*. He can have a look and then he can die."

Oh, Faro. My heart squeezes with terror for him. Thousands of metres of dark water press me down. We are in the Deep and there's no rescue. Why did we come here? Why did we ever believe we could do anything against the Kraken?

Faro swims forward to the mirror as easily as if he's swimming to catch a current. His lips are pressed tight together. It's the only sign of tension and I don't think the Kraken notices. He doesn't know Faro – doesn't know how brave he is and how he's risked his life to come here—

"Faro!" I didn't mean to say it. The word just escaped from my lips. His answering frown silences me.

"Hold up the mirror, little sister."

It is the worst thing I've ever had to do. As I raise the mirror slowly, I feel as if I'm signing Faro's death warrant. Once he's looked into the mirror, the Kraken will kill him. Why did I ever start this?

Faro looks, and even in the lairlight he grows pale. I try to find him with my thoughts, but he's made a wall around his mind and I can't get in. I don't know what he's seeing but I can tell it cuts him to the heart.

The Kraken skitters towards the mirror. Cunningly he positions himself. He's trying to see Faro's reflection, without seeing his own. The Kraken peeps sidelong through the water in a paroxysm of spiteful relish.

"Oh, Merboy! Oh silly silly little Merboy who's not what he thinks he is! How upsetting! How terribly terribly terribly upsetting. But don't worry, silly little Merboy because you're not going to be upset for long. You'll soon be dead dead dead dead dead, and you won't have to worry about your blood because there won't be any."

I feel sick. The Kraken is winning again. No matter how hard we try, he turns everything inside out until he's winning. He's *got* to look into the mirror. But will he, now he's seen that the mirror can hold terrible truths? I've got to persuade him. Tempt him. Convince him that he'll really see something wonderful.

"Poor old Faro," I say callously, and I wink at the Kraken. "The mirror hadn't got much to show him, had it? Not much greatness there!" The Kraken snickers.

"Saldowr will be so angry," I go on, making my voice frightened. "He was terrified in case you—"

"In case I what?"

"Nothing. It's nothing, Kraken. Anyway, he knew you wouldn't look in the mirror. He said you couldn't bear to see your own reflection."

"Did he indeed? Indeed indeed indeed indeed," chatters the Kraken. "Scared of my reflection? Scared of my shadow – did he say that?"

"N-no, please, please, Kraken, I shouldn't have told you—"

"But you *have* told me. You humans are all blibber blabber blibber blabber. Saldowr didn't want me to look into his precious mirror. Ha! *He was scared.* Scaredy scaredy scaredy anemone. Wanting to keep his precious mirror to himself. He's selfish. Selfish selfish selfish selfish. Always trying to cheat the Kraken out of what is rightfully his..."

He's shifting. He's moving closer to the mirror. It's luring him. He wants to see greatness. His vanity is swelling, conquering fear and suspicion. He believes he's going to see greatness.

"Ugly Merboy," he murmurs, "ugly, ugly little Merboy. If I were you I wouldn't even *want* to be alive. But don't worry, you'll soon be dead. Dead dead—"

He stops himself and edges even closer to the mirror's rim. "But before I bother to kill you," he goes on, more quietly than ever in a voice like poisoned silk, "*I'm* going to cheat *Saldowr*. I'm going to have *my* turn with the mirror."

The Kraken dances into position, then whips round. My heart thunders, choking me. He's going to look.

There's a long moment of silence. I wait for him to be blinded, or struck like lightning by the horror of himself. But the moment lengthens, lengthens, and the Kraken continues to stare. He's still a shrimp – yes, but not just a shrimp. Phantoms are bulging out of him and darting towards the mirror. The Claw Creature, the sea serpent, the Portuguese man-of-war, the ravenous shark and the cloud of piranhas. They dart towards the mirror and the mirror throws them back, more real and solid with each reflection. The mirror is making them stronger. It's multiplying all the demons that the Kraken makes of himself. With each shape-shifting the Kraken is gaining power.

My blood feels like ice. What have I done? We're going to die, and there's no hope for the Mer.

"Oh yes yes yes yes yes yes yes," comes the incongruously tiny shrimp voice out of the mass of monsters. "How great I am! How great I am!"

And then the mirror flashes.

CHAPTER FOURTEEN

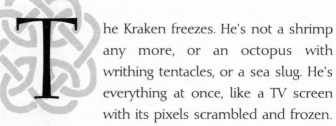he Kraken freezes. He's not a shrimp any more, or an octopus with writhing tentacles, or a sea slug. He's everything at once, like a TV screen with its pixels scrambled and frozen. All the shapes he's shifted in and out of are clamped around him.

I keep holding up the mirror. I don't know what else to do. The lairlight is growing weaker. I can still see Faro and Conor, but the Deep is coming closer, pushing in on us.

"I can't hold it up much longer, Conor."

"Wait."

Conor supports my elbow from underneath. Faro grasps the mirror handle.

"It's getting heavier! It's slipping!"

The mirror weighs like lead. It wants to fall through the heavy, dark water to the ocean floor, and then down and down through sand and rock until it reaches the earth's fiery core. And then it'll melt, and remake itself, and wait for another wizard to conjure it up from the Deep...

"Saph! *Hold it up!*"

I jerk myself awake. I'm so tired. So tired of holding on. Why not let go now and let the mirror do what it wants...

"He's moving, Faro!" calls Conor sharply.

I look up, aghast. The pixels of the Kraken are reassembling themselves, making shapes that are even more monstrous than before because they're not complete. The giant sea slug has a hole in its belly through which the Deep pours through. The cute little shrimp has no head. An octopus tentacle lashes the water, detached from any body. And the mirror's still forcing my hand down, as if a giant magnet's pulling on it from the centre of the earth.

Conor and Faro brace themselves. Muscles and tendons stand out on their arms. We're holding on to one another for support, struggling to keep the mirror from falling. But the Kraken's winning. He's coming back, reassembling all his monstrous selves and getting ready to strike.

At that moment something scratches my leg, like the end of a twig. There's something in my pocket.

Earth and Air surge back to me so powerfully that I almost choke. Salt fills my mouth. I must let go of the Air.

But Earth has come with me this time. I almost forgot

I had the rowan in my pocket. Granny Carne told me to bring the rowan wherever I went, and not to let go of it, because it's full of Earth magic.

But what good is Earth magic in the Deep? As this thought flashes through me, the rowan scratches my leg again, like a signal. It's as if the rowan wants to communicate with me – to help me.

But Earth and Ingo are opposites. Surely it's not possible that Earth wants to help Ingo?

Granny Carne gave me the rowan. Maybe she foresaw something. Maybe Earth has got to join together with Ingo because their common enemy is so powerful...

Thoughts swirl in my mind, so fast that everything seems to be happening inside the beat of a second. Earth joining with Ingo: that's what's happening in me too. Mixed bloods, running together.

The mirror drags at my arm. Veins stand out on Conor's forehead from the effort of holding on to it. It's like a tombstone, tilting down, ready to fall. We can't hold it any longer. Its metal handle slithers through our hands, then the mirror kicks out of our grasp, turns over, and plunges away through the black water. One last gleam of metal, and it's swallowed up in the Deep.

The Kraken rears up in front of us in all his threadbare horror.

"Oh yes yes yes yes yes yes yes yes," he snickers, "you thought you'd beaten the Kraken, didn't you? But nobody beats the Kraken. Nobody wins except me. Your silly silly silly little mirror's gone where it can't hurt anybody ever again. But it did hurt me. Oh yes yes yes yes yes. It nearly made the Kraken cry. And so I'm going to have to hurt *you*, to make it fair. Merboy first, and then you, *myrgh kerenza*."

Conor spreads his arms in front of me. "You'll have to kill me before you touch her," he says.

"Oh yes yes yes yes yes, no need to worry about that, I'll kill you all right. You're all going to die. That's so obvious it doesn't even need saying. Trickety trick trickety trick. What a trio of trite little tricksters. You tried to bamboozle the Kraken and the Kraken doesn't like that. I'll tell you what he does with tricksters and bamboozlers. He munches them up. You'll enjoy seeing it, I promise you. First Merboy, then *myrgh kerenza*, and then when you've had a good look at what's going to happen to you, it'll be your turn, singing boy! And you'll get out of my way when I want you to."

The rowan. The Kraken's voice clack-clacks in my ears like claws. Got to think of the rowan. The rowan brings protection. No evil can pass its threshold.

It's the only thing left. Earth and Ingo joined together. *You've got to try, Sapphire.*

I let my hand drift down to my side, very slowly so as not to attract the Kraken's attention. He'll strike any minute but he wants to gloat over us first. I slip my hand into the wet, tight opening of my jeans pocket. My finger touches something that burns hotly. Salt water hasn't changed the rowan. It isn't soaked with sea water, it's burning hot and dry. I nearly cry out from the shock, but I stop myself and I don't think the Kraken notices.

My fingers close around the spray of berries. They feel as if they're dipped in fire. But there can't be fire in the Deep. It must be an illusion. My fingers aren't really scorching. I bite my lips and force down the sickness and pain. *Don't be such a coward. If you let go of the rowan there's nothing left.*

I bring out my hand, curled, with the spray of rowan hidden in my palm. "Kraken," I say, "Kraken!" I feel like a bullfighter waving his red cloth. "Look, I've got something for you."

This time the Kraken doesn't freeze, but he goes very still. All his eyes glitter feverishly. "Something for me?"

"Yes."

"Like your mirror mirror mirror mirror mirror—"

"No. Not a mirror."

I spread out my hand with the rowan spray in my palm and hold it out. The weight of the Deep presses the burning berries against my hand.

The Kraken stares with his sea-slug eyes and his crab eyes and all the other eyes in his body.

"That's not a Deep something," he chatters. "That's a something that's not allowed in the Deep."

"Like us," I say, staring straight at him. "Humans can't come to the Deep, Kraken. The Mer can't come to the Deep. But here we are."

"Saldowr never gave you that. I'll munch your finger finger finger finger finger if you say he did."

"It's not from Saldowr's treasury. It's not from Ingo. You plant it by the threshold, Kraken. No evil can pass it."

A groan of terrible frustration escapes from the Kraken's many bellies.

"I should have killed you all," he moans, "I should have killed you all when I had the chance."

Conor, Faro and I are side by side, the rowan in front of us. It makes me feel stronger than a siege wall. Its blood-red berries look as if they're bathed in golden fire that spreads outwards, lighting the Deep. The Kraken groans in agony.

"Take it away. Make it not be alive. *No no no no no no no.* Give it to me now and I'll break it into a million million pieces. The Kraken wants it, the Kraken wants it," he mutters.

"No. The Kraken can't have it."

The Kraken looks down at himself, at his slug trail leaking through the water into the oily lairlight, his scandalously detached tentacles and his jumping, headless shrimp tail. He lifts a monstrous claw and passes it over himself. Even the claw shivers when it finds the holes where the Deep has swum through him.

"The Kraken doesn't like it," he moans. "Oh no, oh no, oh no, oh no. The Kraken doesn't want the light."

His voice has changed. It isn't chittering with malice and hatred now. It's keening like someone who's lost the dearest thing in life. "Oh no, oh no, oh no," laments the Kraken. "Don't show me the light. The Kraken never wanted to hurt anybody. The Kraken never did those bad things. Don't show me those things."

Faro folds his arms, and looks at the Kraken coldly. "He's seeing himself," he says.

We watch, chilled to the bone by the horror of it all. And now, in front of our eyes, the Kraken is changing yet again. His many selves are dropping away like old rags. I hold the rowan high. No evil can get past it. No evil...

Dark water swirls around the Kraken, and for a few seconds he's hidden from us. Something is lashing the water. A tail. A strong seal tail, glistening like Faro's. A cloud of hair, glistening like seaweed, eddies around a face that looks...

Human. Mer. Mer and human, mixed. Its eyes are dark, without the silvery gleam of Mer eyes.

"Who are you?" I ask.

A cloak of oily water wraps itself around the Kraken's body, half concealing him.

"I want to go to sleep," he says.

"To sleep?" I echo.

"Cusca, cusca, cusca," moans the Man-Mer-Kraken. "I never hurt anyone. I didn't do anything. I want to go back to sleep."

"Sleep then," says Conor. "Sleep for a thousand years, Kraken."

"But I might dream," moans the Kraken.

"The rowan will put you to sleep," I say. Words rise to my lips like lullabies I've forgotten years ago. "There won't be any bad dreams or nightmares. You'll be safe in the dark. Cusca, cusca, cusca, Kraken. It's time to sleep."

I make my voice soft, as if I'm putting a child to bed. The rowan burns even more brightly, searing my palm. I stretch my hand out, and touch the Kraken with the spray of rowan berries.

The Kraken's mouth widens to a black O. Nothing, nought, nil. Zero with zero inside. The mouth-circle swells. It's as big as a football. It spreads outward, lapping up the monster selves of the Kraken. It's a black cavern and now only a rim of the Kraken shows, stretched around the blackness. The cavernous mouth gapes like in a vast yawn. The Kraken-rim stretches and stretches, growing thinner and thinner like elastic pulled to breaking point. The huge black mouth convulses, and swallows the Kraken.

He'll come back. Any minute now that shrimp will bounce back, jeering at us.

Time stretches. Slowly, as we watch, the black mouth melts into the surrounding dark of the Deep. The lairlight fades to nothing. We are in the solid, comforting darkness of the Deep.

"He's gone," says Conor.

"Yes, he's gone," echoes Faro.

There's a long pause, and then Faro adds, in a different voice, "I hope there will be."

"Will be what?"

"Bad dreams. Nightmares. I hope there'll be plenty of them."

Conor and I say nothing. We've got no energy left. The Kraken has gone, but we can't feel any triumph – not yet. We are in the Deep, alone, hand in hand. The only light comes from the rowan spray in my hand, but as we watch even that melts away, as if it knows its work is done, and we are left in complete darkness.

CHAPTER FIFTEEN

"We'll have to wait for the whale," I whisper at last.

"Are you sure she'll come back?"

I'm trying not to consider this possibility. Of course the whale will come back. How could she not? I'm her friend, her little barelegs...

My thoughts stutter to a stop. The whale has only met me twice. What if she forgets us once she's back on the surface? Or she might decide to dive somewhere else, where there are more giant squid for her to eat. We're not her children. Conor and I are human and Faro's Mer. She has no reason to feel loyalty to us.

No, she has no reason. But the sense of the whale's strong, protective presence flows back over me. I trust her. I don't believe that she'll abandon us. "Of course she'll come back," I say firmly.

We must keep hold of one another. If someone drifts off into the Deep now, they're gone for ever. The thought of it makes me dizzy, as if I were standing on top of a cliff, with the ground crumbling beneath my feet.

Hold on. Faro's gripping Conor's wrist, supporting him. We're close together, like shipwrecked sailors on a tiny island with the tide coming in.

"Conor?"

"It's OK, Saph. I'm here."

The dark tide of the Deep rolls around us. There's nothing to do but wait, and hope that the whale has kept faith with us. If anyone can find us in the pitchy darkness of the Deep, she can. The sperm whale has the best sonar system in the world, I tell myself over and over. She'll pick us up on her whale radar. We'll be three tiny echoes, a long way off, and she'll know it's us and dive towards us.

What if she dives too close? Her weight would destroy us. Even if we survived, we'd be scattered in the Deep.

Don't think like that. I've got to hold on to my courage.

Long minutes vanish into the Deep. I've lost track of time. I don't know how long we've been here. I can't remember what day it is. Mum and Roger and everything at home are shrouded in fog. I daren't even start thinking about Sadie.

"It's like waiting for the bus to St Pirans," says Conor suddenly.

"Bus?" I echo stupidly. My thoughts are so far from

buses that for a moment I have no idea what he's talking about.

"Bus?" asks Faro in the casual voice people use when they don't want to admit they don't know what someone's talking about.

"The bus from Senara to St Pirans only runs twice a day," explains Conor, "and you always just miss it. It's much quicker to walk."

Conor's clear memory of the human world touches mine, and ignites a dangerous flare of memories. The fog that surrounds Earth when I'm in Ingo clears for a moment, and a wave of longing pours through me. If only Conor hadn't mentioned walking. Walking on soft, springy turf in the evening sunlight. Or walking on cold, hard sand after the tide goes out, leaving footprints like the ones Robinson Crusoe found on his island. Or maybe walking on a hot road, uphill, with the smell of tar and dust and petrol...

I mustn't do it. I must let the fog roll back over my memory. The Deep is hurting me now, and I'm scared. I'm so scared. I don't want to be here. The pressure is flattening me and crushing my ribs. *It's your own fault, I tell myself angrily. You started thinking of sand and roads and all those Air things. Conor started and Air got into you. Turn away from it. You're in Ingo. Ingo.*

The whale told me that even the Deep was part of Ingo, the first time I met her. *How can it not be Ingo, where I am?* she said. She was laughing at me, but kindly. I think she thinks I'm much younger than I am. Probably because sperm whale babies weight about a ton, even when they're just born. I must look like a tadpole to her.

The pressure of the Deep has eased off again. I've got Conor here, and Faro, and the whale's coming. That's what I've got to remember and hold on to.

"I'm so tired," says Conor, and suddenly his voice is heavy. "I'm going to have a sleep while we wait."

"No!" says Faro sharply. "Stay awake, Conor!"

"Only a little sleep…"

I'd like to go to sleep too. Now that Conor's said it, I realise how tired I am too. My arms and legs have got weights of lead on them. Just a little sleep, until the whale comes. My eyelids hurt from the effort of keeping my eyes open. The Deep is pressing them shut… Why not sleep, why not let go of everything and sleep – just for a little while –

"No, Sapphire, no!"

"Jus a lil slee Far— Faro, stop it!"

His nails dig into my arm, gouging the skin. *Wake up, Sapphire!*

"Ge off – 'm awake!"

"Lea – leave sis 'lone."

"Leave her alone to *die*, you mean! Is that what you want! We've got to hold on. You've got to stay awake, Conor!"

Faro's voice swells and echoes in my ears, reaches my brain and tears it awake. I see a nightmare vision of

Conor floating away, arms outstretched, struggling to reach me and Faro. Floating farther and farther until he's beyond touch and hearing. Floating for ever through the trenches and caverns of the Deep until even his bones disappear.

I fight free of the clinging net of sleep that has wrapped itself around me. I grab Conor's shoulder and shake him as hard as I can. "Wake up, wake up, Conor!"

"Not you 's well... Stop it, Saph. I'm awake, I'm awake, I'm awake. Can't you get that whale to come a bit quicker?"

Of course I can't. The whale's so huge, and I'm so small. I haven't got any power over her.

How I wish she was here. How I wish I could touch her wrinkled skin, and swim up her vast sides, and hear her voice. Even the worst joke in the world would be welcome. Why did the whale cross the ocean? To get to the other tide. Why was the whale so sad? Because he was a blue whale. What kind of whales fly? Pilot whales. Is that bad enough for you, dear whale?

The Deep stirs. Heavy water surges against our bodies as if an underwater earthquake has set off a giant wave. We cling together desperately as the water buffets us.

"Greetings, little barelegs."

"Whale!"

"Quick, little one, tuck yourself behind my flipper. And your companions must go to my other side."

"But we can't separate. I'll lose the others."

"I must be balanced to carry you through the mountains."

"We've got to be together."

The whale's voice rumbles impatiently. "There's no time for argument. I must rise. Listen. Will you travel inside my mouth?"

"Inside your—"

"Quick. A giant squid attacked me as I came. He'll be waiting. They grow bold in the trenches."

But how can we go inside her mouth? We'll be swallowed. We'll be like Jonah inside the whale – and I can't remember the end of the story. Jonah must have got out somehow, or there wouldn't have been any story, but how?

"Do as she says," cuts in Faro. "She will not swallow us."

"You're sure about that?"

"How can I be sure? I'm as sure as I am that we'll die in the Deep if we stay here, and as sure as I am that Conor and I can't find our way to her other side in this dark."

A giant squid. I'd rather be inside the whale's mouth than meet one of those. I'd even rather take the risk of being swallowed.

We feel the vast movement of the whale as she gets into position. She knows exactly where we are. Water swirls heavily, and then her voice booms so close that it's like being inside her already. "My jaw is open. Swim straight ahead."

Faro's tail carries us forward. My legs barely stir the dark water. I'm so tired and so afraid. We're going to travel inside a whale, like Jonah. I try to remember what the inside of her mouth looks like. She only has one row of teeth, I do remember that, set in her lower jaw. Those teeth can tear a giant squid apart.

"I won't hurt you, little one."

I sense the exact moment when we swim over the threshold of the whale's jaw. Everything changes. We're no longer in the climate of the Deep, but in the climate of the whale's body.

Her vast mouth cavern smells faintly of rotting fish. I try not to notice. It seems wrong to notice the smell of someone when they've invited you inside them. Especially when the whale's trying so hard to rescue us.

We speak in whispers, but our voices echo as if we're in a cathedral.

"Are you all right, Conor? Faro?"

There's a short pause, then, "Never better," says Conor. "Saph, is this the way you came up from the Deep last time? Inside her mouth?"

"No, I wasn't as far down that time."

"So you've never been in her mouth before."

"No, why?"

"I was just hoping there was a precedent."

"Giant squid and sperm whales have been known to fight great battles," says Faro sombrely. "I've seen the body of a whale on the surface, attacked by many squid. I've seen the marks of their tentacles and their beaks."

The whale's voice vibrates along the roof of her mouth. "I am ready, little one."

We brace ourselves, but at first the movement is almost imperceptible. The whale seems to be gliding, swimming fast but smoothly. Sonar echoes roll around us. We must be in among the undersea mountains now. The noise doesn't hurt as it did on the dive down. I expect that's because we're cushioned by her mountains of flesh.

She's going more slowly now. She must be feeling her way cautiously forward between the steep underwater cliffs. The passage will be very narrow now. Even with the whale's blubber to shield us, the noise begins to thunder in my head.

It eases. She must be through the pass. Only a little way farther and she'll be safe to rise.

Suddenly her pace quickens. We're thrown backward, then forward. I lose hold of Conor's hand. The whale rolls and my stomach swoops. Her body judders as if she's fighting her way through giant waves. She rolls again, and takes another blow. I slip and slide. I'm tossed from the ribbed roof of her mouth to her tongue, then against the columns of her teeth. She judders again. My bones shake and my teeth rattle.

"She's being attacked! It must be a squid!" I hear Faro's voice but I can't reach him. We've been thrown way apart. It feels as if she's fighting for her life. But how can she fight without using her teeth? She'll have to open her jaw to defend herself. We'll be sucked out into the Deep.

Another lurch. It's like being in the belly of a plane in a war film, rolling and diving through the sky to get away from an enemy. But the squid keeps coming at her. How long can she hold on without using her teeth?

"Hold on – hold on, little one," comes the distorted boom of the whale's voice.

"Fight them, dear whale! You can't let them kill you!"

"No, little barelegs. Hold tight. I'm ready to rise."

Giant squid only live in the trenches of the Deep. They don't rise. They won't be able to follow her. But what if they've already got their tentacles suckered around the whale?

We're in the heart of the battle, but we don't know what's happening. We can only guess what's going on out there in the Deep. The squid flailing its tentacles, trying to get a grip. The whale lashing her tail, striking her enemy. The Deep churning with their battle, and the whale fighting to get free for just long enough to gather all her strength and plunge upwards, out of the giant squid's reach.

Suddenly the whale goes dead still. We hang in her mouth, suspended. It's killed her. The giant squid has killed her. She's dead, and it's all because of us. She only came back because of us—

And then with a rush like an aeroplane take-off, the whale breaks loose and surges upwards.

CHAPTER SIXTEEN

Blood streams from the wounds in the whale's side, where the giant squid's beak gashed her. There are tentacle sucker marks all over her, and some have pulled off her skin. She looks like a ship limping home to harbour after a terrible battle at sea.

And she sheltered us all the way through. She never opened her mouth.

"Dear whale, we owe you so much. Without your courage, the squid would have torn us to pieces."

I'm swimming by the whale's head, close to her right eye. Conor and Faro are swimming on her other side. We're out of the Deep now. As soon as it was safe to do so, the whale opened her jaw and we swam out, stunned, into open water.

We are in Ingo. The Deep lies far below us, like a giant shadow. Even to look at it makes me shudder. We're still a long way below the surface, but we're beyond the grasp of the Deep and high above the trenches where giant squid lurk.

The whale swims on very slowly.

"Are you badly hurt, dear whale?"

"Not too badly, little one."

"You should have fought the squid with your teeth."

The whale's voice is fainter than usual, but cheerful. "He came off worse than I did. I gave him a blow from my tail that he'll never forget. How could I have used my teeth, little barelegs, when you were behind them?"

"Thank you, dear whale. You saved all our lives. You saved mine for the second time."

"It wasn't hard," says the whale placidly, as if she's quite prepared to save it a dozen times more.

"But, whale – if you don't mind my asking – why is it that you're so – well – so nice to me?"

And so completely uninterested in Conor and Faro, I might have added. I don't think the whale has spoken to them once. But although I'm curious about this too, I'm not going to pry too far.

"You please me, little barelegs," says the whale simply. "You remind me of the past. Happy days, when my children were young, when my daughter played hide-and-seek below my jaw and above my back."

So perhaps it's because I'm a girl and the others are boys that she makes a favourite of me.

"Whale – if you don't mind me asking all these questions – where is your daughter now?"

The whale's eye looks beyond me, into the distance. "Far away, little barelegs, at the bottom of the world. She's safer there. My pod was torn apart by sickness, many seasons ago. Those who were sick could not find their way. They could not dive to find food. They swam into rivers where we whales have never been, and so they died there. My son had left me long before to swim with the other young bulls. But – that was as it should be. My daughter stayed with me, because that is the way for us whales. She would have stayed with me until I saw her children's children, but for this sickness. No one knew where it came from.

"My daughter grew ill too, but I would not let her die. I supported her day and night. You know that a whale can drown, little one, when she's too sick and weak to reach the surface?"

"No. No, I didn't know that." I picture the whale struggling to stop her daughter sinking down, down, down into the fathomless Deep...

"I called on my sisters to dive for food for her," the whale continues. "At last she recovered. I did not dare let her stay here, with the risk that the sickness might attack her again. I sent her away with her cousins, far from the sickness, to the bottom of the world. Our pod was already scattered by death."

"But couldn't you have gone too, with your daughter and the other whales?" I ask her.

"I am too old. I must stay here. I am happy that she is

safe and well. I get news of her sometimes from whales who have made the long journey from the bottom of the world. So it is not a sad story, little barelegs.

"You pleased me when I first met you in the Deep because you reminded me of my daughter. But now I love you for yourself."

No one has ever said such a thing to me before. I put out my hand and touch her wrinkled skin. "Dear whale, I wonder if Elvira could heal these wounds."

"They will heal anyway, with time. We whales are strong. It takes more than a squid to conquer us. Scars don't matter, little one. They are the marks of the battles we have won."

Her words sink deep into my mind. I wish I could be as calm and strong as she is.

We swim on slowly but steadily into shallower water. It's light up there on the surface. Maybe it's still the same day. I feel as if I've been in the Deep for days and days on end, but maybe it was no more than an hour.

"One day, little barelegs, you may go to the bottom of the world too, and meet my daughter," speculates the whale, "when you are old enough to make the Crossing of Ingo."

"But how could I do that?"

"Never mind now, little one," says the whale maternally. "When the time comes it will be soon enough."

This is extremely frustrating, but I don't argue. I don't

want to stop bathing in the dreamy comfort of the whale's presence. We've been through a hurricane together, and now we're in the calm. We've survived. We're out of the Deep, and alive.

And above all, the Kraken is sleeping. *Cusca, cusca, cusca, Kraken. Cusca, cusca, cusca, Kraken. Sleep for a thousand years. Sleep for ever. Don't ever wake again...*

"Look ahead, Saph," shouts Conor. He and Faro are swimming towards me. "The dolphins are coming!"

"And the Mer!" calls Faro. "Look, little sister, my people are coming!"

I'll never forget the last part of the journey. The dolphins and the Mer must have been watching and waiting, hoping against hope for our return. They keep at a safe distance as the whale breaches, then surge in and swim alongside like a guard of honour as she makes her way slowly forward. Blood rolls away from the gashes in her side into the clear water. The dolphins leap and curve, brimming with life, rushing up to the surface, crashing through it and then plummeting back into the water.

It's wonderful to watch the arc of a dolphin's leap from below. I long to ride on one of them but I can't leave the whale now, after all she's done for us. The Mer stay below the water surface, their hair streaming out behind them, their faces glowing in the brilliant light of the sunwater.

"Sapphire, the dolphins want us to ride on them. Come on!" shouts Faro.

The dolphins are so beautiful. Maybe just a short ride. The whale would understand.

She told me last time that dolphins are much cleverer than whales. Cleverer and more playful and more beautiful. She'd understand completely why I'd want to be with them – and she'd try not to be hurt, but it wouldn't quite work.

"Go with them. They will carry you faster," says the whale.

"I'll stay with you."

Conor hesitates for a moment. Then, "Thank her for us, Saph," he says. "You speak her language."

"You tell her, Con."

Conor clears his throat. He looks almost embarrassed, which is rare for Conor. For half a second I see the whale as Conor sees her. Not as a person but as a rough-skinned mountain.

"We are grateful to you," he says at last. "I can't tell you how much. We all know that we owe you our lives."

He hesitates again. Slowly, massively, the whale dips her head in acknowledgment. And Conor's released. He plunges towards the dolphins.

The next moment I see them both, Conor and Faro, mounted triumphantly on dolphins, like young warriors coming home. The Mer swim farther off, driving through the water with powerful strokes of the tail. I peer around but there's no sign of Ervys, Talek or Mortarow. I wonder how Ervys will feel now that we are home safe from the Deep, and Saldowr's mission has been accomplished. He should be glad, because the Kraken's power has been broken, and the Mer children are safe. But somehow I doubt that we'll be getting much thanks from Ervys.

Faro calls back to me over his shoulder, "The Groves of Aleph, Sapphire! We're almost home."

The dolphins leap like horses at the sight of the finishing line. Faro's face is exultant. "Hurry, little sister! You'll be left behind."

I want to be with him. I want to be first into the Groves of Aleph, to bring our victory to Saldowr. Why should Conor and Faro—

Sapphire, get a grip. What does it matter who goes first? The Kraken's sleeping: that's all that matters.

Besides, the whale's pace is slackening. She's swimming so slowly that I have to hold back, or I'll leave her behind.

"This water is too shallow for me," she says at last. "I must leave you here, little barelegs. Go on with the dolphins."

"But you came to Saldowr's cave before. *Please* come. He'll want to thank you. Please, dear whale!"

"No, little one. I am injured, and cannot find my way as well as I could before. I must leave you now."

"But, whale," I say in a panic, "you'll be all right, won't you? You're not going to…"

I can hear the smile in the whale's voice as she says soothingly, "I will fight many more squid before I die, and kill them too. It's a pity that you don't care for the taste of squid, little one. You don't realise what you are missing. Perhaps one day you will let me catch one for you. Life has few pleasures to equal a stomach full of squid."

"Come on, Sapphire!" Faro's impatience swirls through the water. He hasn't realised why the whale has fallen behind. "I see Saldowr's cave!" The dolphin that is carrying him arches its back, hangs for a second in the bright water and then dives.

"Go, little one. Go with them."

"They don't mean to forget you, dear whale. You did so much for us. You saved everyone."

"It was nothing. Your brother thanked me. We'll meet again. And I never told you my joke after all."

"Go on then, tell me."

The whale pauses. Her eye shuts in concentration. The wrinkles in her forehead seem to grow deeper as I wait.

"When is a whale… not a whale…" she says at last, hesitantly.

"I don't know. When is a whale not a whale?"

"When it's a… when it's a… wait a minute, it'll come back to me. I had it just there on the tip of my teeth."

"When it's a?"

"When it's a... When it's having a shark attack!"

There's a pause. I say carefully, "I'm not quite sure why that's funny. I expect it's because I'm human and it's a whale thing."

"No," laments the whale, "it's not because you're human. It's because we whales can't tell jokes. I got the punch line wrong again."

"I'll tell you what, I'll teach you one of Conor's jokes next time." (*A very carefully selected one*, I think.) "We can go over the punch line until you're sure of it."

"I'm sure you can teach me, little barelegs, if anyone can," says the whale.

You can't hug a whale. It's completely impossible. Anatomically impossible, as Faro said to me long ago, the first time we met, when I blurted out something about him being a "mermaid".

All you can do is stretch out your arms as far as you can, and touch as much of her rough, wrinkled skin as you can, and hope that she understands that it means you'll never forget that she saved your life, and you wish her daughter hadn't gone to the bottom of the world and left her alone, and you wish you didn't have to say goodbye.

CHAPTER SEVENTEEN

aldowr is waiting for us in the heart of the Groves. His hands stretch out towards us. Even his cloak seems to have come back to life. It ripples and glistens like living water, although its hem is still torn. He's better! Saldowr's wound has healed and he's come back to us.

We swim closer and I see that it's not quite like that. Lines of pain are still written on Saldowr's face. It's obvious that it must have taken a huge effort for him to swim out of his cave.

But he's done it. He's waiting for us, and his face is illuminated with pleasure as he holds out his hands in welcome. Faro bows his head over Saldowr's right hand, and kisses it. Conor stiffens beside me. *There is no way he's going to do that*, I think, and I'm right. Saldowr doesn't seem to expect it, either. His eyes gleam with sudden humour as he grasps Conor's hand in his, and then turns to me.

"You've done well, *myrgh kerenza*," he says, and his eyes scan my face, searching it. I feel the power in him. It's not like the terrifying destructive power that forced its way into every one of the Kraken's shape-shifts, but it's just as strong.

"The Kraken called me that, too," I say.

Saldowr nods thoughtfully. "The Kraken would have less power over us if he knew less about us," he observes. His eyes are clouded by thoughts I can't follow.

"What do you mean?"

"I mean that the Kraken knows what we are. He knows our fears. He knows our weaknesses and he plays on them. He is similar enough to us to do that."

I think of the Kraken's last shape-shift, before he vanished inside the cave of his own mouth. "Saldowr – is the Kraken – was the Kraken ever Mer?"

A hiss of disbelief comes from the Mer who encircle us. Saldowr sweeps them with a quelling glance, and they are silent.

"I believe that there is Mer in the Kraken," he says, "and maybe even some of the blood of your own people."

I shiver. I want monsters to stay monsters. It's easier to think of the Kraken as a monster than to believe he might be like us. Or even worse, that we might be like him.

"The Kraken is sleeping now," says Faro, tossing back his hair and looking like a young warrior who has brought home the spoils of his first battle. "He will not wake to trouble us for a thousand years."

Saldowr frowns at him mildly. "Beware of hubris, my son. Let it be enough that you have fought the Kraken and conquered him."

Faro bows his head, accepting the rebuke. Conor and I glance at each other. I've no idea what hubris is, but it doesn't sound like a compliment. Faro's just risked his life in the Deep and still Saldowr isn't satisfied. Sometimes the Mer are so – so *rigid*.

Saldowr smiles. The tension flows away. "You have done well, all of you," he says. "The Mer have much cause to be grateful to you."

A murmur of approval comes from the gathered Mer.

"Even Ervys," continues Saldowr easily, sweeping his people with that glance again, "even Ervys has great cause to thank these children. But where is Ervys? Has he not come to celebrate with us? He is so concerned with the fortunes of the Mer that I was sure he would be here to rejoice with us."

Some of the young Mer in the front rank look at each other and smile. I can almost feel Ervys's power over them weakening. *Saldowr has won*, I think exultantly. *He'll get strong again, and he'll lead the Mer, and…*

Out of the corner of my eye I see the dolphins playing out in the bright water above the Groves. I hope the sharks will never come back to patrol here. The dolphins are so intelligent and warm and beautiful. But I suppose

there have to be sharks – or do there? My head is muzzy.
I'm so very tired... It sweeps over me suddenly, like the
tide filling a cove. All the fear, all the dread, all the waiting.
The Kraken's cruelty, the terrors of the Deep, the flaying
tentacles of the giant squid. Everything in me has been
used up. I'm sucked dry. How stupid I am! We'll probably
never have another moment of triumph like this, and all
I want to do is go to sleep.

Someone is holding a cup to my lips. A young Mer
woman, with long red hair and green eyes with that
silvery glint in them. She nods and smiles at me
encouragingly. "Drink. It will put back your strength."

The drink looks like melted sapphires. I take a sip and
it tingles in my mouth. I take another. My exhaustion
rolls back like the tide over the sand. I feel as if I've just
woken up on a fresh, bright morning. I take another
long, deep draught, and then the Mer woman passes the
cup to Conor. But he shakes his head. "I'm all right."

"It's wonderful, Conor!"

"You've had enough, Saph. Don't drink any more.
We've got to go home now."

Home... Of course. Home. I'd almost forgotten again.

I look round the circle of Mer faces. This isn't like the
Assembly chamber, where everyone was seated in ranks,
distant and formal. *My people*, Faro said. He said it so
proudly, as if there could be nothing better than
belonging to the Mer. Knowing that you'll never have to
choose between one world and another.

But Faro went to the Deep and survived, like me, and the Mer can't do that. Faro knows what this means, but he's still fighting not to acknowledge it. He'll fight it if it kills him. He wants to be all Mer, to belong one hundred per cent with heart and mind and body, and never have to face the pain of being different. I know exactly how he feels. I want to belong so much. But where?

"You have our gratitude," says Saldowr at last. "The Mer will never forget what you have done for them. Your dangers shall be our dangers. Your friends shall be our friends. Your enemies shall be our enemies."

A murmur of agreement rises from the Mer. They stretch out their hands in front of them.

The Mer don't clap as we do. Their applause seems strange at first. They stretch out their hands and bang the heel of the left hand down of the back of the right, slowly and rhythmically. The rhythm quickens until the sea beats like a drum.

I've never been applauded before, except for ordinary things like going up to get my swimming medals at school. It's one of the proudest moments of my life but also one of the most awkward, because I don't know if I ought to thank the Mer, or just smile graciously like the Queen, or act as if I'm used to it. Faro looks stern and self-possessed. Conor's colour has deepened but he seems to know what to do. He bows his head slowly, acknowledging the Mer applause. I wish I'd thought of that. Saldowr's watching me, with a gleam of amusement in his eye. I decide that staring straight ahead is probably the best option now.

Suddenly, the applause dies away. A figure is shouldering its way through the crowd.

Ervys. He's come after all. *He's got some nerve*, I think. *And courage too*, I've got to admit it. If he's angry he's hiding it well; his face is stern and self-assured. I can't see his followers but I suspect they're here, somewhere at the back of the crowd, where they hope they'll be well out of range of Saldowr's mirror.

Ervys moves forward alone. The Mer draw back to let him through. The atmosphere darkens and fills with tension as Ervys comes to the front, swims forward and faces Saldowr.

"I hear that the Kraken sleeps," he says harshly.

"The Kraken sleeps," agrees Saldowr, watching him carefully.

"Do you claim this victory for yourself, Saldowr?"

"I claim nothing."

"I see that you've risen from your sickbed to welcome your *saviours*," goes on Ervys smoothly. "As I would, in your place, Saldowr. They have done much for you."

I see what he's doing. He's telling Saldowr – and all the Mer here – that Saldowr is so weak that he has to depend on children. He's trying to turn our victory over the Kraken into some kind of victory over Saldowr. Without quite realising what I'm about to do, I swim

243

forward a couple of strokes. Ervys fixes me with a cold, contemptuous glance.

"You are interrupting, child," says Saldowr, not angrily but with a finality that I hardly dare challenge. Yet I've got to challenge it.

"Saldowr, we've forgotten something. The choice. My father."

Saldowr draws his brows together. He looks stern but not – no, not absolutely forbidding.

"We chose to go to the Deep to help the Mer," I plough on. "Now let my father choose."

Everybody is silent. They must know Dad, I think suddenly. But they'll know him as one of themselves. As – as *Mer*. They won't understand about the life he had before, or what it means to us.

Conor swims forward to join me. "We're not asking the Mer to release our father from Ingo," he says. "All we want is for him to have the power to choose."

The silence continues. It's not so much hostile as baffled. At last a voice speaks out from the crowd. "But why would anyone choose to leave Ingo?" it asks.

There's a swell of agreement. Even Faro nods slightly, without seeming to notice that he's doing it. Saldowr holds up his hand. "It's true that I gave these children a promise," he says. "They have fulfilled their side of our - *agreement* - and I shall honour mine. Your father will have his choice, Sapphire, as each of us must one day choose for himself. But not now. It will come when the time is ripe. To enter or to leave Ingo is not as simple as to open or close one of your doors."

The Mer are looking at one another. They don't like this, but respect for Saldowr keeps them subdued. I hear mutterings: "Door? What does he mean, *door?*" "We've never had *doors* in Ingo, and we're not starting now."

But I don't care. Saldowr's words throb in my mind. *Your father will have his choice.*

Conor and I glance at each other. He gives me the slightest, most fleeting of winks.

But we've forgotten Ervys. "So," he says bitingly, "I see that it is human children who decide the laws of Ingo now. When did they earn such power?"

Saldowr refuses to get angry. "These children have earned some credit in Ingo, Ervys," he says calmly. "Without them, the Kraken would still prey on us. This is why we show them our gratitude."

"Are you telling me that thanks to your guardianship, our people must depend on creatures like these? They are not Mer. They are no part of our lives and they never will be. Why are they here, except to make bargains in exchange for their 'heroism'?

"And maybe you will tell us, Saldowr, why you take for your *scolhyk* and your *holyer* this boy whose Mer blood is compromised?"

Faro's face flares into rage. He thrusts forward, dodging the arm that Saldowr holds out to stop him.

"Faro," says Saldowr in a measured voice, "such words are not worth your thoughts. You have proved yourself before all the Mer." His gaze sweeps the crowd of Mer. "Which of you has faced the Kraken?" he demands, and his voice rolls out like thunder.

There's a low muttering from the Mer, but Ervys seems completely unmoved. Arms folded, he continues to stare straight at Saldowr.

"You are my *scolhyk* and my *holyer*," says Saldowr more quietly, speaking directly to Faro. "Remember what I have taught you."

"You have taught him to usurp privileges which do not belong to him," challenges Ervys.

Still, to my amazement, Saldowr won't react. It's clear that he's holding Faro back too. Faro would love to charge into Ervys, but even though Saldowr isn't touching Faro, his grip on him is like iron.

"Wish he'd show Ervys the mirror again," Conor murmurs in my ear.

But the mirror is lost in the Deep. I keep my face impassive. I can't be as bold as Conor. I'm afraid of Ervys, deeply afraid.

"Ervys," says Saldowr evenly, "all you show here is your lack of understanding. You think to insult Faro. You fail to understand that I am preparing my son for the future, not for the past."

"Your son, Saldowr! Do you dare to say that in front of all of us?"

"Yes, my son," repeats Saldowr. He beckons to Faro and draws him close to his side.

Faro brings himself up proudly, his tail strongly curved, his hands clenched at his sides. Saldowr continues, "Not my son by blood, but the son I have chosen for myself, Ervys, as I have the right to do."

Ervys's cruel words echo in my head. *One whose Mer blood is compromised.*

Little sister, that's what Faro's always called me. Maybe we're more alike than he knew.

Don't mind so much, Faro, I want to tell him. It's not so terrible to be partly one thing and partly another. At least, I don't think it is. The Mer can be so inflexible, though. They want life to follow set patterns. Maybe, if you don't belong in the patterns, they cast you out. *Don't be hurt, Faro. Saldowr has claimed you as his son. That means something, doesn't it?* I try to reach Faro with my mind. My thoughts touch on his, and recoil from the pain and confusion there. Outwardly Faro keeps his cool. He won't let Ervys know how his words have cut him to the heart.

"Yes, my son," repeats Saldowr again. "The one I have chosen to guide the Mer when I am gone, and to receive my inheritance. But calm your hopes, Ervys, I shall be with you for many years yet. I speak of time as I know it, and as Faro will come to understand it, not as you know and understand it.

"To become a Guardian of the Tide Knot, and wise among the Mer, is not the work of one of your lifetimes.

You think my power is here to be seized, Ervys," says Saldowr, and his voice is suddenly resonant and forbidding. "You try to overcome me, and take my place, but my place cannot be taken by force. Understand me, Ervys, I did not choose to be what I am. It chose me. I think that one day it will choose Faro, too."

Faro's face is proud and solemn as he listens to Saldowr's words, but those words chill me. Is Saldowr saying that Faro will become like him one day, able to see far back through the past and far ahead into the future? If that happens, Faro won't be Faro any more. At least, he won't be the Faro I know. I can't imagine Faro being wise and mysterious like Saldowr, wearing a long cloak and living on his own in a cave and having the kind of powers that Saldowr has. I won't be able to be Faro's friend any more, not as I am now.

I don't want Faro to have a magical destiny. I just want him to stay the same, calling me his little sister and teasing me and being a bit vain and incredibly courageous, and doing the best somersaults I've ever seen, and pretending he knows everything about life on Earth when really all he knows is what the seagulls tell him.

I'm not the only one who doesn't like Saldowr's prophecy about Faro. Ervys looks thunderous. Fury flashes from his eyes like lightning. "So I am to call another Assembly and tell the Mer that they will never be free to choose their own leader," he says.

I expect Saldowr's anger to flash back at Ervys, but it doesn't. Saldowr sighs deeply. He looks weary. "Ervys, will you never be able to content yourself?" he asks. "Will you never choose to use your strength for the common good? The Kraken is sleeping. Our children are safe. These children have given the Mer everything that they longed for."

"For now."

"For now. Can't that be enough for you? There are no promises, Ervys. *For now,* the Kraken sleeps."

The atmosphere has changed. The Mer faces surrounding us look troubled and uneasy. The feeling of victory has vanished. Ervys knows how to destroy things all right.

At that moment there's a movement behind Saldowr. I recognise the man who challenged Ervys in the Assembly chamber. Karrek. He makes his way forward and bows his head briefly to Saldowr in greeting.

"Greetings, Karrek," says Saldowr.

"Greetings, Saldowr. Since there is no Speaking Stone here, I must speak as I find, and hope that you will forgive my boldness."

"All may speak freely here, as Ervys has already discovered," says Saldowr drily.

Karrek looks round at the others. There is pent-up anger in his voice as he starts to speak. "It seems to me that we have quickly forgotten how anxiously we waited and watched and hoped, just a short while ago," he says.

"We had no hope of defeating the Kraken by our own effort, and so we sent these children to the Deep, because nothing else could help us. It seems to me that we have already forgotten that they did for us what no one has done since the time of Mab Avalon." His voice cracks out suddenly, making me jump. *Are the Mer so ungrateful? Are the Mer so forgetful?* We should remember what has been done today for a thousand years. Our children are safe. Our mothers and fathers will not have their hearts broken. What else matters, besides that? Why are you listening to Ervys, when Ervys could not save your children?"

A murmur of agreement runs through the crowd: "He's right. Yes, Karrek speaks for us, Saldowr. His words are our words."

Faro glows with pride. I'm dreading that the clapping will start again, and Conor obviously just wishes the Mer would all go away now. Ervys is watching, gauging the mood, planning his next move. Even though Saldowr's here and we're under his protection, I'm still very afraid of Ervys.

"Karrek speaks for you, does he?" says Ervys at last, smoothly and coldly. "Very well. Let him speak for you. Let Saldowr speak for you. Let the Mer live like a shoal of sprats scared by every mackerel's shadow. I thought that the Mer were fit to live freely and choose their own leaders, but it seems that I was wrong. *For now.*" and he stares straight into Saldowr's eyes, challenging him, before he turns with a powerful swish of his tail and plunges through the ranks of the Mer. They part to let him go, and I think I see some of them peeling away from the crowd and following him, but I can't be sure.

The tension dissolves. In small groups the Mer begin to drift away, talking in low voices, each one saluting Saldowr as he or she leaves. Some call to the dolphins, others swim away through the Groves. We watch the undersea light flicker on their shining hair and their strong, smooth tails. One moment the Groves of Aleph are full of life and movement. The next, the Mer have gone.

CHAPTER EIGHTEEN

Saldowr needs to rest, and Faro goes with him into the cave. A few moments later, a figure appears in the dimness of the cave mouth. I think it's Faro coming back again, but Conor knows who it is straightaway.

"Elvira!"

She swims forward, cradling something in her arms. A baby. A Mer baby, curled so that his tail lies over her arm.

My mind goes dizzy. Elvira hasn't got a baby... has she?

"Elvira!" says Conor again. There's a soft, annoyingly eager expression on his face. She smiles at him with equally annoying warmth as she swims towards us.

"Whose baby is that?" I ask her. But as soon as I ask the question, I know the answer. Feathers of black hair, wide eyes, and a look that is so familiar it makes me feel as if someone's got their hands round my heart and is squeezing as hard as they can.

It's the baby I saw in Saldowr's mirror, way back last year. He was lying in his rock cradle, with Mellina bending over him. My – my brother.

"My brother," I say aloud, and to my amazement I find that I'm smiling at him. It's not because I *like* him or anything. It's just because you can't help smiling at babies.

Elvira comes close. The baby waves a fat fist through the water, greeting me. It feels as if there's just Elvira, the baby and me, and everything else has melted away.

"Where's his mother?" I don't want to say Mellina's name. It makes her seem like a real person.

"She's gathering kelp, so I'm looking after him."

Hmm. I don't think that's the real reason our baby brother has suddenly appeared, just when everyone knew we were in the Groves. Mellina must have wanted us to see the baby. Saldowr must have wanted it too, because he let Elvira bring the baby here, to his cave.

I don't even let myself think about what Dad must have wanted. There's no point. I cling to Saldowr's promise. The time will come when we know what Dad truly wants.

"Do you want to hold him?" asks Elvira in her soft, sweet voice. Elvira is so exactly like a beautiful mermaid in a fairy story that it makes her seem unreal. Conor can't take his eyes off her. I'm still wary.

"I – I don't know."

"He won't cry. He likes being held."

He's my *brother, not yours,* I think. *Stop telling me about him.*

"Oh, all right then. Give him here," I say grudgingly.

I'm not sure how to hold a baby. In fact I can't really remember ever holding one, although I must have done. And this baby has a tail, which makes it even more of a challenge. I try to copy the shape of Elvira's arms. Elvira smiles her radiant, irritating smile.

"Not like that, Sapphire. Curve your arms more, and bring them close to your body, then he can't slip away into the water. He can't swim very well yet. That's it. Hold still like that, and I'll give him to you."

I panic for a moment as Elvira gently lifts the baby and puts him into my arms. What if he floats away? What if he's all slippery? What if he doesn't like me, and starts screaming?

None of these things happen. The baby's eyes are fixed on mine, serious and a bit unsure, but he doesn't cry. I smile tentatively. He feels much heavier than I expect. His tail is very smooth and soft, not like the tail of an adult Mer. I rest it over my arm, as Elvira did. I can't believe this is happening. It's one thing to know that you've got a little Mer half-brother. It's completely different to hold him in your arms. He's so solid. So *real*.

My brother. His little tail twitches. It's like silk against my arm. He looks so... so *Mer*. If I didn't know, I wouldn't guess that he had a drop of human blood in him. And yet he's still my little baby brother.

Sometimes, when I was little, I used to nag Mum

about having another baby. I wanted to be the big sister. I used to imagine a little baby in our cottage, sitting in a highchair, then learning to crawl and learning to walk while I held his hand. But Mum said two children were quite enough, and gradually I realised that no matter how much I nagged, it was never going to happen.

It's happened now, but it's completely different from everything I ever imagined. My baby brother is never going to crawl, or walk. He won't do the things Conor and I did. He'll never scramble up and down the rocks to the cove, or make fires and cook sausages on the sand. He won't go to school or take a boat out, or eat chips, or play football. He's Mer. He'll do everything that Mer children do when they're growing up. I'll have to ask Faro more about what it's like to be a little Merboy. What games they play, what they're scared of. He'll never taste sweets or ice-cream. I wonder what kind of treats Mer children have.

I don't even know his name. How bad is that? My own brother, and I don't know his name.

"There you are, little Mordowrgi," says Elvira to the baby. "Say hello to your big sister."

"Mordowrgi – is that his name?"

Elvira shakes her head. "No, it's just what we call him. He'll have his real name later on. We can't name him until we know what he's like, can we?" and she laughs as if the idea is ridiculous.

"We're given our names when we're born," I say.

"How strange your human life is. What use is a name that doesn't fit the person? Look, he's smiling at you."

It's true. The baby – Mordowrgi – is smiling a wide, toothless smile and reaching out for my hair.

"Don't let him pull it. He's strong; it really hurts," Elvira warns me.

I turn to Conor excitedly. "Look, Conor, he's smiling at me! Maybe he knows who I am."

But Conor just shrugs. "Babies smile at everyone."

"Do you want to hold him, Con?"

"No."

The smile is widening on the baby's face. He's staring very intently at me, as if he thinks he knows me. The thing is, when a baby smiles at you like that, you can't help smiling back.

I glance up and see Conor's face so cold and critical that it makes me jump.

"Careful, Sapphire, you're squeezing the baby."

Oh no, the baby's face is crumpling. He's going to cry.

"Don't cry, Mordowrgi, I didn't mean to hurt you, don't cry."

Mordowrgi gulps and stares at me piteously, but at least he's not crying. I hand him back to Elvira and she rocks him gently as she swims up and down, up and down, a little way off from us. Conor can't take his eyes off her.

"At least we've got Saldowr's promise, Conor."

"What?"

"About Dad. About Dad getting the chance to choose whether to be Mer or human."

"Yes."

"You could try and sound more pleased about it. It's the whole reason we went to the Deep."

"Was it?"

"Of course it was, Conor! We agreed about all of it, you know we did. We wanted Dad to have the chance to choose. It wasn't just my idea, it was yours as well—"

"Listen, Saph," says Conor, "I know. But now I'm not sure. You know when we were in the whale's mouth? I thought that was it. The end. We'd never see home or Mum again. And it was..." Conor pauses, thinking it through, "It was *unbearable*, Saph. That Mum would think I'd wanted to leave her, just like Dad already had.

"Dad's already chosen, Saph. Face it. He chose to leave us. He wasn't forced to go. I'm sure you're right and he's got loads of regrets, but he *chose*."

"But, Conor, Dad never had a proper choice! He didn't know – he thought he'd be able to come back to us."

"Did he?" Conor nods towards the baby in Elvira's arms. "So where did *he* come from?"

"I don't know what you mean."

"He's Dad's son. Dad chose to have him. He chose a Mer wife and a Mer child. Face it, Saph. That's what's happened, and you can't undo it."

"But, Conor, we agreed it wasn't fair. Dad never had a real choice."

"Fair," says Conor bitterly. "No, it wasn't fair. None of any of it is fair. But it happened."

I don't believe that Conor is right. He hasn't seen Dad and talked to Dad the way I have. He hasn't seen the misery and conflict in Dad's eyes.

"You can't make this baby not exist, Saph. Even if Dad did come back, you've got to think about what it means. Do you want Dad to abandon this kid as well?" asks Conor. "When he's old enough to understand, he'll feel just as bad as we do now. There's no point in messing up any more lives. Dad's here. Mum's got Roger. We're... well, we've got used to it, mostly, haven't we? I just hope Dad's happy with his choice."

"You know he's not."

"I don't know anything. All I know is that Dad should have stopped himself a long time ago, before he fell in love with that – that woman."

Even though Conor's words pierce me, I'm not going to accept that they're true. There's still hope. Who would have believed we could defeat the Kraken? If that can happen, anything can happen. Saldowr has made a promise.

Elvira swims up and down, singing a lullaby to my baby brother. The trouble with babies is that you feel you've got to put them first. But why should I? *We* were first, me and Conor. We were Dad's babies long before Mordowrgi came along. Conor might be willing to give up and accept that Dad won't come back, but I'm not. I haven't got used to anything. I haven't accepted anything. I'm going to keep on fighting.

Conor's eyes are still following Elvira. I feel a stab of alarm. *He should have stopped himself a long time ago, before he fell in love with that - that woman.* It's all right to look back and know what Dad should have done, but Conor ought to think about himself. Elvira's just as much Mer as Mellina, and Conor doesn't seem to be stopping himself...

Then you'll just have to stop him, won't you, Sapphire? I smile to myself. If I can survive in the Deep, and win the battle against the Kraken, then I should be able to win my brother back from Elvira.

We see Saldowr for a few minutes before it's time for us to leave with Faro. Everything has that late feeling, like the end of a party. There's so much to think about, but I need to be home to think about it. Home is starting to become more real in my mind. Time is passing, passing – Mum will be waiting for us...

Saldowr looks very tired, but not even Ervys would dare to say now that he's ready for Limina. You can tell that he's going to live. Maybe he won't ever be as strong as before, but the raw wound on his shoulder has closed. It's an ugly scar, but it's definitely healing.

Maybe Saldowr's getting better because Ingo is

healing itself, too. The Tide Knot is sealed again. The storm damage was just as bad here in Ingo as it was on land, but surely the scars will disappear in time. Things will come back to how they were. And the Kraken is sleeping. *There might be peace in Ingo now*, I think hopefully, but then I remember Ervys's expression of fury, and I'm not so sure. Ervys is not defeated.

Faro sits on the sandy floor of the cave with his tail curled under him. He's sewing up a tear in Saldowr's cloak with a fishbone needle and a thread which must be angel's hair seaweed. Nothing else could be as fine. The needle flashes through the water and in and out of the cloth. Faro looks as expert as a sailor mending a net. I didn't know Faro could sew. There are still so many things I don't know about him, or about the rest of the Mer. They don't let you into their lives easily.

Time to go. I feel as if we've been here in Ingo for a hundred years, but maybe it's only a hundred minutes.

"I held the baby," I say to Saldowr, knowing that he already knows. "He smiled at me."

"You have done well, my child," says Saldowr gently. "You, Conor and my own Faro. You braved the terror of the Deep for the sake of the Mer, and the Mer will remember it, as they remember Mab Avalon." His words of praise do a little to ease the sore emptiness inside me. I still feel separated from Conor, and soon I'll be separated from Faro too. I wonder if the day will ever come when we can all be together.

"Saldowr, do you think – do you think that Dad will stay here for ever?"

Saldowr shakes his head slowly. "I cannot tell."

"But you can, Saldowr," I say boldly. "You can look back and forward through time. You must be able to see what happens to Dad."

"Time has its secrets, even from me. You think that the Mer are holding your father prisoner, but it is not as simple as that. Prisoners can be released by their gaolers. But if you are your own gaoler, who is going to release you?"

I don't really understand what he's talking about, so I say nothing. Conor looks angry and rebellious, but he says nothing either.

Saldowr continues, "I make very few promises, but I can promise you that you will see your father again, and soon."

"When?"

"Where?"

"At the next Assembly, when the young Mer who think they are ready to make the Crossing of Ingo will come forward. All the Mer will be there. Your father will surely be there. I know in my heart that he will be strong enough. He will not miss a ceremony which is so important to us."

The Crossing of Ingo. The words sound familiar. Yes, of course, I've heard them before. The whale said that when I was old enough to make the Crossing of Ingo, I might meet her daughter at the bottom of the world. But how can I do that? I'm not Mer. I don't really know what the Crossing of Ingo is, or why I feel such a thrill of excitement and fear.

"But Saph and I won't be at that Assembly," says Conor. "We're not Mer."

Saldowr doesn't answer for a while. Now I'm the one who feels rebellious. Conor can't answer for me like that. I look down at my bare toes. My body is definitely a hundred per cent human. I'm not so sure about my mind, though. My Mer blood is strong. Why shouldn't I go to the Assembly?

I watch Faro's bone needle flash in and out of the cloak. *The Crossing of Ingo... the Crossing of Ingo.* Longing overwhelms me. I've got to be there. Conor's wrong. I can't just say "I'm not Mer" and leave it like that. Inside me I've been growing more and more Mer ever since that first day when I met Faro in the cove.

It must have started long before that, only I didn't know it. I wanted to be in Ingo even before I knew what Ingo was.

I've got to go to that Assembly. Dad will be there, but that's not the only reason. I need to be there for myself. I've got to test myself, or I'll live the rest of my life never really knowing how strong my Mer blood is. Never knowing where I truly belong.

"Faro," I say quietly, "will you make the Crossing of Ingo?"

"It's not for me to decide, Sapphire," answers Faro, glancing up from his task. "I'll present myself to the Assembly, and declare myself ready and willing. Then the decision is for the Assembly. Some are chosen, some are left behind. You can present yourself year after year, and never be chosen."

Faro's face is set. He doesn't have to say how important this is to him. He's got to be chosen, especially now that he knows he's not a hundred per cent Mer. I'm quite sure now that Faro has got human blood in him, maybe from far back in the past. So many clues are starting to fit together. Faro's always visited the shore more than most of the other Mer. He can stay in the Air for a long time. And then there's his curiosity about the human world. He's always asking me questions. He mocks the way human beings live, but he can't hide his fascination.

His dark eyes have no Mer silver in them. There's no Mer tinge of blue to his skin. Once I start to think about it, it's obvious.

I'm equally sure that Faro will hate having even a single drop of human blood. He won't see it as a bond between us, but as a weakness. I won't risk asking him about it. Faro only wants to belong in Ingo.

"Faro..." I say hesitantly, scared that he'll refuse, "Faro, when you go to the Assembly chamber, can I go with you?"

Faro drops the fishbone needle and stares at me. A

long stare, as if he's reading my thoughts. And perhaps he is. I'm not stopping him.

A brilliant smile lights up his face.

"Yes, little sister," he says, "you can come with me."

CHAPTER NINETEEN

I'm so used to Faro swimming alongside Conor, and Conor holding on to Faro's wrist, that I think it's still happening even when it isn't. I don't notice that there's clear water between the two of them. We're close to land, travelling not far below the surface. I look across to ask Faro how far it is now, and see that there are more than two metres of water between Faro and Conor. They haven't separated by accident. Conor's not struggling. He's swimming strongly.

"Conor!"

He turns. He looks completely normal, not pale and pinched and blue around the lips. He's not fighting for oxygen. He's drawing it from the water, just as Faro and I do.

"Conor, you're not holding Faro's wrist!"

"I know. Good, isn't it?"

I can still hardly believe it. Conor, swimming without

support and as much at home in Ingo as I am. But why, after all this time? Something must have changed, but what?

"I expect it's because you have the talisman my sister made," says Faro confidently.

"No, it can't be the talisman," I argue, "because Conor was wearing it earlier, before we went to the Deep. He still had to hold on to you then."

Faro shrugs. He's swimming with his hands clasped behind his back, using only his tail to drive him through the water. "What does it matter?" he says carelessly, in the way people do when they want to drop an argument they're going to lose.

"Do you feel OK, Conor?" I ask him anxiously. "Really OK?"

"I feel amazing," says Conor. He shakes his head in disbelief. "Why didn't you tell me how incredible it feels? I'm going to try what you're doing, Faro."

He puts his hands behind his back, clasps them and starts to swim quite differently, moving from the waist as Faro does. His legs are together, his feet joined. It looks weird, as if…

As if Conor has a tail. And he's going so fast. Too fast. I can hardly keep up with him.

"Don't, Con!"

"What's the matter, Saph?"

"Don't swim like that."

"But it's amazing. It's so much faster than the way we

normally swim. I can't believe I didn't ever try it like this before. It's like wearing fins!"

I plunge after him. "Maybe that's how Dad started, Con. Maybe he kept swimming like that and when he wanted to go back to swimming normally, he couldn't. Maybe it's part of... you know... *changing.*" I'm whispering because of Faro. He'd be mortally insulted. What could be better than becoming Mer?

"Don't be crazy, Saph, nothing like that's going to happen to me. *You're* much more likely to end up with a tail than I am."

"All right, Conor, but please don't do it. *Please.*"

"Saph, you are so neurotic. You know I'm never going to become Mer. But if it keeps you happy..." Conor unclasps his hands, and begins to swim a smooth, effortless crawl. Relief washes over me.

"What is that kind of swimming, Conor?" asks Faro with apparent innocence. I guess that there's a sting in the question somewhere.

"Front crawl."

"Crawl – what is *crawl*, exactly?"

"You know, Faro, going along like a – like a..." I search my mind for a sea-creature that could be said to crawl."...Oh, I don't know, Faro, it's just a stroke."

"What a lot of effort you humans put into 'strokes'. We Mer prefer just to swim."

Conor's so elated by discovering that he can travel alone in Ingo that he doesn't react to Faro's teasing. For the first time he's fully part of Ingo. I think back to the day two years ago when I first let go of Faro's wrist and knew I could survive underwater. Conor's right, it's an amazing feeling. It changes you.

"Thanks, Faro!" Conor calls.

"What for?"

"For all the times you took care of me. Now you won't have to do it any more."

"No, you are my brother now," says Faro. His mood seems to have changed completely. He's suddenly very serious. "You are my brother, and Sapphire is my sister. We are bound for ever by what we shared in the Deep. Our lives lay in one another's hands, and we did not betray ourselves."

"I'd never do that," says Conor.

I know it's true. Conor has such strength. He doesn't even gossip behind people's backs at school – he never has. People trust Conor. If he says he'll do something, it's done.

I've spent too much of my life wishing I was like Conor. Maybe it's partly because I always thought there was a look in Mum's eyes that said, *What a pity that you're not more like your brother.* But it's not only that. Conor has qualities anyone would want.

"For a long time I was not sure," Faro says thoughtfully. "Sapphire, I was sure about her from the first day. But you – no. Even when you sang to the seals, even when you read the Keystone, I still wasn't sure.

But now Ingo has rewarded you because of what you did in the Deep. Ingo has given you a sign that you belong here."

Conor frowns quickly. He hates people telling him what to do with his life. "We're not slaves," he says. "We don't belong to anyone. Or anything."

But we do, Conor. You're wrong. I'm not going to say it, though. It would just lead to an argument. Faro doesn't argue either, but this time I don't think it's because he's afraid of losing.

The human world is coming closer. We pass below a red buoy, and then another. They mark the lobster pots.

"We can't be far from the cove now," says Conor.

"No."

Suddenly I remember Sadie, not in the foggy way that I remember Air and Earth when I'm deep in Ingo, but with all my feelings alive again. I feel a surge of joy at the thought of putting my arms around Sadie's warm neck and hugging her while she pants with excitement and tries to lick my face. It's like waking up and remembering that it's my birthday. And Mum...

But with the thought of Mum and Roger, problems come rushing back too. I wish I didn't always have to hide things from them. Half my life is a secret from

Mum. I've also got a horrible feeling that Mum hides things from me, too. She doesn't really trust me, not as she trusts Conor.

Sometimes I think you're growing away from me, Sapphy. Mum said that about a week ago. I didn't know what to answer. I could have said, *Sometimes I think the same about you*, but Mum would have been so hurt that it wasn't worth it. I wish Mum could say the things the whale said. *You please me.* Of course I know Mum loves me really. The trouble is that there are so many things about me that she wants to change and improve.

My chest hurts. There's pain tightening its way around my ribs. *You're still in Ingo, remember*, I tell myself. *Don't risk thinking of the human world.* Ingo's wild and dangerous and it can kill you, but it doesn't hurt you the way the human world can hurt you.

Faro swims up close to me. "You're leaving me again, little sister," he murmurs. "Always coming and going, coming and going. When are you going to learn that you can't live in two worlds?"

"I have to, Faro. I don't have a choice."

"You always have a choice. You just haven't made it yet."

But I'm too tired to want to think about this. Faro doesn't understand what it's like to feel that you belong in the human world and that you belong in Ingo too. He's determined not to face the fact that he's probably got human blood in him. He takes it as an insult. I'm sure that's wrong. You have to accept what you are, instead of fighting to pretend you're something different.

In a way I'm growing more Mer – I know I am. I don't even have to think about whether I understand what the whale is saying; I just do. But at the same time I'm not as desperate to escape from the human world as I was just after Dad disappeared. Home seemed so empty, even with Conor there, but now it's filling up again.

There's Sadie. No one can feel empty when a dog is pouring love all over them. I've made friends with Rainbow. And Granny Carne gave me the rowan. She didn't give the rowan to Conor, even though he's got so much more Earth in him that I have.

"Did you mean what you said about the Crossing of Ingo?" Faro's voice hardly stirs the water by my ear, but Conor hears.

"No, she didn't," he says sharply. "She's going home now, Faro, back where she belongs. Come on, Saph, we're almost there," and Conor kicks out strongly, increasing his speed until he overtakes us both.

I'm not going to argue. I'd have to yell if I wanted to speak to Conor now, anyway. He's powering towards the shore, as if he can't wait to get home.

Faro and I drop back. The water is still deep enough and salty enough to be Ingo. Ingo has its arms wrapped around me. Maybe it's only when you have to leave somewhere that you really know how much you love it.

There's sand beneath us now, and the sea turns turquoise.

"Faro?"

"I'm here."

There's no hurry. We've been to the Deep, and returned alive. The Kraken's voice is silent. That's enough for now. Faro smiles, as if he knows what I'm thinking. He probably does.

"We must make a bracelet of our hair, Sapphire," he says.

"What?"

"It's what we Mer do as a sign of friendship. We each cut a lock of our hair, and then we weave the hair together so tightly that the water can never separate it. There are many weaving patterns. We must choose one which has meaning for us."

I look at Faro's long hair, swirling around his shoulders in a cloud. The colour is not very different from my own. If his hair and mine were woven together, you probably wouldn't be able to tell where one ended and the other began.

"What do you cut your hair with?" I can't imagine that there are scissors in Ingo.

"The edge of a clam shell."

"There isn't time to do it now, Faro." But I'd like to. Part of me would always be in Ingo then.

"Next time I see you, then." Faro's eyes glow with eagerness. "Let's make our bracelets before the Assembly,

Sapphire. We'll wear them there. It'll be a sign that when they choose one of us to make the Crossing of Ingo, they'll have to choose the other as well."

Sometimes Faro's confidence is outrageous. He turns every "if" into a "when". But I like it, too. I love the way he makes me feel that anything could happen, and the only thing that could stop me is myself.

"But are you sure you want me to come, Faro? You might have a better chance without me."

"Better chance!" Faro scoffs. "Why are you so timid, little sister? We'll make our own chances."

CHAPTER TWENTY

o one comes to our cove. Well, they do, of course, but not often. The climb is too steep, and you can't carry stuff down, and the tide sweeps in too fast. Nearly everyone prefers Morvrinney Cove, about a mile down the coast.

But there's someone there now, on the flat white sand up by the rocks, as Conor and I swim up through the surface. At first I don't notice. I'm busy fighting for breath. I've been in Ingo too long.

"You OK, Saph?"

I turn on my back and take great painful gasps of air. My lungs feel like paper bags which have been scrunched into a tiny ball. They don't want to expand.

"It'll be better in a minute," Conor comforts me.

"I know, I—"

"Don't talk."

I float until my breathing settles. As soon as I look a bit better, Conor says warningly, "There's someone in the cove, Saph. We're going to have to be careful."

We roll over and start to swim in. At least whoever it is can't have seen Faro: he didn't even enter the cove this time. It may seem eccentric to go for a long swim in April, but that's our business. The trouble is that whoever it is probably knows Mum, because only local people know the way down here.

We swim slowly to shore. The cold of the sea is starting to bite. In Ingo you don't feel it, but as soon as you leave Ingo the protection leaves you too. My arms and legs feel as if someone's sticking needles in all over them.

"Can't wait to g-get into dry clothes," says Conor.

"It's so cold!"

"Freezing."

I stagger as I come out of the water. The tide is lower than it was when we left the cove. That was morning, and by the sun's position it's late afternoon now. The tide's been out, and now it's coming in again. I shake my head to clear it. I feel as if I've been away for years.

Conor left our stuff high up on the rocks, so it should still be dry.

The figure waves but doesn't move towards us. For a terrible moment, I think it's Mum, but then I shield my eyes, peer, and see that it's Gloria Fortune.

It can't be her. Gloria couldn't climb down to

the cove on her crutches. She'd never risk such a fall.

"Hi, little mermaid," calls Gloria Fortune, and swings down the sand towards us.

"Don't say anything, Saph," whispers Conor. "Let me handle it."

But luckily Gloria is only joking. She thinks we've been for a freezing-cold swim because that's the kind of stupid thing that kids do, and as soon as she notices how much we're shivering she tells us to get changed quick before we catch pneumonia.

Why is she here? What does she know?

I grab my bundle of dry clothes, go behind a rock, pull off my wet clinging stuff then rub myself hard with the towel until some life comes back into my body. The dry clothes feel strangely hard and cardboardy, compared to how easy and flowing everything feels in Ingo. And the air is so thin and noisy. Gulls screeching, a helicopter way up in the sky making for St Pirans, water slapping against rocks, waves swashing up on to the sand...

It's pandemonium. Why do people think we live in one of the most peaceful places on earth?

I stuff my wet clothes into the bag with Conor's, and we emerge to face Gloria Fortune. The best tactic is to start asking questions before she can – real questions, like, *Did you fly down that cliff?*

"You must be wondering how I got down here,"

understates Gloria. "Richard brought me round from Morvrinney in the Tregerthens' *Seagull*."

"Oh. Is he – is he still here?"

"He's coming back in half an hour. I wanted to be – well, I wanted to be here on my own. I've always wanted to visit this cove." She pauses, frowns and then goes on more uncertainly, "This is going to sound weird. I know this cove is your place and you probably think I shouldn't be here. But I keep feeling I've *got* to be here. As if the cove is pulling me down to it." She tries to smile, but it doesn't reach her eyes.

"I don't think you should be here on your own," says Conor, with such conviction that he sounds as if he's the adult, not Gloria.

I don't think she should be here on her own either. Half an hour sounds a short time, but it's long enough for a shining head to appear above the water, or a figure to be suddenly there, sitting on the rocks by the cove entrance, wearing a wet suit pulled down to the waist. Or at least, that's what it will look like, until you get close. And once you're close, it's all too late. Once I'd seen Faro and I knew that what everybody else thinks is a myth or a fairytale is hard, cold fact, then there was no way of returning to the life I'd been living five minutes before.

Her husband won't guess that it's dangerous to leave her here. He won't sense that this cove is a gateway to another world. He won't realise that Gloria sometimes has a look of Ingo on her face.

"Don't stay here on your own," Conor repeats, frowning. Gloria rubs her hands over her eyes as if she's trying to rub something away.

"I meant to go and see Granny Carne today," she says in a puzzled voice. "I can't think why I didn't."

I can. Her Mer blood wants her to come here, to the cove, not to Granny Carne's cottage.

"You two were swimming a long way out," Gloria goes on. "I thought this coast was meant to be so dangerous."

"It is," says Conor. "Saph and I know the currents."

"Do you always go swimming with your clothes on?" Gloria asks, laughing.

"It's... it's warmer."

I wish her husband would hurry up and fetch her. He was stupid to leave Gloria here. What if the weather changes and he can't bring the boat round? People from upcountry don't understand how quickly the sea can change here. Gloria could be cut off by the tide. She'd never struggle to safety up those cliffs on her crutches.

"You really should go to see Granny Carne," says Conor with a seriousness that makes Gloria stare at him. I can almost see the wheels of her mind working. Any minute now she'll come out with a question that we won't be able to dodge—

"There's the *Seagull!*" I exclaim, my voice loud with relief.

"Where?"

"Out where I'm pointing."

"I see it!" Gloria leans on her left crutch, slips her right crutch free, lifts it and waves it over her head. "Richard! *Richard!*"

She looks as if someone has switched on a light inside her and it's shining out through her eyes. She must really love him. He seems quite dull to me, compared to Dad or even Roger, with his job in Exeter and his files of paperwork and his pale city skin. Nice, but dull.

He's not using the engine. He's rowing *Seagull* in, and she's riding easily over the swell. I've got to admit he knows how to handle her. I hope he knows how tricky it'll be to bring her alongside at the landing-place at this state of the tide. He must do, because he's not even going to try. He's bringing her in on the beach, and suddenly I realise why. Gloria wouldn't be able to use the ladder. He glances behind him, sees Gloria waving the crutch, and waggles his left oar in salute. He's laughing. He looks a bit less dull when he laughs.

Suddenly I'm overwhelmingly glad that she is still here, waiting for him. Ingo hasn't taken Gloria. I've got to stop her coming to the cove again. I'm going to talk to Granny Carne.

They've gone. The shining sea is empty again. I wanted to stay until *Seagull* was out of sight, even though Conor's desperate for a hot shower. I wanted the cove to be empty again, and ours.

"Come on, Saph, Mum'll be back from work soon."

It must be still the same day, or Gloria would have known we were missing. Mum will think we've spent the day down here.

You can't see a blow coming from behind but there's a millionth of a second when you feel the air rush towards you. A gull slices the air above my head, so close that its claws comb through my hair. It swoops almost to the sand, screeching, then swings upwards over the water. And then it straightens out, drops, rolls and comes round again in a wide circle. It's passed me. It's behind me and then—

"Look out, Saph!"

The gull dive-bombs me again. I duck, throwing my arms up to protect my head, and when the gull has gone there's a broad scratch on my hand from which blood starts to well.

"You OK, Saph?"

I'm shaking. "It – it attacked me."

"It's gone. Look, there it is, flying out to sea."

I watch in case it sweeps back on itself again, but it

disappears into the distance.

"It must have thought you'd got a pasty," jokes Conor. If you're eating outside in St Pirans, gulls dive close to scare you and make you drop your food, and then they snatch it.

But I don't think this gull was after food. I shake my hand disbelievingly. It hurts, and blood drips on to the sand.

"Wash it in the sea, quick. You can put a plaster on at home."

I don't say anything more until we've climbed to the top of the cliff. But I'm thinking hard. Gulls see everything. They know what happens in the human world. They'd make good messengers. If they were on Ervys's side – if they were able to report back to him about what we were doing and where we were going...

Maybe the gull was telling me something. *We know where you are. We can still find you, even when you're not in Ingo. Don't think that Ervys has forgotten about you.*

I shiver. I can't forget the cold, hard anger on Ervys's face. It's the kind of anger that will keep for years without ever weakening. My hand stings from the blow of the gull's claws and the salt water.

"Nearly home, Saph," says Conor encouragingly, as if I'm five years younger than him instead of only two.

"M'OK, Conor. Don't *fuss*."

Conor puts his arm round me and suddenly I'm

281

glad of his help. "For someone who's OK, you don't look too good, Saph. We'd better get your hand sorted out before Mum sees it."

CHAPTER TWENTY-ONE

The barbie didn't happen yesterday after all. By the time Conor and I got home it was well after six. I thought Mum would be back from work, but she was late too, which gave us time to clean up my hand. We washed the scratch again with disinfectant. I had a crazy idea that maybe Ervys had put poison on the gull's claws. Conor found a plaster big enough to cover half my hand, and although Mum noticed it she accepted my explanation that I'd scratched myself on some brambles.

Mum didn't even mention rolling out the Super-Antipodean. She asked us if we'd had a good day, and after a short pause we said yes.

Mum seemed preoccupied. She kept glancing at us as if she wanted to say something, and then quickly filling the kettle or folding washing. I cooked a big omelette and chips for everyone. Roger came in so late that his share was leathery from being kept in the oven, but Mum didn't get cross with him. She seemed to be not quite with us.

When I was wiping down the surfaces, I heard something I wished I hadn't. The door from the kitchen to the living room was open.

"Did you get a chance to tell them, Jennie?" That was Roger.

"No. It wasn't the right moment. They were out all day and Sapphy looks exhausted."

I clattered a pan and they went quiet. I didn't want to hear any more, or think about what "telling us" might mean. I wasn't in the mood to talk to Conor about it, either. Conor's suspicions might turn out to be the same as mine.

I was so tired that I went to bed before eight. Conor had already gone up. I didn't dream or even move, and I didn't wake until almost nine this morning.

So the barbie is happening today. Mum's coming back from work early, and Roger, with typical efficiency, had the food ordered ready for pick-up from St Pirans first thing this morning. It isn't going to be a simple sausage and burger barbie: no, it's going to be like restaurant food. I asked him if he wanted some help, but he said, "Relax. This is my treat."

I don't think I've ever spent such an empty day. I got

up slowly, wandered around with a mug of tea, watched the spring sunshine glittering on the horizon and didn't want to go anywhere or do anything. Conor was still in bed; he didn't get up until two o'clock. I think we both felt as if everything that happened in the Deep was hitting us, now that we were safe.

I kept seeing flashes of the Kraken changing shape, or the battle inside the whale. They were so real it felt as if the whole thing was happening again. I kept having to remind myself that it was all over. The Kraken was asleep. He couldn't do anything to us. And Ervys was in Ingo, far away. I'd have to think about him one day soon, but not now.

The sun was warm in my sheltered spot and Sadie flumped down on my feet, curled up and closed her eyes. Her warm heaviness was comforting. I felt drowsy even though I'd slept for nearly thirteen hours. I kept thinking I ought to go and see Granny Carne. There was so much I needed to talk to her about. The rowan berries, the Kraken, Conor and Elvira, and Gloria Fortune. I had to find a way of keeping Gloria away from Ingo.

But I couldn't find the energy to walk across the garden, let alone up to Granny Carne's cottage.

I drifted into the kitchen to see how Roger was getting on. He'd already prepared kebabs, marinated steaks and made a beautiful salad. Now, to my amazement, he was whipping up homemade lime mayonnaise.

"Are lots of people coming?" I asked. I thought maybe he'd invited some of his diving friends.

"No. Just us."

"All that for just us?"

Roger nodded, and got on with chopping herbs for the steak. "Keep Sadie out of the kitchen, Sapphy," he said as I turned away. The steak must have cost loads, I thought.

I had a slow shower while Sadie did her thing of lying across the bathroom doorway, as if she thought someone might come in and stab me through the shower curtain. I washed my hair and then went into the garden with Sadie to dry it in the sun. She settled herself to sleep again. I shut my eyes and thought of nothing, and suddenly it was two o'clock and Conor came out with his duvet wrapped round him and a mug of coffee.

"You don't need your duvet, Conor. It's really warm out here."

"I need my comfort blanket. Budge up, Sades, give me room to sit down."

But Sadie had already moved away from him. She doesn't like the talisman, and Conor hasn't taken it off since we got back. Even Mum noticed it last night.

"That's nice, Conor, did you buy it at the craft fair?"

Craft fair! Sometimes I wonder how Mum thinks we spend our time.

"Someone gave it to me," said Conor vaguely. I could

see Mum thinking, *Oh! Has Conor got a girlfriend?* and then deciding to be tactful and say nothing. Mum is so obvious when she's being tactful.

Conor's eyes were still puffy with sleep. He finished his coffee, snuggled into the duvet and looked as if he was going to drop off again. "I'm still aching all over," he mumbled.

"From – from the Deep?"

"Yeah. Don't let's talk about it now, Saph."

We both felt the same. Don't let's talk about anything.

After about another hour, Conor hauled himself up and made us some cheese and pickle sandwiches.

"Roger's making strawberry shortcake," he reported from the kitchen.

"Strawberry shortcake! I didn't know Roger could cook stuff like that. He's always going on about Mum's cakes as if they're miracles."

"He's doing it step by step from a recipe book. I can't believe how much food there is. Is anyone else coming besides us?"

"He says not."

"Weird."

I thought about mentioning the "Have you told them" conversation, but decided not to. Why spoil the afternoon?

The Super-Antipodean may be a gleaming alien stainless-steel monster, but I have to admit it works. Today Roger cooks juicy lamb kebabs with red pepper and tomato chunks, sizzling rib-eye steaks coated with crushed peppercorns, and barbecued sardines with rosemary for Mum because it's her favourite. Roger's as efficient as the barbie and everybody has a plate of food in about quarter of the time it would take me and Conor to cook a couple of mackerel over a driftwood fire.

The barbie isn't as beautiful as a driftwood fire. You don't get leaping, crackling flames which burn down to a heap of soft red ash, and you don't get the wonderful wood-smoke taste in your food. But when there are five of you all wanting food at once, the barbie is a pretty good substitute. I'm counting Sadie as one of the five. She's the greediest of us all. The cooking smells excite her so much that she trembles all over and whines in ecstasy, and I have to restrain her from jumping right into the food as soon as it comes off the grill, and burning her nose.

I feed her the best titbits from my plate as well as her own portion. I'm not supposed to do this because Roger says there's nothing worse than a dog that makes a nuisance of itself begging while people eat. I see his point, so I've explained to Sadie that tonight is an exception.

Sadie's still wary of Conor because he won't take off the talisman. I suggested he could put it under his pillow, but he refused point-blank. It's got to stay round his neck day and night, even though we're a long way from the Deep now. However, I'm not going to argue with him. Any criticism of the talisman is like a criticism of Elvira. It will just make Conor more and more stubborn.

I'm hoping it's just a phase. It used to drive me mad when Mum said that. Now, though, I find the idea reassuring. I've never seen Conor so… so *melted*. Elvira is much too beautiful and gentle and gifted and generally perfect. A person like that could never fit into our family. And then there are all the other obstacles – such as her tail…

Nearly all the food has gone. There's just one slice of strawberry shortcake left, and Sadie's got her eye on it. It's quite chilly now. Even a warm spring day quickly changes into a cold night. In a minute I'll offer to start clearing up. Mum and Roger have drunk a bottle of wine between them and now they're staring romantically into the dying glow of the Super-Antipodean.

"Shall we tell them, Jennie?" asks Roger abruptly. Conor and I snap to attention while Mum looks panicky.

Oh my God, I think. *They're going to tell us they're getting married. They can't do it! Dad isn't dead.* You can't get married when your husband is alive and you're not divorced or anything. Mum would be a bigamist.

"Do you think this is the best time?" asks Mum in a thin nervous voice. Maybe she doesn't want to marry

Roger, but she can't think of a way of telling him. *Don't worry, Mum, we'll help you.*

"You know I told you I was born in Australia, but we had to leave when I was a kid?"

Conor and I mumble something. Maybe Roger thinks he needs to run through his autobiography to convince us that he deserves to marry Mum.

"It's a great country. A fantastic place. Beautiful scenery, friendly people, a great attitude to life."

Roger sounds like the Australian Tourist Board, but it's clear that he really means it. His face glows with enthusiasm.

"I've always wanted to go back. A diving job has come up on the Queensland coast. A mate of mine emailed me last week. It's for three months."

Roger's going away! It's what I hoped and prayed for every night when Mum first met him. But now – well, I suppose I must have got used to him. I don't feel the joy I would have felt even a few months ago. I glance at Mum, wondering how she's going to cope.

"I've got some savings which will pay for the fares," Roger goes on, "and I can't think of a better use for them. It seems to your mum and me that this is a chance that won't come again. If we wait, Conor will be in his exam year and he won't be able to take time out of school.

"There's a house that goes with the job. It'll be pretty basic but we'll give it a lick of paint and get hold of some more furniture. We won't have a load of money but your mum would get a bar job out there. What do you reckon? How do three months in Australia sound to you? We can add on a bit of holiday after the job's done – we might even go down to New Zealand if we can get the money together.

"You kids could go to an Australian school for a term if you want, but your mum and I don't think it would do you any harm to miss a few months. I can train you up to do some diving with me, Conor, if you're interested? And, Sapphy, you're going to love the coast and the outback and the wildlife – it's a different world out there."

Conor and I just stare at him in blank silence. It's so far from what I've been expecting that I can't take it in. *Australia – three months – maybe add on a bit of holiday – bar job – New Zealand…* Roger's words whirl in my head but fail to make any sense.

Mum's face is turned to us, anxious and eager. Sadie senses that everybody's distracted, snatches the last piece of strawberry shortcake and wolfs it down.

All at once I understand. The barbie is meant to be a celebration. Roger's hoping we'll jump at this chance of a lifetime.

"When would it be?" asks Conor at last.

"We'd leave in September."

There's another long silence. I remember what the whale said. Her daughter is at the bottom of the world. She said that maybe one day I could go there and meet her daughter. But not like this. We were talking about the Crossing of Ingo, not flying thousands of miles in a jumbo jet.

I've never even been in a plane. None of us has, not even Mum. There was never enough money. I keep quiet when kids at school talk about going to Thailand or Greece. Mum has always wanted to travel, just as she's always wished she'd stayed on at school, listened to her teachers and got some qualifications. But Dad never wanted to go outside Cornwall.

"*Australia,*" says Conor at last, slowly and wonderingly. It's just one word, but it's enough. Even Elvira won't be enough to hold Conor back. He's still looking stunned, but once his mind gets to work on the idea, he'll want to go.

"We'd go straight from summer here to summer in Australia," says Mum. Her eyes shine. "It's a once-in-a-lifetime opportunity, all of us going together. They have some of the best surf in the world."

But do they have Ingo? Does Ingo open her gateways at the bottom of the world?

I feel as if there are already thousands of metres of air below me, and I'm freefalling. *Leave home.* Leave our cottage when we've only just got it back. Leave the cove, and everything we know. Leave Faro—

Sadie whines, picking up my tension.

"Oh my God," I say slowly, "Sadie."

Sadie can't go. There's quarantine and all sorts of rules about animals leaving one country and going to another.

Three months, or maybe even more with the holiday added on. I couldn't do that to Sadie. She'd be so scared in quarantine with loads of other dogs, all homesick and miserable. She'd think I'd abandoned her. She'd look for me and look for me and at first she'd be all hopeful and then slowly she'd despair—

"Sadie would be well looked after," says Roger quickly. "Jack's family would be glad to take her for three months. She won't forget you, Sapphire."

You've already asked them, I think furiously. *You've already checked it out, without even telling me.*

"I know it's hard about Sadie," says Mum, "but she'll be here when you come back. Dogs don't forget."

Keep calm, Sapphire. Don't let it all burst out. It won't do any good, it'll just make them angry and then they won't listen to anything you say. You've got to be like Conor and make them respect you. Sadie's too important to risk by losing control now.

Sadie huddles close to me. I stroke her mechanically while my mind races. Mum's looking at me nervously, waiting for me to explode. Waiting for me to get angry and shout and maybe cry, and there'll be a storm with thunder and flashing lightning. And then clear sky again. That's the usual pattern. Mum knows it, because it's what she does, too. I'll shout, and then Mum will shout, and then...

I'm not going to do it. I'm going to do what *they've* done: make my plans and not tell anyone until I know exactly what I'm doing.

"I'm really tired," I say at last. "We were in the sea too long yesterday. I think I'd better go to bed."

"We can talk it all over tomorrow," says Mum quickly. "Don't worry, Sapphy, we'll work it all out."

I don't catch her eye. I don't respond to her pleading stare.

"Night everybody. Thanks for the barbie, Roger, the food was amazing."

I don't even look at Conor as I walk to the cottage door, with Sadie pressing against my side.

CHAPTER TWENTY-TWO

I'm on my way up to Granny Carne's. I didn't tell anyone I was going, not even Conor.

The reason I wanted to talk to Granny Carne in the first place was because of what happened in the Deep, and Gloria. Now so many other things have crowded in. Granny Carne will understand that I can't leave Sadie. Sadie belongs to Earth, and so does Granny Carne.

The sun isn't just warm today, it's hot. People are saying this is one of the warmest Aprils there's ever been. I keep a wary eye on the footpath as I climb towards Granny Carne's because this is just the kind of day for adders to come out of their hibernation holes and lie on the path to sun themselves. They're still slow after the winter and not so good at getting out of people's way. I keep Sadie close to me, on her lead, because I don't want her investigating any adders.

I hear a clop of hooves on the bridleway below me.

"Sapphire! *Sapphire!*"

I turn round. It's Rainbow, with a riding hat crammed over her bright short hair.

"Rainbow! What're you doing up here?"

"Come down; I can't bring Treacle up that path."

Treacle, what a ridiculous name for a pony, I think as I scramble down the steep path I've just climbed. But when I get close up I see that it suits her. She's dark brown and short and fat and wide. Rainbow's legs look much too long for her.

"I didn't know you liked riding," I say, stroking Treacle's muzzle. I kneel and unclip Sadie's collar from the lead. "Sit, Sadie girl, sit down over there in case you scare Treacle."

"Hi, Sadie, how are you doing? She's my friend's pony, Sapphire. I said I'd exercise her while Kylie's on holiday."

"Kylie Newton?" That figures. Kylie Newton is our age but the top of her head only just comes up to my shoulder. Treacle would suit her perfectly.

"Yes. Where are you going, Sapphy?"

"Oh, just for a walk with Sadie."

Rainbow laughs. "Don't tell me then."

She's bound to guess where I'm going. The footpath is well worn by people taking their troubles to Granny Carne's cottage.

Treacle stands as stolid as a post. I *could* tell Rainbow. I couldn't tell her all of it, but she might understand about Australia. She might think of something I can do.

I don't look at Rainbow while I tell her. I just keep on stroking Treacle and breathing in her comforting smell of horse. I tell Rainbow about Sadie going to Jack's to be looked after for three whole months, and how Roger and Mum think it's the best present they could ever give us: a trip to Australia! But I don't want to go.

Rainbow's quiet for a while after I've finished talking. Treacle twitches away a couple of flies, and Rainbow steadies her. Sadie seems to be snoozing. I feel light and empty, as if nothing matters any more and there's nothing I can do anyway. It's all going to happen. I'm going to lose Sadie, and travel to the other side of the world. It all seems like someone else's life, not mine.

"You could stay here," says Rainbow at last. "They could go, but you could stay."

"In the cottage on my own? That's not going to happen. Mum would never let me."

"No, maybe not in the cottage. It'd be too much for you to look after everything on your own. And it'd be lonely at night, even with Sadie. But you could stay with someone else. Listen, Sapphy, you could stay with me and Patrick, if you didn't mind sharing my room. Sadie would settle in all right, as long as she had you there. I know you're not crazy about St Pirans, but at least you'd be with Sadie."

I understand why Rainbow thinks it's natural for kids to manage without their parents. Her mum and step-dad seem to go off to Denmark for weeks and weeks, and she and Patrick cope fine. They do all the shopping and cooking for themselves, and Patrick works in a surf shop as well as studying at the sixth-form college.

"Mum would never agree," I say wearily.

"Why not? Why shouldn't she agree? Your mum's going to Australia because she wants to. So's Roger. What about Conor?"

"I think he's probably going to be all right about it too."

"Well then, *they're* all doing what they want. It's not as if they've *got* to go to Australia. They're choosing to go because they want to. My mum does the same – she's always going off to Denmark because she really loves it there. But I don't, and nor does Patrick. We don't know anyone, and we don't even speak Danish. We'd rather be here. They go and we stay, and everyone's happy."

It sounds so logical, but...

"My family doesn't live like that," I say.

"Maybe you should start," says Rainbow, and her eyes flash. "You didn't want to come to St Pirans, did you? And they made you. You were really happy when they said you were coming back here, to your old home. Now they've decided to go somewhere else and you're supposed to leave everything again, even though you'd rather stay here. It's stupid."

"You should talk to my mum."

"Hmm. Maybe I will." Rainbow's face is bright with purpose.

"I wasn't being serious," I say hurriedly.

"Maybe you should be, Sapphy! What's the point of being angry and miserable and not even trying to change things?"

I have plenty of time to think over what Rainbow has said because when I knock on Granny Carne's cottage door there's no answer. She'll come back soon. Granny Carne has a way of knowing when people have come in search of her.

Sadie and I wander past the cottage, on to the top of the Downs. Granny Carne's beehives are up here, but I'm not going that way. The bees don't like me. I pick my way through the heather roots and the new young shoots of bracken to the standing stones.

There are a lot of stories about this broken circle of stones. It's not a big circle, like the Merry Maidens. There are only three complete stones and a few stumps, and the rest are gaps. But you can easily see where the circle was. People say there were sacrifices held here once, long ago, before Christianity came to Cornwall. Other people say that there are still gatherings here on nights of full moon. Nobody knows exactly how long the stones have been standing, or who raised them up in the first place, but they were probably Bronze Age people.

The stones are full of old Earth magic. It's bad luck to

go inside this circle, and I never have. Sadie doesn't want to either. I keep her close to me.

There's so much age and time up here. The stones have weathered, but granite doesn't easily wear away. There's a place on one of the stones that girls used to touch on the day before their wedding. I've seen an old photo of a crowd of girls coming up with the bride. She was wearing a crown of flowers that was probably homemade and was a bit lopsided on her curly hair. I don't think it ever happens any more. Girls are too busy having hen nights and getting their legs waxed.

A few cabbage-white butterflies blow in and out of the stones. There's a pattern on that stump of fallen stone, like a coil of twisted grass.

I look again, and the coil moves. It's an adder, sunning itself on the stump. I don't move. Adders won't hurt you unless you corner them or step on them. This one looks relaxed and peaceful. It must be wonderful to soak up the sun like that after a long winter hidden away in the earth. I scan the circle to see if there are any others. Yes, at the base of one of the standing stones, facing south, there's another slackly coiled snake.

I know adders won't hurt me unless I scare them. But a shudder goes through me all the same. People used to bludgeon adders to death and bring them into the pub, dangling over a stick.

Sadie's ears are pricked, her body rigid. A low growl rumbles in her throat.

"No, Sadie, you're not going after snakes. Come here, you daft girl, don't you know they could hurt you?"

But the growl rumbles on. Sadie scents danger, and she's determined to protect me. I kneel and put my arms round her, breathing in the warm smell of her coat. "It's all right, girl. Stay, Sadie."

A hand rests on my shoulder. I turn and it's Granny Carne, in her earth-coloured clothes and her scarf which is as bright as rowan berries.

"Step careful, my girl," she warns me. "Nadron are all around these stones. Follow me."

"Nadron?"

She points at the snakes. I turn and walk in her footsteps around the edge of the circle until we come to the tallest of the three standing stones. There are rough tussocks of grass among the heather. Granny Carne sits down, and so do I. Sadie settles beside Granny Carne.

"I was thinking you'd be coming to see me," says Granny Carne. "Did you keep those berries safe that I gave you?"

The rowan berries. In one way it seems like a hundred years since Granny Carne gave me the spray of berries on the dark road. In another way it could be just five minutes ago. I can remember exactly how they burned in my pocket.

"I haven't got them any more," I begin, and Granny Carne nods encouragingly. It's warm and peaceful here. I trust Granny Carne. While the bees buzz and the adders sun themselves, I start to tell the story, slowly at first and then faster until it pours out like the tide pouring over rocks.

"Mind your foot, my girl," says Granny Carne when I've finished speaking.

I look down. An adder is coiled, almost touching my trainer. A low growl comes from Sadie's throat, but Granny Carne quiets her. "Like I told you, nadron are all around these stones. Don't move sudden. Keep still now, both of you."

Granny Carne whistles gently, then more loudly. The adder uncoils itself and slides into a tangle of heather root.

"So you went to the Deep, my girl, and learned what lies there. Let me show you something. Hold the dog close and stand there."

Granny Carne stands. She looks taller than ever as she raises her right hand and strikes the standing stone, as if she's knocking on a door. Deep within the earth, I think I hear an echo. Granny Carne listens. "We can enter now," she says. "Follow behind me. Don't step outside my shadow."

She walks to the edge of the stone circle. She's going to go inside.

"But, Granny Carne, I can't!"

"Yes, you can, my girl, when you're with me."

When we cross the threshold of the circle, it's like walking into an invisible room. The air changes and grows colder, even though the sun is just as strong. Granny Carne's shadow falls sharply over me and Sadie. Sounds thicken around us. It's like a blacksmith's forge, or a workshop. Clangs of metal, the whizz of a blade being sharpened, a hiss of steam. I can hear voices, muffled and confused. Granny Carne pushes aside something that I can't see.

"There's a lot of time trapped in here," she says. "Best take no notice of it."

I am cold. I think I'm frightened too but I'm not sure. Sadie is panting as if she's been running on a hot day.

Granny Carne reaches the centre of the circle. "Come forward, Sapphire," she says, "but mind you keep in my shadow." She glances behind her. The entrance to the circle is behind us, and as we stand now the sun is directly ahead of us.

"Sun and gateway, make a line," murmurs Granny Carne. "Belly of the earth, open."

She steps back from the grassy centre of the stone circle. A knot of darkness appears in the grass. It spreads, opening, until it's as big as a fist. Then wider and wider, until the darkness is lapping at Granny Carne's feet. I think of the Kraken swallowing himself in his own yawn, and of the tides coiling inside the Tide Knot.

"Look down," Granny Carne commands me.

Far, far down, an infinite number of miles inside the earth, a fire burns, ruby and scarlet and yellow-gold. Fire, or maybe jewels. I know that the earth is full of jewels.

"Fire," says Granny Carne. "Fire lives in the Earth. Fire feeds Earth. Don't move out of my shadow or the circle will suck you in."

The deep, hot smell of Earth drifts up to me. It catches at the back of my throat. It's so dark down there, terribly dark, but deep in the heart of the blackness fire is playing like jewels. I take another breath and start to cough.

"Step back, step back now."

We step backwards. Sadie cringes in Granny Carne's shadow. There seems to be a haze over the grass, shimmering. My eyes blur, and when I next look the dark hole has closed over without a trace.

We back out of the stone circle.

"Many a one would walk through that gateway and into the Earth, years gone by," says Granny Carne, "but no one looks for it now. Remember that sun and gateway make a line and you'll always find it."

I shudder. I certainly don't want to find it again. "You should have shown that to Conor, not me," I say. "He's much more Earth than I am."

"He's mixed, like you are. Not as equal as you, but mixed all the same. You know that. He could let his Earth self grow strong and crush his Mer self, just as your Mer self could drown everything else out of you if you let it.

"You and Conor and Mathew and how many others

nobody knows, you're all mixed. That's why I can show you what I've just shown you. I wouldn't want your friend Rainbow to look through the Earth's navel, for she'd walk right into it. She belongs to the Earth and Earth would claim her. But your Mer blood holds you back.

"You think the Kraken's sleeping and all's well. You're wrong, my girl. Earth has never stood so close to danger, nor Ingo. The Tide Knot breaking was only a sign of it. Saldowr knows that. He knows his element as well as I know mine. Floods and fires and poisoned seas are only a sign of it.

"You think that the choice lies in being Mer or being human. You're wrong, my girl. That's not the way to healing. Be this or be that and you'll be safe. No. It's people like you who hold the key to the future, and now look at you. You want to push your Earth self aside."

Granny Carne is changing before my eyes. She's no longer an old woman in shabby brown clothes. She stands as tall as a prophet. Her amber eyes flash and for a moment I see what I've seen once before: her body straightens, her hair turns dark and lustrous, her skin grows smooth as satin. She bends down, as supple as a young girl, and picks up something coiled at her feet. It's an adder.

I want to cry out and tell her to be careful, but I stand frozen. The adder's head rises from the coil. They're face to face, the adder and Granny Carne. Its tail winds around her wrist for support. The adder's head sways a little. Its mouth is open, showing its forked tongue. The tongue flickers.

Granny Carne says nothing, but I'm sure some silent conversation is passing between the two of them. A moment later Granny Carne bows down to the earth and the adder pours away on to the ground, and vanishes into a hole at the base of the standing stone.

The familiar shape of the Granny Carne I know returns. I blink, and shiver.

"Don't you ever try that, my girl," says Granny Carne. "Those who can't talk to the bees won't ever talk to nadron, who are the children of Earth."

Conor can talk to the bees... "Granny Carne, could Conor ever do that with a snake? Hold it, like you did?"

"You don't want to go calling her 'snake'. She has her proper name just as you do. Yes, your Conor has it in him to talk to my lady there, should he think of wanting to do it."

He'll get plenty of chances in Australia, I think grimly. Everyone says Australia is full of snakes, the most poisonous ones in the world. And poisonous spiders and crocodiles. No doubt Roger will plan trips to see them all.

We walk back to Granny Carne's cottage, and I fill a bowl of water for Sadie while Granny Carne puts her kettle on to the fire. I don't want to sit down at the table, but there's a silent pressure that makes me do so. I'm not comfortable here. I never have been. The cottage is too closed in. Too earthy. The night I once spent here was one of the worst of my life.

I wish Granny Carne hadn't shown me that tunnel deep into the Earth. When I shut my eyes I can still see it. I don't want to know about Earth things. I want wild water foaming over black rocks. I want the taste of salt and the slap of waves. I don't want Granny Carne to try and change me.

I glance suspiciously at Granny Carne, who is slicing a malt loaf. "Fetch me the butter from the larder, Sapphire."

Granny Carne's larder is on the north side of the cottage. It is cool and dark and there's a marble slab where she puts milk and butter and cheese. Granny Carne has never had a fridge or a freezer. I fetch the butter, and take a deep breath. *Remember, Sapphire, you didn't come here to think about snakes and Earth things. You came because of Ingo: the Kraken, and what's going to happen now that Ervys is locked in combat with Saldowr. And Gloria Fortune.*

"Gloria mustn't go to Ingo," I say as I put the butter down on the table.

Granny Carne looks at me quizzically. "Mustn't go to Ingo?" she asks. "Not when you think Ingo's next door to heaven?"

"If she goes, it'll be like Dad going. I mean, Gloria's got Richard and they really love each other. What would he do without her?"

Granny Carne shakes her head. "You came here for

307

your own sake, Sapphire. Leave Gloria Fortune to tell me her own story."

"But I've got to help her!"

"You may think that if you want, but the truth is you came for yourself. There's too many folk that rush round helping others so they won't have to look at what needs help in themselves."

Granny Carne makes tea, and spreads the malt bread with butter. As she hands me a plate she observes, "Australia's a fair old distance, Sapphire, near at the bottom of the world."

Did I even mention Australia? I'm sure I didn't.

"You ever seen those old maps they used to draw, with whales spouting and mermen and ships falling over the edge of the world, before they thought that the earth was round?"

"No."

"Course we've come on since then." Granny Carne smiles ironically. "We've even got those satellites taking pictures to tell us what the Queen keeps in her back garden. We know everything about the Earth now, except how to keep her alive."

I munch my slice of malt bread. It's sticky and full of plump raisins. Granny Carne's tea has a faint taste of smoke in it, maybe because her kettle hangs directly over the fire.

The tea is good. I feel more relaxed now. "I don't want to go to Australia," I say.

"Best you don't go, then," says Granny Carne equably.

"But Mum will be so upset and miserable. She'll say she won't go without me."

"I reckon she'll go," says Granny Carne, "knowing Jennie. Long as she's sure you'll be safe and happy, she'll come round to going. What about your Conor? Does he want to go?"

"I don't know – I think so."

"Question is, my girl, will your Conor go without you?"

"That's the trouble. I don't want to mess everything up for him. He ought to be able to go to Australia if he wants."

I say it as firmly as I can because I know it's right, but I can't imagine spending three months without Conor. Conor's always been there. I can't really even imagine a week without Conor.

I suppose at least if he goes to Australia, it means he'll be safely away from falling more and more in love with Elvira. Look on the bright side, Sapphire...

But none of the sides seem very bright.

Rainbow thinks I can do it if I want to. Change things, I mean, instead of always being changed by them. She thinks I should tell Mum and Roger what I want to happen, instead of waiting until they tell me what's going to happen. I wish I had as much confidence in myself as Rainbow seems to have –

"She's a fine girl, Rainbow," says Granny Carne meditatively, as if we've just been talking about her. "She'd do for your Conor, I'd say." I stare at Granny Carne in shock. Conor and Rainbow! Conor and Rainbow? But Conor's besotted by Elvira, and anyway Rainbow's my friend, not Conor's. Conor and Rainbow...

I think it over. Rainbow's warmth and kindness, her good sense, her strength and independence. Rainbow isn't mysterious, she's as transparent as sunlight. Her short, bright hair is the opposite of Elvira's floating locks. When I think of Conor with Elvira, I always see them with their backs turned, swimming away from me. I see Elvira taking Conor away from me. I don't think Rainbow would do that. Rainbow and Conor – could it ever really happen?

"But Conor's going off to Australia," I say aloud.

"It's a funny thing how everyone wants to go to the bottom of the world," says Granny Carne, watching me closely.

Her words echo and echo in my head. They have such power that they make my skin prickle. The whale said that the Crossing of Ingo would take me to the bottom of the world. *One day, little barelegs, you may go to the bottom of the world, and meet my daughter.* I'd love to meet the whale's daughter. It sounds odd, but I think it would be almost like meeting a sister.

I don't want to go to the bottom of the world on a jumbo jet, crammed in with hundreds of people. That's not travelling. I want to surf the Great Currents past continents and islands. I want to be in living water, not in dead aeroplane air. I want to meet all the creatures of Ingo. I want to be with the Mer.

"Earth needs ones like you, and Ingo needs ones like you," says Granny Carne. "You understand what I'm saying, Sapphire? Sometimes I reckon you think it's a curse, the way your blood's equal. You've got your human blood pulling you one way and your Mer blood pulling you the other. Your Mer blood's pulling you strong now, am I right? You want to belong to Ingo. You think you can belong there. Is that it? Am I right, my girl?"

"Yes," I say quietly.

"But you can't belong in one place," says Granny Carne. "That's not what's written for you in the Book of Life."

That's horrible. She makes it seem as if everything's predestined, and I don't have any freedom. I won't believe that my future is already written down in some book, particularly in one which I never want to see again because it's so scary. Words swarming at me like bees – ugh.

"Maybe the Book of Life is wrong," I say rebelliously.

Granny Carne gives a crack of laughter. "Never thought I'd sit here and someone would dare say that to my face."

"Well, it could be."

"You're thinking wrong. You're thinking it's like a recipe written down for the future. No. My Book of Life shows what's there, like flour and salt and fat and honey, not what you make of them. But it shows what's not there, too. You can't make sweetness where there's no honey, or salt where there is no salt.

"You can't belong, my girl, neither here, nor in Ingo. But you ones who can't belong are what the future needs. You ever seen a boulder lifted by a lever? That's how they raised those standing stones."

And you probably watched, I think. I can easily picture Granny Carne standing on the hillside, wrapped in an earth-coloured cloak, watching Bronze Age people heave and sweat to raise the stones. I bet those Bronze Age people used to come up here and tell her their troubles, too.

"The lever doesn't look like much, compared to a granite boulder that's heavy enough to crush a dozen men," Granny Carne goes on. "But it'll lift that boulder. You don't look many, you ones with your blood mixed between Earth and Ingo. But you're the only chance that one day someone'll learn how to put Earth and Ingo back together, so that we find an end to destruction. That's why there's no easy answer. Yes, I know you could slip into Ingo easy as this – " She snaps her fingers. " – just like Mathew did. And one day you'd look down at yourself and you'd be Mer, like him. But I don't know that it would make you any happier than it's made your father."

She sounds sorrowful. I remember how Dad and Granny Carne were always good friends. He taught me to take no notice when other kids said she was a witch, and that if I showed her respect, she'd be good to me. I can hear him saying it.

Dad's trapped. He's not happy. Granny Carne knows he's not, and I do too. When he came to meet me that night, down at the Lady Stream pool, his face was full of suffering.

Don't. Don't think of it. Dad's going to get his freedom. I know Saldowr says you can't force people, but if I can see Dad and speak to him, then this time I'll be strong. I'll find out whether he is still our Dad in his heart, or if Conor and I are as vague as dreams now, and only Mordowrgi and Mellina are real. I've got to be brave enough to see Dad face to face, not in a mirror or in a pool. The only place I can ever see him face to face is Ingo. The only place where this tangle of belonging and not belonging can ever be untangled is Ingo.

"I've got to make the Crossing of Ingo," I say.

Granny Carne's face sharpens. "Do you know what that means?" she demands.

"I – I think so."

Granny Carne draws herself up to her full height. Her eyes blaze like an owl's eye when it sights prey far below.

"You think so?" she repeats.

I'm afraid. It's like a veil lifting, showing me a depth of power in Granny Carne that's like fire blazing in the centre of the earth. I want to turn and run all the way down the hill to the safety of our cottage. My heart thumps like racing footsteps. *Be brave, Sapphire. You've got to be strong now. If you start running you'll never untangle all the knots that bind you. You'll just pull them harder and tighter.*

I stare back into Granny Carne's eyes and for a second I think I see flames leaping in their depths. My skin prickles.

"Be very sure," says Granny Carne harshly, "that you understand what you're doing before you bind your fortune so close to the Mer."

"I'm not sure," I say slowly, "I can't be sure. But I've got to do it."

"You won't travel with my rowan this time."

"I know."

Granny Carne's face relaxes. Her wrinkles are like the deep cracks in a dried-up riverbed as she smiles.

"You know, do you, my girl? You go on then," she says, "you go on like you're bound to do whatever I or anyone else on Earth tells you, come hell or high water. You go on and make that crossing, and then you come back here, my girl, and tell me what you know."

CHAPTER TWENTY-THREE

nd now everything's changed again.

Conor isn't going to Australia. I came home from Granny Carne's and told him I'd made up my mind that I wasn't going to go. I was going to live with Rainbow instead.

"No, you're not," he said.

Before I could get angry, he explained. He'd been thinking too. He'd talked to Roger and Mum about all their plans, and then he'd gone for a long walk to think things through.

"I went up to Granny Carne," I said. "I had to talk to her."

"I had to be on my own. It's got to be my decision, not anyone else's. I'm older than you, Saph."

Conor told me the things he'd been weighing up in his mind. Australia had sounded amazing at first. Travel and new experiences and learning to dive with Roger. But something was nagging at him.

"It didn't feel right to me, the four of us going out there as a family. I like Roger, you know I do. I was never against him like you were. But he's not Dad and we're not a family, not really. I mean we get on fine here most of the time, but out there we won't have our friends, or school, or anything. Just them. If I was five and you were three, then yes, we'd have to grow into a family. But it's not like that.

"Mum should go, not us. She deserves a good time, after everything that's happened. And you know what, Saph, I think Mum will have a better time if we're not there, as long as she knows we're fine back here and she doesn't start feeling guilty."

"You know Mum. She's bound to feel guilty if we don't go."

"Not if we handle it right."

We talked about it all for nearly two hours, going back and forwards over all the arguments. I was worried that Conor wasn't telling me the whole truth, and that he was really giving up Australia because of me. It must have been obvious right away that I didn't want to go, even though I tried to hide it. But Conor said it wasn't because of me.

"We're in the middle of things here. We can't just leave. There's Dad."

"I thought you'd given up on Dad."

Conor flushes. "I'll never do that. OK, I don't think he's a prisoner the way you do, but I want to – you know – see him. Talk to him."

And there's Elvira, I think. "Maybe you can still get to Ingo from Australia," I say aloud.

Conor sighs impatiently. "That's not the point, Saph. What I mean is that these are our lives here. Our home's here. All the really crucial things that have happened belong here. Rushing off to Australia isn't going to solve anything.

"Anyway, I'd rather travel later on, when I've finished school. I'd rather go with friends, and get a job, and be independent. It's not long to wait. I like Roger, don't get me wrong, he's a really good bloke even though you don't think so."

"I don't hate him any more, Conor. I even..."

"Even what?"

"Even think I'd really like having him around, if it wasn't for Dad."

"Yeah, Roger's all right. But I don't want to have to depend on him."

"As long as it's not me holding you back."

"You don't hold me back, Saph. You're a nightmare sometimes, but you don't hold me back."

"When are you going to tell them?"

"Tonight."

That was when the real difficulties began. Mum didn't shout: she cried, and that was much worse. Roger didn't cry, naturally, but it was just as hard in a way. He looked so *disappointed*. As if he'd bought a fantastic present for us both and we'd refused even to open it.

Conor put his arm round Mum and kept it there. I let him do most of the talking because I knew he'd be more convincing. Mum clearly thought at first that Conor was just being a loyal brother and giving up a wonderful opportunity because I didn't want to go. But he made it clear that wasn't true.

We kept saying that Mum and Roger had got to go. They didn't listen at first, and even by the time we all went off to bed, exhausted, Mum hadn't budged on the question of going without us.

"It's impossible. What kind of mother do you think I am?"

"The best," said Conor, "but that's not what we're talking about."

Mum smiled up at Conor, then her face creased again as she started listing more reasons why she couldn't go without us.

The next day was better. Mum was up at dawn, pacing the kitchen, talking to Roger. She called in sick at work, which she never, ever does, and they went for a long walk together (taking a detour to avoid the pub where she works). By the time they came back, halfway through the afternoon, Mum seemed calmer. Roger announced that we were all going to sit down together and discuss the possibilities, and then Conor and I knew that the boulder was beginning to move.

Mum's going. She's not going for the full three months, but she's going. She and Roger will fly out together, and she'll stay for six weeks. Conor argued that it was crazy for her not to go for the whole time, but she wouldn't budge.

Maybe, though, Conor says, she'll stay a bit longer once she realises we're doing fine back here. He wants Mum to have the chance of doing the whole trip with Roger, and going to New Zealand too.

I think it was Granny Carne who really changed Mum's mind. Mum went up to see her. She was away the whole evening, and when she came back she looked different. The worry lines on her face were smoothed out.

Mum wouldn't tell us everything she and Granny Carne talked about, but she said that Granny Carne thought Mum was doing the right thing to go with Roger, and let us stay here. Mum has huge faith in Granny Carne's judgement, and she also knows that Granny Carne's opinion counts for a lot in the village. Granny Carne told Mum she'd be our guardian while she was away.

When I heard this, I saw an owl hovering over its nest with fierce amber eyes and spread talons ready to slash at any predator. But of course Conor and I aren't fluffy owlets. The idea of having Granny Carne as a guardian is about as scary as it's reassuring.

Conor and I are staying here in the cottage with Sadie. Mary Thomas, our closest neighbour, says we're to come straight over, day or night, if there's a problem. And she'll call in every day. Gloria Fortune reminded Mum that she's always around if we need anything, because "with this leg, I'm not going anywhere". However, I suspect it might be us watching out for Gloria, rather than the other way round.

Rainbow hasn't said much. She hugged me when she heard the news, and said, "I knew you could do it, Sapphy."

Jack's Mum says we can come up to Sunday dinner every week. Hmm, that could be a bit restrictive... But I noticed Conor's eyes lighting up. Jack's Mum makes great roast dinners.

Even the vicar came and had one of his lengthy cups of tea with Mum and said to tell us that he was always there, apart from his week's holiday in Rome in November. The vicar is a very literal man.

We're all going to help raise money for their trip, because it'll be hard for Mum and Roger to find enough to keep us here, on top of all the expenses of going to Australia. Roger says he'll work all the hours God sends between now and September. Conor's going to help me work on the vegetable garden. If we get the whole plot dug over, we can grow all the fruit and veg we need this summer, and sell the surplus at the top gate to summer visitors. People pay a lot for organic veg and fruit.

Mal's dad says Conor can help out with the fishing trips this summer too. He doesn't pay much but it's something, and Conor will be bringing home plenty of mackerel and maybe sea bass too. I'm still thinking about more ways to earn money.

"Guided tours of Ingo?" Conor suggested.

I don't mind cooking and washing and cleaning and stuff like that while Mum is away, as long as Conor does his share. I do loads already, as Mum had to admit. I have done ever since Dad left.

So it's more or less settled. Mum is beginning to sound just a bit excited about Australia again, although she still brings up several new worries a day. If It weren't for Granny Carne being our guardian, she'd never have dreamed of considering it, she says. And she trusts Conor to look after me. We've got to email or call Mum every day. Roger will set up his computer so we can make free international calls, and there'll be no excuse for being out of touch.

I haven't let myself think about missing Mum. They're leaving at the beginning of September. Less than five months. Four months. Three months now. Time picks up speed as the date of their flight comes closer. A couple of lines from Dad's song keep going through my head:

But since it falls unto my lot
That I should go, and you should not...

Yesterday Mum came in to show me her new bikini and sarong. Sadie and I were lying in a heap on the living-room floor, watching TV. The sarong was all different pinks, some faded, some hot and vibrant. Very Australian. Mum wound the sarong into a few different styles to show me, and then she said abruptly, "At least with Sadie here I don't have to worry so much."

"She'd soon scare off the burglars," I agreed.

"I didn't really mean burglars," said Mum slowly, and then she was speaking to Sadie, not me. "You'll keep my Sapphy safe, won't you girl?"

She was only half joking.

"Mum, I—"

But then I couldn't think what to say. *Mum, nothing's going to happen. Mum, I'll be fine, you know I will.* I can't promise either of those things. *You're the best Mum in the world, I hope you have a wonderful time.* Conor can say things like that, but I can't.

"Look after her for me, girl," Mum repeated, her voice low and intent. Sadie was really listening now. "You keep her safe, till I come home."

Faro holds the sharp edge of the clam shell steady.

"How much hair do you need for the bracelets, Faro? I can't have too much cut off, or Mum will notice."

Faro separates a lock of my hair from the mass that floats around me like seaweed. "This will be enough. Keep still."

The clam shell saws at my hair, pulling it. They definitely need scissors in Ingo – but I suppose scissors would rust.

My head jerks. The lock of hair is in Faro's hand. Very carefully he binds the ends tightly together with what looks like cotton thread but is really three strands of angel-hair weed woven together for strength. Then he tucks it into his belt.

"Now you."

I grasp a lock of Faro's hair, close to the roots. Maybe that's too much. I don't want to make him look as if I've scalped him. "This much?"

Faro squints at it. "Yes, that's enough."

I start to saw. The clam shell isn't very sharp, or else I'm not using it right. Faro makes a face. "You're pulling my hair."

"I know, I can't get this shell to cut."

"Turn it sideways a bit."

Ah, that's easier. I smile as the strands of hair begin to separate. We are tucked away in calm water, in an underwater cove only about a mile down the coast from home. It's the first time I've seen Faro since the day we got back from the Deep, and he seems changed somehow. There's no sparkle in his eyes.

"Is anything the matter, Faro?"

"Nothing new, little sister. Only that Ervys continues to gather followers, even though he has looked into Saldowr's mirror. Many of the Mer are dazzled by his promises."

"You mean Talek and Mortarow are still with him?"

"Talek and Mortarow! They are like the tip of a rock showing at high tide when the underwater mountains are hidden. Most of Ervys's followers stay hidden. They won't declare themselves yet. But they exist. And so even though the Kraken sleeps and the Tide Knot is healed there is still *trystans* in Ingo."

"*Trystans*...? Oh, yes, I understand." As soon as the word is in my mouth, I understand it. Sadness. Grief. Division. Ingo isn't healed yet.

"How is Saldowr?"

"Better," says Faro guardedly, then glances round as if to check that no one's spying on us.

"There, it's done." The last strands of Faro's hair are severed. I give the lock to him carefully, and he binds it as he did mine.

"I will weave them into bracelets," he promises.

"You know you said there were lots of patterns? What are they like?"

"There is one which will belong to us alone. It's woven as closely as the scales of a fish. No one can see where two hairs join. It's called *Deublek*."

"*Deublek*..." I try out the name. "What does it mean?"

"Two together. And strong, as we were strong in the Deep. Next time you come the bracelets will be finished and we will put them on. After that, we will always wear them."

And Mum will ask me if I got mine from a craft fair, I think.

Faro's face brightens. "And then, little sister, we will present ourselves to the Assembly, and say that we are ready to make the Crossing of Ingo."

The words send a familiar tingle through me. They are pulling me as hard as the cove pulled me when I first heard the voice of Ingo calling. *The Crossing of Ingo. The Crossing of Ingo.* But I can't leave Conor behind. Conor's staying in Cornwall partly because of me; I'm sure of that even though he denies it. I can't repay him by vanishing with Faro to make a journey that might take weeks... or months.

"Conor must come with us," I say.

"Conor?"

"Yes. I can't go without my brother."

"But I'll be with you, little sister. Why do you need two brothers?"

"No, Faro. It doesn't work like that. You and me, but Conor too."

"And what about my sister?" Faro's eyes are malicious and knowing. "You'd like her to be there too, wouldn't you, Sapphire?"

"If it means that Conor comes, then yes, I would," I say steadily.

Elvira too... Oh well, maybe it wouldn't be too terrible. At least I'd be able to keep an eye on her and Conor, and maybe spoil a few of their more romantic moments. And we'd have the benefit of Elvira's wonderful healing powers, I suppose, which could come in handy if the Crossing of Ingo is as dangerous as it sounds. Thinking about Elvira always makes me mean. Why should anyone be so annoyingly perfect?

"I will make us the most beautiful bracelets that have ever been seen in Ingo," boasts Faro.

I haven't told him yet about Mum and Roger going to Australia, and Conor and me staying back here. It seems a bit... risky. Faro would be very glad to know that there were no adults to stand in my way. There'd be no limit to his plans for us.

Ingo is so close. With Mum away and no Roger, there'll be no one to stop us when the sea calls. And there'll be no need to hurry home, in case Mum's waiting and getting frightened for us.

Granny Carne says that I could become Mer. One day I could find that my body had changed, just as my mind had changed.

I look down. There are my feet, wavering through the

water. I can see why the Mer think toes look ridiculous, but I still quite like mine.

"All right, then," says Faro, twisting through the water so that his hair swirls and his tail glistens in the light filtering down to us through ten metres of water. "All right, then, you and me and Conor. And my sister, to balance it. The four of us will travel together. We'll swim past the Lost Islands, and take the first of the Great Currents.

"I've heard such stories, Sapphire, from those who have made the Crossing. Some have dived under icebergs and met ice bears with claws like the hooks you humans drop for fish, but a hundred times more powerful. Strong enough to rip out your spine if you turn your back to them. Some have fought killer whales, and either won or left their bones drifting to the Deep. Some have come close to islands where the trees drop down into the water and there are beautiful humans singing and calling to the Mer, trying to tempt us out to drown in Air.

"There are fish that fly and fish like rainbows and fish that walk on the floor of the sea, and whales bigger than any we see in these waters. There are lost cities too, Sapphire, which were in the Air once and which sank down into Ingo long before our great-great-great-grandmothers went to Limina. Think of it, little sister! We are going to the bottom of the world."

Faro's eyes blaze with excitement. He catches hold of

my wrist. I remember how I dug my fingers into his wrist long ago, the first time he took me into Ingo. I was so scared then that I didn't care if my grip hurt Faro. I knew nothing except that I couldn't breathe underwater. And then Ingo opened, and let me in.

There's still so much I don't know. But if Faro and I make the Crossing of Ingo side by side, then we'll be equal at last. Faro and I, Conor and Elvira.

"You will be truly my sister then," says Faro. "And once I have made the Crossing of Ingo, no one will dare to say that I am not truly Mer."

"No one else can tell you what you are!" I say hotly. "Not Saldowr, not Ervys, not anyone. You're the only one who knows. The only one, Faro!"

Faro laughs. "Such wisdom!" he mocks me. "Saldowr will take you for his *scolhyk* instead of me."

The shadow of pain doesn't leave his face, even when he's laughing. Faro hasn't even begun to come to terms with his human blood yet. How cruel Ervys was to taunt Faro, as if having human blood was some kind of curse – or a contamination. Perhaps that's what all the Mer think. I hope not—

Faro waves his hand in front of my face. "Come back, little sister," he says. "Listen, you may be so wise that Saldowr will be coming to you for advice soon but, can you do somersaults like me?" He flips over, churning the water, his tail driving him faster and faster until his body is a perfect circle bound by his flying hair.

"It's not a fair competition. You've got a tail," I point out, once the display is over and he's facing me again. Faro just looks at me with bright eyes and raised eyebrows, teasing, questioning.

"No, Faro," I say firmly. "Don't look at me like that. *No.* It's not going to happen. Not ever."

"Never say never," murmurs Faro. "Who would think that water could grind a rock to sand, or wear away a cliff, unless they'd seen it with their own eyes? Never say never, little sister. Who can tell what the future will bring?"

INGO

Helen Dunmore

Everything is wet and shining with
mist. The rocks hidden, the sea hidden.
Everything slippery and dangerous...
the sea pulling me like a magnet.

Swimming, surfing, exploring – Sapphire and her
brother Conor enjoy life by the sea in Cornwall. But why
does Conor start disappearing for hours on end? And
who is the mysterious girl talking to him on the rocks?

Following Conor down to the cove one day,
Sapphire discovers Ingo – an exciting and dangerous
world beneath the waves, where all you breathe is
adventure...

www.harpercollinschildrensbooks.co.uk

HarperCollins *Children's Books*

THE TIDE KNOT

Helen Dunmore

I can't go back in the house. I'm
restless, prickling all over. The wind
hits me like slaps from huge invisible
hands. But it's not the wind that
worries me. It's something else,
beyond the storm...

Sapphire and her brother Conor can't forget their
adventures in Ingo, the mysterious world beneath the
sea. They long to see their Mer friends once more. But a
crisis is brewing far below the ocean's surface, where the
wisest of the Mer guards the Tide Knot. And soon both
Sapphire and Conor will be drawn into Ingo's troubled
waters...

www.harpercollinschildrensbooks.co.uk

HarperCollins *Children's Books*